THE NATIONAL TRUST BOOK OF
ENGLISH
DOMESTIC SILVER
1500–1900

Timothy Schroder

VIKING
in association with
THE NATIONAL TRUST

VIKING

Penguin Books Ltd, Harmondsworth, Middlesex, England
Viking Penguin Inc., 40 West 23rd Street, New York, New York 10010, U.S.A.
Penguin Books Australia Ltd, Ringwood, Victoria, Australia
Penguin Books Canada Ltd, 2801 John Street, Markham, Ontario, Canada L3R 1B4
Penguin Books (N.Z.) Ltd, 182–190 Wairau Road, Auckland 10, New Zealand

First published 1988

Copyright © Timothy Schroder, 1988

Typeset in 11/13 Monophoto Palatino
Printed in Great Britain by Butler & Tanner Ltd, Frome and London

British Library Cataloguing in Publication Data

Schroder, Timothy
The National Trust book of English
domestic silver, 1500–1900.
1. Silverware—England—History
I. Title
379.2'3742   NK7143

ISBN 0–670–80237–9

Library of Congress Catalog Card Number: 86–512 02

To
Ellen

Contents

Preface

The serious study of English silver is usually dated from Octavius Morgan's lecture on hallmarks delivered to the Society of Antiquaries in 1853. Subsequent generations have produced successive historical surveys, such as W. J. Cripps's *Old English Plate* (1878), Sir Charles Jackson's *Illustrated History* (1911), Charles Oman's *English Domestic Silver* (1934) and Gerald Taylor's *Silver Through the Ages* (1956). In more recent times these classic titles have been augmented by a number of books focusing on specific periods.

The more recent of these books still stand as perfectly valid surveys of the range of silver objects in use at different times and the stylistic development of the main categories of plate. This book is not intended, therefore, as an updated survey in that tradition. While it touches on much of the same territory, it is also concerned with the role that plate played in the lives of its owners, the reasons patrons had for acquiring it, and the sort of financial commitments that having it involved. It also attempts to give some account of the relationship between silver and base metals, especially pewter, and to consider silver as one material among several that were all competing for different shares, and in some cases for the same share, of the market.

Wherever possible I have chosen illustrations from the holdings of the National Trust. These are substantial, but considerably less representative of the development of the subject than the Trust's houses or their furnishings are of theirs. Little early English silver survives in the houses for which it was originally made, and most of that illustrated in the opening chapters of this book is in the custody of Oxford and Cambridge colleges, parish churches and City livery companies. However, a number of important collections from later periods are in the care of the Trust, among which the most notable are the late seventeenth-century silver furniture at Knole, the early and mid eighteenth-century domestic silver at Dunham Massey and Ickworth and the Regency ambassadorial plate at Attingham Park.

Many people have helped me to see the wood in addition to the trees during the preparation of this book. To Philippa Glanville of the Victoria and Albert Museum I am especially grateful for reading the manuscript and saving me from many errors of fact and interpretation. I have particularly benefited from conversations with the latter on silver of the Tudor period, and with Vanessa Brett, Peter Hornsby and Belinda Gentle on the relationship between base metal and silver. In this connection I should also like to thank Major J. M. Halford, Clerk of the Worshipful Company of Pewterers, for improving my negligible knowledge of the subject by generously allowing me to examine the company's important collection of pewter.

Finally, I should like to express my thanks to my publishers for their great forbearance in respect of an embarrassingly overdue manuscript; to the National Trust, Christie's and Sotheby's for contributing a large number of the illustrations; to Jeanette Hanisee for preparing the glossary; and to my secretary, Lori Kaplan, for transforming a barely legible manuscript into a thoroughly revisable 'floppy disc'.

Timothy Schroder
Los Angeles
July 1986

$$\text{Illustration Acknowledgements}$$

Her Majesty the Queen 263, 265
A.D.C. Heritage Ltd 279
Worshipful Company of Armours and Braziers 23
Admiral Blake Museum, Bridgwater, Somerset 94
Ashmolean Museum, Oxford 43, 184
James Austin, Cambridge 121, 151, 155, 211
J. H. Bourdon-Smith Ltd 3, 47, 84, 136
Brand Inglis Ltd 12, 145, 201, 285
Trustees of the British Museum 24, 48, 57, 70, 126, 149, 156
Christie's 6–8, 10, 83, 88, 99, 104, 105, 108, 115, 125, 129, 131, 132, 134, 135,
    146, 147, 158, 160, 161, 170, 171, 174, 175, 185, 186, 192, 195, 197, 198, 202,
    204 (top), 205, 208, 218, 219, 229, 233, 237, 247, 250, 271
The Master and Fellows of Christ's College, Cambridge 27
Cirencester Parish Church (Bryan Berkeley) 32
Michael Clayton, Edinburgh 67
Corpus Christi College, Cambriidge 29
Peter John Gates, London 76, 133, 144, 169
Worshipful Company of Goldsmiths 36, 59, 65, 267, 277
The Controller of Her Britannic Majesty's Staitonery Office 54
Worshipful Company of Ironmongers 45
Kremlin Museum, Moscow 74
Los Angeles County Museum of Art 5, 9 (bottom), 17, 33, 37, 58, 63, 68, 73, 91,
    96, 103, 109, 191, 193, 217, 248, 252
Mary Rose Trust, Portsmouth 39
Metropolitan Museum of Art, New York 66, 69, 77, 117, 130, 203
Museum of Fine Arts, Boston 35, 107, 214, 235
Museum of London 42, 46
National Trust 4, 9, (top), 11, 79, 118–20, 123, 150, 154, 159, 164–8, 172, 189,
    194, 199, 206, 207, 209, 215, 216, 245, 246, 249, 257, 261
National Trust for Scotland 240, 254–6, 264

One

SILVER:
THE METAL AND THE CRAFT

In common with other metals, silver has been used for making domestic or decorative artefacts since very early times. It is attractive and has certain physical and chemical properties that make it ideally suited to being worked into objects with a wide variety of functions. But it has historically been invested with a further property, irrelevant from the point of view of the metallurgist, and which it has until recent times shared only with gold:[1] the fact that it is precious. The softness and rarity of gold has meant that it has seldom been used, even by the very wealthy, for utilitarian domestic objects and these two properties, practicality and preciousness, have together invested silver with an ambiguity that is seen throughout the history of its use and that accounts both for its similarities to and differences from objects made in other materials.

The earliest evidence of silver artefacts is in the form of jewellery dating from the third millennium B.C. Domestic objects are not known in any quantity before those made by Mycenean craftsmen during the second millennium and later. These are mainly in the form of dishes and drinking vessels, although the range of objects expands dramatically among the Roman hoards dating from the early years of the Christian era. All of these were deliberately buried, presumably at times of crisis, and must therefore represent only a minute fraction of what was actually made. But both the extent of these finds and the quality of their craftsmanship suggest that there was a high consumption of silverware in late antiquity. The main sources of silver in the Roman world were Spain and the Middle East. During the Middle Ages Austrian and German mines were exploited, but evidently less successfully, and domestic plate would not seem to have been produced again on the same scale until the import of large quantities of bullion from the New World in the sixteenth century.

Silver is a soft, highly conductive and malleable metal, capable of being

— 1 —

worked into a variety of forms and decorated with numerous different techniques. When polished it takes on a brilliantly reflective surface which, combined with its relative scarcity, inevitably made it desirable. In most cultures it was considered precious, some even attributing supernatural or religious qualities to it. Unlike gold, it is rarely found in its pure state and the technical problems encountered in extracting the metal from its ore almost certainly account for the late start made in the production of silver artefacts when compared with gold. In practice, however, pure silver has seldom been used for making objects of adornment or practical use; it tends to be too soft for most purposes, and even when the problems of extracting the element had been overcome most silver was deliberately alloyed with a small proportion of other metals, such as copper, in order to improve its strength and durability.

Various techniques have been used in the manufacture of silver artefacts, or plate, such as casting molten metal in a mould or stamping silver sheet in a mechanical die. But until the mid eighteenth century the only practical means of making most basic vessel shapes involved forming a workable sheet of silver by repeatedly hammering an ingot until it was reduced to the desired thickness. For 'hollow ware', which, as its name implies, includes all vessels and containers, the basic form was usually produced by 'raising'. This is an extremely slow process whereby the silver sheet is gradually shaped by being hammered over an anvil or stake until the appropriate form has been achieved. It is complicated by the fact that the process tends to induce a hardness caused by the molecules of the metal becoming misaligned and which would in turn cause the silver to crack under further hammering. To correct this it must be subjected at frequent intervals to annealing, in which it is heated until red hot and then plunged into cold water. This has the effect of realigning the molecules and returning the silver to its characteristically malleable state.

However, while the production of other domestic metal wares, such as bronze or pewter, generally required comparatively few processes, even fairly plain silver ware normally involved a number of separate stages and techniques. The basic form of a typical eighteenth-century pear-shaped coffee pot, for example, would be raised from a sheet, first producing a hollow, bowl-like form and then gradually raising the sides until the appropriate shape was achieved. The foot and spout would be cast separately and soldered to the body. Other parts, such as the cover, finial, hinge and handle sockets, would all be raised or cast separately and

Coffee pot, silver, 1769, maker's mark of St John Barry; $11\frac{1}{2}$ in. high.

assembled together. The basically finished pot could then be decorated in a wide range of styles or techniques, including engraving, embossing, gilding or the addition of further cast ornament.

Most of the techniques involved quite different skills and although the goldsmith would generally be expected to be in command of all those necessary to his craft, in practice most workshops employed specialist workmen for all these different tasks. In addition to those who prepared the metal and raised the forms, these included chasers, engravers, makers

Castwork: Wine cistern, silver, 1701, maker's mark of Philip Rollos; 25½ in. long (National Trust, Dunham Massey, Cheshire).

of cast ornament, gilders, wire pullers and so on. Aspects of production which did not warrant the full-time employment of a specialist would be performed by 'outworkers' or sub-contractors. This system was described in 1747 by R. Campbell, who wrote in *The London Tradesman* that 'the Goldsmith employs several distinct Workmen, almost as many as there are different Articles in his Shop ... He employs, besides those in his Shop, many Hands without.' Even in the sixteenth century the hand of a particular engraver, or castings from a common source, can be recognized on objects with a variety of makers' marks. Many of the basic techniques practised in the eighteenth century had been developed at least by the Middle Ages and were essentially the same as those described in the twelfth-century treatise by Theophilus, called *De Diversibus Artibus*.[2]

Sophisticated cast ornament was produced by the lost wax process, in which a clay core was covered with wax and modelled to the shape of the finished piece. It was then encased in plaster of Paris and baked. The melted wax having run away through carefully placed channels, the cavity was filled with molten silver. But this was a complicated process and most simple

*Castwork: Basin (detail), silver, 1742, maker's mark of Paul de Lamerie
(Gilbert collection, Los Angeles County Museum of Art).*

mouldings would normally be produced by sand casting. In this technique a carved wood model was impressed into a bed of fine, slightly damp sand and the resulting impression again filled with molten metal. Hollow elements, such as spouts and handles, would be made in two halves and soldered together.

Cut-card work: Coffee pot, silver, 1709,
maker's mark of Richard Bayley; $10\frac{1}{4}$ in. high.

Even quite plain silver ware would require substantial finishing after its basic form had been assembled: hammer marks would have to be erased with the broad-headed planishing hammer and then polished with soft red sand, and the rough surfaces of castings chased and burnished before the surface acquired its characteristic reflective quality. All these processes were,

Engraving and piercing: Caster, silver, 1672,
maker's mark WC; $5\frac{1}{4}$ in. high.

to the modern mind, extraordinarily time-consuming. An ordinary sauceboat on three feet, for example, took as long as sixty hours to make and required polishing for as many as twenty hours before it was ready for sale. The basic manufacture of a tapering cylindrical coffee pot, the body of which would be made from a seamed sheet, would take between forty and sixty hours prior to polishing, whereas that of the more sophisticated pear-shaped type described above would take as long as 200 hours. Likewise, as many as forty hours would be needed for a typical mid eighteenth-century cast candlestick and 160 for a bullet-shaped teapot.[3]

Other than casting, the principal forms of decoration were engraving and embossing. The former produces a two-dimensional, linear design by means of cutting into the metal with a sharp instrument and making a fine groove in the surface. Although there were brief periods when it achieved great brilliance, such as the late sixteenth century and the early eighteenth,

Engraving: Salver (detail), silver, 1732, maker's mark of Augustine Courtauld.

it was never a particularly important feature of English silver and was usually restricted to little more than heraldic decoration. It is easily confused with a less common technique that was particularly popular during the early and late seventeenth century, known as flat-chasing. The flat-chaser uses a series of fine punches to produce a linear design by means of slightly denting the surface of the metal. The result is a comparable, but more stylized, less precise and less versatile form of decoration than engraving. The technique, which, unlike engraving, does not involve the removal of metal, can always be distinguished by the fact that the impression of the pattern can be seen on the inside of the vessel.

TOP: *Flat-chasing: Monteith bowl, silver, 1689, maker's mark TA; 13 in. diameter (National Trust, Erdigg, Clwyd).*

BOTTOM: *Embossing: Layette basket, silver, c. 1670, unmarked; 25 in. long (Gilbert Collection, Los Angeles County Museum of Art).*

Embossing is a generic term for the techniques known as *repoussé* and chasing. The two are often used together, hammering a pattern in relief from behind and sharpening, or chasing, the details from the front. It is obviously particularly suited to malleable metal of a thin gauge which can be raised in high relief to produce elaborate sculptural decoration. The work

Embossing: Plate, silver-gilt, 1787, maker's mark of William Pitts;
7½ in. diameter.

is usually carried out on a bed of pitch, which is sufficiently firm but yielding to support the object without preventing the formation of the decoration. Another special technique was described by Campbell for making small embossed medallions of silver which were sometimes let into the main body of mid eighteenth-century plate: 'a Mould is made of Clay ... into which is run Plaister of Paris ... A Piece of Plate is beat out very thin of the Figure of the Plaister Mould.' The silver sheet is then hammered with small punches over the plaster to reproduce the exact design.

Cut-card work and casting: Ewer, silver, 1715, maker's mark of David Willaume; 11½ in. high (National Trust, Attingham Park, Shropshire).

Bright-cut engraving: Cream jug, silver, 1788,
maker's mark of Daniel Smith and Robert Sharp.

Embossed decoration seems only to have been particularly popular in England during periods of strong continental influence, such as the late sixteenth, late seventeenth and mid eighteenth centuries. Although also subject to occasional periods of relative disfavour, a more consistently popular form of decoration was gilding. Silver-gilt is silver covered with a thin layer of gold, and was usually done to create a more opulent effect. Until the invention of the electrolytic process in the nineteenth century, it was a hazardous process that involved mixing ground gold with mercury under heat in the proportions of about one part gold to two parts mercury. The resulting paste was then applied to the silver and fired so that the mercury evaporated, leaving the gold alloyed to the surface. The dangers of the process, however, were well recognized in the eighteenth century, and Campbell, having described the process, goes on to observe that 'gilding is a very profitable business; few of them live long, the Fumes of the Quicksilver affect their nerves, and render their Lives a Burthen to them. The Trade is in but few hands.' Although gilding was normally applied all over an object, it was sometimes used to highlight selected areas in a technique known as 'parcel', or partial, gilding. Even with completely gilded pieces, however, it is unusual before the eighteenth century for areas not normally seen to be gilded. Gold was very much more expensive than silver (during the sixteenth century about ten times as much) and was used sparingly. When an area such as the underneath of a base has been gilded, it is usually an indication that the gilding is later.

At different times additional forms of decoration have enjoyed varying degrees of popularity, some of which, such as 'cut card' ornament and 'bright cut' engraving, are discussed in later chapters (pp. 143 and 225). The broadest range of techniques was in vogue during the sixteenth century, when sophisticated commissions called for enamelling, niello (a compound of silver and sulphur fired to the surface and resembling black enamel), etching and so on, in addition to all the more standard techniques. Many of these were revived during the second half of the nineteenth century. During other periods, notably the second half of the seventeenth century, more restrained techniques, such as matting, were also considered fashionable. This type of decoration was produced by repeatedly striking the surface with a small punch and was designed to produce a texture which contrasted with the burnished silver.

Silver and gold plate share with other metals the characteristic that, unlike ceramics, they are reusable, and when damaged, worn out or surplus to requirements can be melted down and reworked into a new object.

Sometimes this would merely involve heavy repairs or modifications, but more often it would mean melting down and making a wholly new object. Customers would frequently turn in quantities of old pewter to be remade, but silver plate – and gold even more so – was subject to quite separate pressures from those which have led to the destruction of other

Matting: Tankard, silver-gilt, 1676, maker's mark of
Francis Leake; 8¼ in. high.

domestic metalwares. The ambiguity of silver as a material for ordinary domestic objects consists not in its expense, for European glass and porcelain in their early days were also expensive, but in its recoverable value and the fact that it represented actual wealth, rather than being merely the product of wealth. This was always reflected in the price of plate, which was calculated at so much per ounce for the metal and so much per ounce for the work, or 'fashion'. The former would be relatively fixed at any one time, while the latter would vary according to the style and decoration that was agreed between the goldsmith and his patron.

Until the development of the stock market in the eighteenth century, the two principal forms of wealth were generally considered to be land and precious metal. Plate was regarded as a suitable form in which to hold gold and silver which was surplus to immediate needs, and at times of extraordinary expenditure, such as war, it was accepted that it would be melted down and converted into coinage. The added cost of having precious metal fashioned into plate was more than compensated for by the fact that, at least until the seventeenth century, it was considered important that wealth should be visible. The function of the 'buffet of plate', the display of rows of vessels that enriched medieval and Renaissance dining halls, was to display to the world the extent of the wealth, and hence the power, of its owners. But it was also intended to display their taste and their awareness of current fashions. Antiquarianism and an undiscriminating enthusiasm for old things hardly existed before the eighteenth century, and to display outmoded plate would be taken as a sign either of deficient taste or that funds to have it reworked were not available. Consequently inventories, domestic accounts and goldsmiths' ledgers until the end of the eighteenth century contain repeated references to plate being handed over to gold-smiths for remaking. It is for this reason that there is so little early silver in the care of the National Trust.[4] Great Elizabethan and Jacobean houses such as Hardwick, Blickling and Hatfield still exist, and many of them still contain at least an element of their original furniture and pictures. But their rich appearance and the vital role that plate played in their overall effect is almost impossible to recreate.

The pressures of personal finances and fashion, then, both contributed towards the periodic recycling of plate. But the pattern was also affected by economic factors of a more general kind. Until fairly recent times most economies and currencies have been closely keyed to precious metals, and from the Middle Ages to the eighteenth century there was a recurring tension between demand for new plate and the need to keep gold and silver coinage in circulation. Most European countries operated a dual system in which coins of both precious metals were in circulation, and at times when gold coinage was preferred large numbers of silver coins would be taken out of circulation and made into plate. At certain stages, such as the second half of the sixteenth century, when silver from the New World was flooding into Europe, the large-scale manufacture of plate did not have a serious impact on the economy; at others, notably in the late seventeenth century, so much silver was being hoarded in the form of plate that it was impossible for the economy to function properly and government pressure was exerted to reverse the tendency (see chapter 5, p. 142).

Most ordinary plate was made in response to needs that would normally have been served by other materials. Cups to drink from, plates to eat off, and so on, existed in overwhelmingly greater numbers in cheaper materials, such as pottery, pewter or brass, and even though few of these may survive today, it is argued in a number of places in the following chapters that utilitarian objects in precious metals were almost certainly modelled on forms already established in base metals such as pewter and brass. But equally, because of the prestige and expense associated with plate, means of substituting and imitating precious metals were devised from an early date. The most successful and well known of these was Sheffield plate, which was produced in the late eighteenth and early nineteenth centuries. Other substitutes had been available much earlier, including gilded or silvered bronze or brass and, from at least the seventeenth century, 'close plating'. The latter is a process in which the metal is dipped in molten tin, then overlaid with silver foil which is fixed to the surface by remelting the layer of tin with a soldering iron and then burnishing the silver foil.

Both the existence of such substitutes and the fact that the value of plate was obviously dependent upon the purity of the alloy presented a clear need for legislation to protect the consumer, and these have been the motives behind most hallmarking legislation over the last 500 years. The first known attempt to regulate the standard of plate in England copies earlier French legislation and dates from 1238.[5] The act entitled 'De Auro fabricando Civitate Londinium' presupposed that it was already mandatory for wrought plate to be of equal fineness to the currency, for it provided for the Mayor and Aldermen of the City of London to appoint six goldsmiths to ensure that this standard was maintained. It also specified the price of gold, ruled that gold should be 'no colour but its own' and that copper and latten should not be gilded.

The act clearly failed to prevent fraud, however, and was replaced in 1300 by a new act which introduced the first mark to be struck on plate. It also reaffirmed the essence of the previous act by ordaining that 'no goldsmith ... shall from henceforth make or cause to be made any manner of vessel, jewel or any other thing of gold or silver except that it be of the true alloy (that is to say), gold of a certain touch, and silver of the Sterling alloy ... and that none work worse silver than money, and that no manner of vessel of silver depart out of the hands of the workers, until further, that it be marked with the leopard's head'. The 'Sterling alloy' is a reference to the silver pence in circulation which were known as sterlings and which were the only currency of the time. They were composed of 92.5 per cent pure silver, alloyed with 7.5 per cent other metals, and this has been the standard known as sterling ever since.

Hallmarks: From left to right: leopard's head for London, date-letter for 1742–3, maker's mark of Paul de Lamerie, lion passant for sterling standard.

Presumably because of the difficulties that continued to arise in detecting fraud, a statute of 1363 introduced a second mark, the maker's mark, by requiring that 'each Master Goldsmith shall have a mark to himself, and which mark shall be known to those who shall be assigned by the King to supervise their works'. The final refinement to the system consisted of the addition of the year mark in 1478. This mark consisted of a letter of the alphabet; its purpose was to enable the warden responsible for marking a substandard piece to be identified, and it was to be changed every year on 19 May, the feast of St Dunstan, patron saint of goldsmiths.

Various modifications to the system have since been made from time to time, the most significant of which was the addition of the lion passant mark in 1544. No official record survives of the purpose of this new mark, but it has been suggested that this was in connection with the appointment by the crown of two officials, independent of the authority of the wardens, whose task it was to supervise the administration of the Goldsmiths' Company on behalf of the King.[6] Since then these four marks – the leopard's head, maker's mark, date letter and lion passant – have remained the marks of the London assay office, although the system was changed between 1697 and 1720.[7] Further marks have from time to time been struck in addition to these, the most important of which was the monarch's head, which was used from 1784 to 1890 to show that the duty of 6d an ounce on hallmarked plate had been paid.

The earliest method by which plate was assayed seems to modern eyes extraordinarily primitive and inexact. Known as the 'touch', this involved the use of a set of 'touch needles', each of which was alloyed with a known proportion of base-metal. The object under assay was scratched against the abrasive 'touch stone' in such a way that a small deposit of metal was left on the stone. This was then compared with a similar mark left by the touch needles. More a matter of experience than scientific analysis, this method allowed the assay master to judge whether or not the object in question was up to sterling standard by its softness or otherwise and the colour of the mark it made on the touch stone. The chief advantage of this technique was that it was quick and convenient when most assaying was carried out by the wardens in the goldsmiths' workshops. After the act of 1478 all assaying in London took place at Goldsmiths' Hall, and thereafter the much more exact method known as 'cupellation' was adopted. In this process scrapings are taken from the object, carefully weighed, and wrapped in a small sheet of lead. This package is then melted in a porous bowl of bone ash until the lead and alloying metals have been fully oxidized and absorbed into the bowl, leaving a small ingot of pure silver. Comparison of the weight of this with that of the original sample allows the exact percentage of alloy in the plate to be calculated.

The London hallmark, together with those of the other assay offices subsequently set up in towns such as Chester, Exeter, York, Birmingham and Sheffield, has rightly been regarded as the greatest tradition of consumer protection in the world. Hallmarks have also incidentally been an invaluable tool to historians of silver, in that they make it possible to identify the place and time that the object was assayed and very often the goldsmith in whose workshop it was made. But the convenient existence of such a tool has arguably led to a certain complacency among historians of the subject, who have not always made sufficient allowance for its limitations. The maker's mark, for example, is often assumed to be the equivalent of an artist's signature, whereas it should more properly be thought of as the sponsor's mark and is intended to identify the master who presented the object for assay and who represented it as being of sterling standard; similarly, the date letter was introduced to record when the object was marked, so that the assay master responsible could be identified in the event of a dispute subsequently arising. They were never intended to imply that the object was actually made at that time or by that master – although it was normally expected that goldsmiths should present their own works for assay – and there is plenty of evidence of plate having been hallmarked at a later date, such as when it appeared on the market as second-hand, and of goldsmiths striking their own mark on plate made by another master but which they were offering for sale. It has also been tempting to regard the earliest surviving hallmarked example of a particular form as evidence of when that form was first introduced. However, the earliest survivals are seldom prototypes, and inventories, especially in the sixteenth and seventeenth centuries, often make it perfectly clear that certain categories of plate had been in currency long before the date of their earliest known representatives.

With the exception of a few periods of political isolation, the history of English silver, as of other crafts, has been one of repeated compromises between the assimilation of continental influences and the assertion of peculiarly English characteristics. The vitality of the former has been all the greater because of a long history of refugee craftsmen, often victims of religious persecution, settling in England, and while the degree of assimilation or the strength of self-assertion has varied from time to time, continental influence has seldom been hard to find, especially at the top end of the market. Generally the Englishness of English silver has been expressed through its native robustness and individuality of form while the impact of the Continent has been in technique and decoration. A sixteenth-century writer's comments on Flemish weavers could equally be applied to goldsmiths when he wrote that 'we ought to favour the strangers from whom we have learned so great benefits ... because we are not so good devisors as followers of others'.[8] But in time the settled strangers became strangers no longer; in any event, the role of the craftsman was always that of servant to his patron and, enlightened servant though he may have been, his career would hardly have been successful had he not been prepared to comply with the typically English demands of his customers.

Two

THE EARLY TUDORS

The sixteenth century was a period of dramatic change in England. Politically this appeared as a pattern of recovery after the Wars of the Roses, followed by flamboyant and expansive diplomacy during the reign of Henry VIII and cost-counting, economically hard-headed retrenchment during the second half of the century. Socially it was expressed through the changing life-styles of the aristocratic, merchant and developing 'professional' classes, through the contents of their houses and their steadily improving material expectations. For the lower orders of society – agricultural workers, artisans and servants – relatively greater or lesser poverty remained the only serious expectation in life, with actual conditions changing little or even worsening somewhat towards the end of the century.

The same patterns are clearly reflected in the development of the gold-smith's craft and the expansion of his trade. For much of his reign Henry VIII (r. 1509–47) was the richest monarch in northern Europe. The evidence we have suggests that plate made for the King and the aristocracy during the second quarter of the century was as fine as any made in Europe, but that during the second half of the century there was a marked decline in the standards of craftsmanship of London goldsmiths. A visiting Venetian remarked in about 1500 that 'the riches of England are greater than those of any other place in Europe',[1] but by the beginning of the following century complaints were being made by the Goldsmiths' Company of declining standards and the failure of most journeymen to have mastered even the basic skills of the craft.[2] At a lower level, however, while quality may have declined, quantity certainly seems to have increased. Inventories of ordinary domestic silver and base metal over the century show a gradually growing supply, with an ever expanding range of items in silver and pewter penetrating an increasingly broad section of society. On the other hand, domestic metalwork beyond the most basic implements and vessels played a very limited role in the lives of the lowest social ranks. Before the effects of industrialization made themselves felt during the second half of the eighteenth century, the history of silver and base metal in England is essentially concerned with the middle classes and above. A silver spoon in the mid sixteenth century would have cost 4s., the equivalent of the relatively high wages paid to a worker in the building industry for about a week and rather more than would have been earned by a skilled craftsman. The possession of something even as modest as a silver spoon was, therefore, essentially a middle-class aspiration.

The study of domestic silver from the sixteenth century and earlier is hampered by the fact that the physical evidence we have is very inadequate. Most of the information available is in the form of inventories and wills rather than surviving objects, and the great rarity of silver and metalwork from the Tudor period, especially from the first three quarters of the century, makes it very difficult to form a clear view of the range and appearance of objects that were in daily use. Nor are surviving objects a fair sample of what was actually made, since time has dealt unevenly with different categories of plate. Gold and silver of the very finest quality would all have been in the possession of the King, the wealthiest aristocratic families and the pre-Reformation monasteries and cathedrals. But while old plate belonging to the Church would generally (until the Reformation) have been reasonably sure of preservation, that in secular possession would always have been the first asset to be liquidated at times of financial necessity and was liable to periodic replacement by more fashionable vessels: of this category virtually nothing remains. For example, one of the greatest early houses in the possession of the National Trust, Hardwick Hall, still contains furniture and works of art which were originally made for the house, but not a single piece of the enormous collection of silver listed in the inventory of 1601.[3] Henry VIII's Jewel House contained over 800 items of gold and silver plate, but only a solitary piece, the medieval royal gold cup in the British Museum, is known to survive.

At the other end of the scale, ordinary domestic plate was subject to the additional pressures of wear and tear and was less likely to be preserved by later generations on grounds of sentimental or antiquarian interest. Although made in vastly greater quantities, therefore, the material on which to base a survey of the most common categories of plate in the early sixteenth century is limited to a few chance survivals. The middle range of plate, on the other hand, has fared considerably better. This is the type, usually decorated and often of a ceremonial nature, that has been preserved through ownership by stable institutions such as Oxford and Cambridge colleges, City livery companies and parish churches. The temptation, however, is to treat such a numerically predominant group among surviving plate as a fair sample, when in fact it is representative only of one category of plate of the period.

The relative cultural backwardness of England at the turn of the sixteenth century is indicated as much by the style of plate as by its range. By 1500 Italian artists had been working in the Renaissance style for approaching half a century, but in England and other northern European countries it failed to make any general impact for another two decades. There, the fashionable style was still gothic. The application of this familiar style to plate is illustrated by the very few works of art in precious metal that survive from the medieval period, such as the so-called King John Cup in King's Lynn, which dates from the fourteenth century.[4] The forms are architectural, attenuated and complex and the surface is lavishly decorated with polychrome enamel and precious stones. Its effect is more akin to jewellery on a large scale than to plate.

Objects such as this, however, would always have been exceptional. Typical of more standard late medieval display plate is the early sixteenth-century Richmond Cup in the collection of the Armourers' and Braziers' Company. It is of an organic form in which shape and ornament are unified. There is no clear division between the different elements of its construction; the line between the bowl and the cover is unbroken and the impression is one of a single plant-like form. This is enhanced by the ornament of the cup, which is also derived from nature. The pronounced spherical finial is a characteristic feature of the period, a common alternative taking a hemispherical form with the donor's or owner's coat of arms engraved on the top.

The Richmond Cup is influenced by German design and reflects the strong presence of foreign goldsmiths in London during the sixteenth century. It has been estimated that by the year 1500 no fewer than 3,000 alien craftsmen were settled in London, which was as much as 10 per cent of the male population.[5] By 1540 their numbers had swelled still further, giving considerable concern to the authorities. The impact of such numbers on goldsmiths' work was inevitably dramatic, and throughout the first half of the century the evolution of design for fashionable decorated plate was dominated by ideas of continental origin. A further channel for continental influence was the introduction of printed 'pattern books'. These engraved designs for vessels and ornament intended for use in the workshop were

Richmond Cup, silver-gilt, early sixteenth century, maker's mark a wreath;
12½ in. high (Armourers' and Braziers' Company).

produced in centres such as Frankfurt, Nuremberg and Antwerp and were
known in England from at least the second quarter of the century.

The assimilation of continental ideas in England was undoubtedly accelerated by the presence at court of the German artist Hans Holbein (1497–
1543). His sophisticated Renaissance style is illustrated by his design for a

gold cup made to celebrate the marriage of Henry VIII to Jane Seymour in 1536.[6] This drawing is a work of art of the highest order and is no more representative of the kind of plate ordinarily made at the time than the King John Cup is of its period. But in a diluted form its essential stylistic features are reflected in lesser plate of the second quarter of the century.

Rochester Tazzas, silver-gilt, 1528–31; $8\frac{1}{4}$in. high
(British Museum, London).

Two standing bowls and covers of 1528 and 1531 in the British Museum are typical of the early Renaissance style as applied to fashionable but practical domestic plate: they are constructed in a rational manner, with feet, stems and bowls strictly zoned and a strong emphasis on the horizontal rather than the vertical. The range of ornament, too, is quite different from earlier plate, taking its inspiration from the abstract repertoire of Renaissance architecture rather than from nature.

Although these are not in the court style of the King John and Seymour Cups, they are certainly vessels of prestige which would have lent dignity to their owner. Status and the ranking of society was an important aspect of medieval life which in no way diminished during the Tudor period. It was reflected in carefully regulated customs, concerning matters such as the number of attendants it was proper for a nobleman of one rank or another to have in his retinue, or the quality of fur or cloth that it was permissible for him to wear. Status was also integral to the buffet of plate. In fifteenth-century Burgundy a sovereign and his consort were entitled to a *dressoir*, or buffet, of five tiers, a prince to four, a countess to three and nobles of lesser rank to one or two.[7] Similar customs, if not actually enforced by law, regulated what was proper for any individual to display in Tudor England. The few glimpses we have of the buffet of plate, such as the illustration of the Duc de Berry dining, taken from his *Très Riches Heures*,[8] suggest that these were decorated but functional vessels, rather than sophisticated jewelled or enamelled pieces. Their prestige would, however, usually be enhanced by gilding, which was fashionable throughout the sixteenth century but added considerably to the cost of the finished article. These higher costs are reflected in the (second-hand) values placed on plate in many surviving inventories, such as that of Archbishop Parker, dating from the middle of the century, which valued silver at 4s. 8d. an ounce and silver-gilt at 5s. 4d. an ounce.[9] In 1614 the Earl of Northampton's silver was valued at 5s. an ounce, as against 6s. for silver-gilt.[10]

The buffet was not generally intended only for a fixed display of plate, but was used also as a sideboard on which vessels in use during the meal were kept and from which cups and flagons would from time to time be taken and then returned. In this, as in other things, Cardinal Wolsey (d. 1530) was the exception to the rule. George Cavendish describes the banquet given by the Cardinal for the French Ambassador in 1527, in which 'there was a cupboard made, for the time, in length, of the nether end of the same chamber, six desks high, full of gilt plate, very sumptuous, and of the newest fashions ... This cupboard was barred about that no man might come nigh it; for there was none of the same plate occupied or stirred during this feast, for there was sufficient besides.'[11]

With the exception of unusually splendid banquets such as this, status was expressed not only in the buffet itself, but in the kinds of vessels that were in use during the meal. Cups with covers tended to be reserved for the master of the house or important guests, and the provision or absence of a cover was an indication of the status of the intended user. In 1572 the Mercers' Company possessed plate 'necessary for Company suppers', including ten gilt covered cups for the Court, twenty-four sets of goblets or bowls with four covers for the Livery and eight dozen drinking pots with two covers only for the rest of the guests.[12]

From the point of view of prestige and ceremony, the most important type of plate during the early sixteenth century was the standing cup and cover. Odd survivals, such as the Lacock Cup of about 1450 in the British Museum,[13] as well as frequent references in medieval inventories, show that this was an established form well before the Tudor period. But it is only from the late fifteenth century that sufficient numbers survive for a survey to be attempted. Until about 1520 one of the most usual basic formulas consisted of an inverted bell-shaped bowl and thick cylindrical stem on a spreading foot. The cover was generally of a shallow, stepped conical form and with a large finial. The Richmond Cup, the astonishingly plain Anathema Cup of 1481 at Pembroke College, Cambridge,[14] and the highly decorated Leigh Cup in the collection of the Mercers' Company[15] are all of this type. But although goldsmiths seem to have had a fairly standard approach to shape, the decoration of these cups shows great inventiveness and variety. The Richmond Cup is decorated with entirely abstract embossing, the Warden's Grace Cup of about 1480 at New College, Oxford,[16] is chased with a closely packed design of fruits, and a cup of 1520 at Christ's College, Cambridge,[17] is flat-chased throughout with scalework.

As far as we can tell from surviving examples, this approach seems largely to have been reversed during the second quarter of the century, with decoration becoming gradually more uniform, and form more varied. It is difficult to trace the exact course of this development, although it is clear that by around the middle of the century the formula which had gained general acceptance, possibly under the influence of continental printed pattern books, was the highly adaptable vase shape. The few standing cups to survive from this transitional period show a striking variety, as native, medieval designs reacted with new ideas from Europe. The Scudamore Cup of 1529 in the Victoria and Albert Museum (see p. 34) is of conservative shape, although its decoration betrays its date. The Howard Grace Cup of 1525[18] is in complete contrast, with a much stronger horizontal emphasis in its construction. At the same time, bowls tended to become deeper and more straight-sided. A cup of 1553 in the collection of the Armourers' and Braziers' Company[19] represents the standard formula for a moderately decorated mid-century cup.

Throughout the sixteenth century a special ceremonial role was played by the salt cellar. Salt was a costly and important commodity during the Middle Ages, but in England it was also invested with a social significance that accounts for the prominence of the grandest plate made to contain it. Since medieval times the salt cellar had reflected an obsessive concern with the proper ranking of society and had been used to mark the place of the host or important guest on the high table. The expression 'to be below the salt' has its origins in this custom. In decorative terms it performed a similar function to the table centrepiece of a later period, and the grandest examples

Hour-glass salt, silver-gilt, c. 1500, unmarked; $9\frac{1}{4}$ in. high
(Christ's College, Cambridge).

were used as vehicles for elaborate sculptural fantasies by the late medieval goldsmiths. Very few of these survive, though the late fifteenth-century Giant Salt and Monkey Salt at All Souls and New College, Oxford,[20] are both examples of this form, while contemporary inventories testify to many more.

We have no clear idea of the appearance of the most imposing salts of the first and second quarters of the century, such as were commissioned for the King or Cardinal Wolsey. As with other categories of plate from this period, surviving examples even of more standard types are so rare that any conclusions based on this tiny sample are at best tentative. However, it would seem that towards the end of the fifteenth century a new form evolved, known, from its shape, as the hour-glass salt. The term is not new and occurs in records of the period. One of the earliest known is a highly elaborate silver-gilt openwork salt of about 1500 at Corpus Christi College, Oxford,[21] while a pair of simpler examples is at Christ's College, Cambridge. All have been preserved because they were part of the plate bequeathed by the founders of the colleges, Bishop Foxe (d. 1528) and Lady Margaret Beaufort (1443–1509), mother of Henry VII. Together they show the two extremes of elaboration or plainness in which this form seems to have been produced and, in view of the importance of their original owners, it is reasonable to suppose that both would have been regarded as acceptable in the greatest of households. Although decorated in quite different ways, these and other surviving examples conform to the same basic formula: a waisted construction, symmetrical about its large knop, with a shallow receptacle for the salt and generally with a cover. The status associated with a ceremonial salt of this kind would have made a cover indispensable and it may safely be assumed that surviving coverless examples were originally supplied with one.

The latest hour-glass salts date from the second quarter of the century, and a new formula does not seem to have won general acceptance until about 1550. Between about 1520 and 1550 our knowledge of ceremonial salts is virtually a complete blank, although one or two odd survivals, such as a salt of 1522 in the collection of the Goldsmiths' Company,[22] give some idea of the experiments that were being conducted with form. The formula that eventually prevailed was the drum, or pedestal, salt which appears to figure in inventories from as early as the 1540s. The chances of survival, however, have spared no examples of this important category from the second quarter of the century, and it is impossible adequately to document its development during this crucial period before about 1560, after which known examples are relatively numerous.

The third major category of ceremonial plate in the Tudor period was the ewer and basin. This also had a practical role, and as such remained one of the most important items of plate throughout the Middle Ages and until the mid seventeenth century. Even during the reign of Elizabeth I (1558–

1603) the fork was far from usual in England. The Royal Jewel House inventory of 1574[23] lists only thirteen silver forks, and elsewhere they were regarded with suspicion. As late as 1617 the traveller Fynes Moryson observed with some disapproval 'a custom in all those Italian cities and towns through which I passed that is not used in any other country that I

Ewer and basin, silver-gilt, 1545, maker's mark a queen's head;
diameter of basin 18 in. (Corpus Christi College, Cambridge).

saw in my travels ... The Italians ... do always at their meals use a little fork when they cut their meat. The reason for this their curiosity is because the Italian cannot endure by any means to have his dish touched by fingers, seeing all men's fingers are not alike clean.'[24] The ewer and basin was consequently essential to civilized eating, and diners would be given the opportunity of rinsing their fingers between courses.

Its prominence and size made the ewer and basin an ideal item for display, and throughout the century they were lavishly decorated in the latest styles. But just as they were essential before the arrival of the fork, so equally they were made redundant by its adoption, and their substantial bullion content has ensured that very few survive. English examples from the sixteenth century probably amount to less than a dozen. The enormous extent of this destruction is put in perspective by the fact that an equal number are listed on the 1601 inventory of Hardwick Hall alone. The earliest basin to survive is apparently one of 1493 at Corpus Christi College, Oxford,[25] while the earliest paired ewer and basin, hallmarked for 1545, is in the collection of the college of the same name in Cambridge, presented by its benefactor Archbishop Parker (1504–75). Our knowledge of the formal development of the ewer during the first half of the century is therefore woefully inadequate. Its form, however, is suggested from a number of sources, such as contemporary paintings, base-metal ewers and small altar cruets. These follow a surprisingly uniform pattern and are generally of an elongated pear form with a foot and stem similar to those of contemporary cups. The form of the 1545 ewer is quite different from this and it is impossible to know when it first appeared, although a ewer of 'helmet facion' referred to in a royal inventory of 1520 was probably of this type.[26] Its inspiration is unquestionably Flemish, since it is almost identical to a contemporary ewer with basin in the National Museum of Wales, bearing marks for Bruges,[27] and the same form is also found in Flemish paintings of the period. Although translated into another form, it has all the characteristics of the Renaissance style that were discussed in relation to cups: in particular a strong emphasis on horizontality and a clear visual separation of its various parts.

The range of ornament which would have decorated much of this lost plate can be surmised from smaller objects which survive in rather greater numbers. Native traits still in vogue during the first quarter of the century included the use of naturalistic foliage, embossed spiral flutes, sun-rays or scalework that avoided the disciplined exactitude of the Renaissance style. Surfaces were enlivened by embossing, die-stamping or piercing and motifs derived from gothic architecture such as trefoils, quatrefoils and friezes which were all designed to break up, rather than consolidate, the sense of line and form. A number of these features characterize the silver-gilt cup of 1524 at Charlecote Park, the only example of early Tudor plate of any importance in the National Trust's collection.

The changes in design which become noticeable from about 1525, on the other hand, were mainly of continental origin and were due in part to the influence of Holbein. But their rapid dissemination had much more to do with the circulation of printed pattern books which were becoming available for the first time. New decorative motifs which appeared during this period can also be traced to the same sources. One of the most influential of these was published in Frankfurt by Hans Brosamer under the title *Ein New Kunstbüchlein*[28] and was evidently familiar to the maker of the 1536 Boleyn Cup at Cirencester Church. It contained a number of designs which, in addition to sharing carefully ordered construction, reflect new motifs, such as the use of loosely classical medallions and a pattern of abstract scrolling foliage. Because of the scarcity of early Tudor plate, we

Charlecote Cup, silver-gilt, 1524, maker's mark a mullet; $4\frac{3}{4}$ in. high
(National Trust, Charlecote Park, Warwickshire).

have very little evidence for the use of the latter pattern, but it was probably quite common around the middle decades of the century. It is engraved, for example, around the lip of the Boleyn Cup and embossed on the body of a small casting bottle of 1553.

A major type of engraved ornament first found on English plate around 1540 is known as the 'moresque' or 'arabesque'. As its name suggests, this abstract foliage decoration is of Hispano-moresque derivation. It appears in

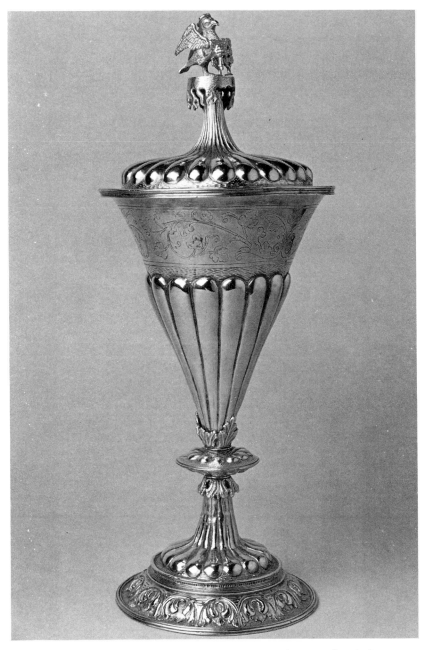

*Boleyn Cup, silver-gilt, 1536, maker's mark three flowers; $12\frac{3}{8}$ in. high
(Cirencester parish church, Gloucestershire).*

Holbein's design for the Seymour Cup and was probably already creeping into the general repertoire some time before the publication in 1548 of Thomas Geminus's *Morysse and Damashine Renewed*.[29] Strapwork, too, derived from the plaster decoration of Francis I's (r. 1515–45) palace at Fontainebleau, was used by Holbein but popularized by the printed designs

Casting bottle, silver-gilt, 1553,
maker's mark a device; $5\frac{3}{4}$ in. high
(Gilbert Collection, Los Angeles).

of Balthasar Sylvius, published in 1554.[30] This proved to be one of the most successful motifs of Tudor decorative art; by the second half of the century it had become quite ubiquitous and there is virtually no plate of the period on which it does not feature.

Early Tudor plate of a utilitarian nature has fared even less well than its ceremonial counterpart. It is impossible to give a reliable account of the development of different forms prior to the middle of the century, though such survivals as can be traced do enable some sort of picture to be pieced together. Although the early part of this chapter implies a clear distinction

Scudamore Cup, silver-gilt, 1529,
maker's mark a merchant's mark; $8\frac{3}{8}$ in. high
(on loan to the Victoria and Albert Museum, London).

between ceremonial and utilitarian plate, this needs some qualification. The division is blurred by the fact that the possession of drinking vessels or dishes in silver rather than pewter conveyed status in itself, and even objects of a quite unpretentious character could, in this sense, be used in a ceremonial capacity. Thus, for example, plain domestic font-shaped cups of the early sixteenth century were sometimes provided with a cover, as would have been proper for the master of the house. At the same time elaborate

Hour-glass, silver-gilt and glass, c. 1540, unmarked;
7 in. high (Museum of Fine Arts, Boston).

decoration did not necessarily imply purely a ceremonial role, and practical plate was often quite elaborately decorated.

Plate from the first half of the century falling into this category includes, among others, goblets, bowls and decorative spoons. Odd survivals such as the instrument case belonging to the Barber-Surgeons' Company[31] or an hour-glass in the Boston Museum of Fine Arts testify to the wide range of objects made by goldsmiths which have almost completely disappeared. But rare though decorated plate is, it tends to have survived in considerably larger numbers than the severely plain, which is almost completely un-represented from the first half of the century.

Cressner Cup, silver-gilt and verre églomisé, 1503,
maker's mark a crossbow; 6⅜ in. high (Goldsmiths' Company).

The font-shaped cup is the only type of secular hollow ware to survive in significant numbers. Even though only about a dozen examples are known, they share a family likeness which suggests that it was a standard form of the day. One of the earliest is the Cressner Cup of 1503 in the Goldsmiths' Company Collection. It has a shallow bowl with straight sides, a stunted tapering stem and a heavy ring moulding applied for strength to the foot. The cover is of fairly flat profile and with a disproportionately large finial which is decorated with a coat of arms. With or without a cover, this is basically the formula for all these cups, although they were subject to a wide variety of decorative treatment. These vessels were presumably intended for wine. Certainly the shallow, stemmed bowls of the second half of the century had that use, and a transitional stage in the evolution from one to the other can probably be recognized in the Charlecote Cup of 1524

Beaker, silver, 1525, maker's mark a device; 4 in. diameter
(Gilbert Collection, Los Angeles).

and a cup of 1557 in the Kremlin.[32] These have wider, shallower bowls than the font-shaped cup, but the same characteristic straight sides.

Possibly also connected with wine-drinking is a type of two-handled covered cup which survives in very small numbers, including two hall-marked for 1533 and 1555, at the Corpus Christi Colleges in Oxford and Cambridge.[33] These extraordinary little vessels appear to have no precursors, although their successors might perhaps have been the so-called 'ox-eye' or 'college' cups of the early seventeenth century (see p. 101).

More mundane domestic plate survives in odd instances, but on far too small a scale for a proper view to be formed: a beaker of 1496[34] and another of 1525 can be cited, for example, but no domestic silver bowls or plates from the first half of the century have yet come to light. The form of the 1525 beaker is apparently unique, but it is closely related to German *Waldglass* 'Maigelein' cups and it possibly represents a type that would have been quite common at the time. The likely appearance of certain types of plain domestic plate can, however, probably be inferred from other sources. Whereas fashionable decorated plate tended to originate in pattern books or drawings by artists, plate of a more mundane nature, which was only exceptional in so far as it was made of silver, was almost certainly derived from similar objects in more ordinary materials. In the sixteenth century this was principally pewter. This conjecture is given some support by comparisons such as that of a plain silver drinking pot of 1556[35] with an almost identical pewter example dated 1545 which was recently excavated from the wreck of Henry VIII's flagship, the *Mary Rose*.

While the export of precious metal was forbidden during the fifteenth and sixteenth centuries, English pewter enjoyed a considerable reputation abroad. As early as the late fifteenth century an Italian visitor wrote of 'vessels as brilliant as if they were made of fine silver, and these are held in great estimation'.[36] Writing in the third quarter of the sixteenth century William Harrison echoes the same sentiment: 'In some places beyond the sea a garnish of good flat English pewter of an ordinary making ... is esteemed almost so precious as the like number of vessels that are made of fine silver.'[37] This was undoubtedly due in part to the high quality and strictly controlled alloy used in England, but it also reflected technical advances, such as the introduction of bronze moulds, which improved both the quality of castings and the rate of production, or the fly wheel which improved the finish of objects. These technical advances placed the industry in an excellent position to respond to the enormous social changes of the middle of the century which form the subject of the next chapter. Although still out of reach of the poor and far more expensive than alternative materials (a single substantial item of pewter in the middle of the sixteenth century would still have cost the equivalent of a whole day's average wage), it was enormously cheaper than silver. During the early sixteenth century finished pewter cost in the region of 4s. for 12 lb.,[38] which was approximately the price of a single ounce of finished silver. At a rough approximation, therefore, the cost of plate during the first quarter of the century was something of the order of 160 times that of pewter. In practice this gap would admittedly have been narrowed to some extent by the fact that pewter is heavier than silver, object for object, but the difference would still have been vast.

The softness of pewter together with its hard daily use has made examples from the sixteenth century even rarer than silver. Nonetheless, a few chance survivals have been found, mostly in excavations, which throw some further light on the likely appearance of contemporary utilitarian plate. Whereas plate in early sixteenth-century use seems to have related both to eating

Drinking pot, pewter, dated 1545; 6 in. high
(Mary Rose Trust, Portsmouth).

and drinking, most pewter was used for eating. As much as 80 per cent of items described in inventories comprises objects such as plates, dishes, chargers and saucers.[39] Other groups were candlesticks, pots and flagons, but until quite late in the sixteenth century these were not of great numerical significance. A dish in the collection of the Pewterers' Company,[40] excavated from the foundations of Guy's Hospital in 1899 and tentatively dated to the early sixteenth century, has a plain rim of about one-seventh its diameter and a slightly raised centre. A small saucer of about five inches diameter, recently excavated and evidently lost when still quite new, has the same characteristics on a smaller scale. Its virtually mint state also preserves its

Porringer, pewter, early sixteenth century;
diameter of bowl 6½ in. (Pewterers' Company).

original finish and the marks where it was turned on the lathe. Exactly the same form is displayed in a late sixteenth-century silver dinner service, some fourteen plates and dishes of which are still preserved in a private collection in Scotland (see p. 80),[41] a similarity which illustrates not only the kinship between silver and pewter forms for domestic wares, but also the relative irrelevance of fashion to non-decorative plate.

A category of pewter represented by several examples is a small single or two-handled bowl known as a porringer. They are first referred to in the records of the Pewterers' Company in 1556, when it was ordained that 'no person shall make or cause to be made any eare dishes ... except such eares be cast in the moulde together with the body of such dishes so made, and not to be sontered [soldered] to the body as heretofore they have done'.[42] The purpose of these dishes is not entirely clear, although it would seem likely that they were made to contain some sort of gruel. It is almost certainly significant, however, that while a number survive in pewter from the sixteenth century, the earliest known examples in silver do not occur until well into the seventeenth. Moreover, when they do occur in silver, they closely follow the pattern established in pewter between half and three-quarters of a century earlier. The most reasonable inference, therefore, is that the pewter version was the innovator and silver the imitator.

Other significant categories of pewter during the first half of the century that might relate to silver forms of the period are candlesticks and spoons. The latter compare very closely with datable silver spoons and have an equally wide range of finials. We can be less certain when inferring from pewter candlesticks to silver ones, since, although wills and inventories show that they were quite plentiful, none survives in silver and virtually none in pewter. An almost solitary survivor is in the Museum of London. This was excavated from a mid fifteenth-century deposit in London. It has features in common with early sixteenth-century continental brass candlesticks, such as a cylindrical stem with moulded details and a circular foot with sunken centre. While certainly not constituting proof, therefore, such comparisons probably provide the best clues available to the form of standard silver candlesticks of the period.

Two other categories of domestic plate, on the other hand, have survived in rather more representative numbers and both, at least in part, for the same reason: the small bullion content of silver-mounted pieces and spoons made their usefulness relatively greater than their financial value and they were correspondingly less likely to be melted down. A silver spoon, as we have seen, would be worth about 4s. and the mount to an ordinary wooden mazer bowl not much more, whereas standing cups or other more substantial plate would have realized several pounds when melted down.

Vessels were mounted with silver, or 'trimmed', to use the term found in contemporary inventories, for a variety of reasons. Sometimes mounts were provided in order to make a broken or impractical piece usable, sometimes to enhance its appearance or to add dignity to a rare artefact or natural 'curiosity', such as ceramic, glass, nautilus shell or rock-crystal. But the fashion for mounting objects extended beyond the rare and curious, and the largest categories of mounted pieces were in fact those made of quite common materials. Foreign visitors regarded this as something of an English eccentricity, and Etienne Perlin remarked in 1558 that 'the English use much beer, both double and single strength, and drink it not in glasses, but in earthenware jugs, whose handles are of silver, and also the lids; and this is what is done in houses where they are fairly well to do'.[43]

The most common surviving mounted objects from the late fifteenth and early sixteenth century are turned mazer wood bowls. Before glazed pottery

Candlestick, pewter, early sixteenth century;
4 in. high (Museum of London).

became generally available the commonest material for bowls and plates, or 'trenchers', was wood. Wooden bowls with silver mounts are known to have been made since at least the early Middle Ages, but only survive in any numbers from the fourteenth and fifteenth centuries. Earlier examples tend to have comparatively deep bowls and narrow lips with decoration generally confined to the 'print' — the small circular boss in the centre of

Standing mazer, silver-gilt and turned wood, 1529,
maker's mark IC with orb and cross; 6½ in. high (All Souls College, Oxford,
on loan to Ashmolean Museum, Oxford).

the bowl – which might be embossed, engraved or enamelled. Late fifteenth-
and early sixteenth-century mazers begin to have broader flaring lips,
usually with stamped or engraved decoration to the border and occasionally
embellished with an inscription.

A grander and more formal version of the same vessel was the standing
mazer. The late fifteenth-century 'Three Kings Mazer' at Corpus Christi

College, Cambridge[44] (so called because of the names Jasper, Melchior and Balthazar engraved around its lip), is of this type, and another of 1529 is in the collection of All Souls College, Oxford. In 1528 Cardinal Wolsey presented his college in Ipswich with a 'standing Masar with a cover and foote silvar and gilte standing upon iij [three] Lyons'.[45] The only standing mazer to survive with a cover is the Barber Surgeons' Cup of 1543, the original bowl of which was presumably wood and has been replaced by silver. But while financial considerations must have been a significant factor in having simple mazers 'trimmed' with a band of silver, the saving of expense can hardly have been a serious motive in the more imposing covered standing mazers such as this, where the wooden bowl actually makes up a fairly small part of its overall mass, and it must be assumed that such improbable combinations of the mundane and opulent had their origins in tradition.

Other than mazers, the most frequently mounted material during the late fifteenth and early sixteenth century was coconut. Its shape and non-porous nature made it ideal for mounting into drinking vessels and it continued to enjoy periods of popularity until as late as the latter part of the eighteenth century. Continental goldsmiths, especially later in the sixteenth century, frequently took advantage of its decorative potential by carving relief scenes in the outer wall of the nut, but in England they were generally left plain or polished.

The fashion referred to by Etienne Perlin for drinking from silver-mounted earthenware pots seems to have developed during the second quarter of the century. The Rhenish stoneware pots that became so ubiquitous later in the century first appeared with mounts from about 1530, and two *façon de Venise* glass pots of similar form in the British Museum[46] and the Museum of London, hallmarked for 1546 and 1548, may give some indication of the state of glass-making in England, although it is possible that the glass, like the stoneware, was imported. The form of these vessels, with their characteristic bulbous bodies and cylindrical necks, is quite novel and was perhaps derived from Persian metalware which may have found its way to Europe.

A smaller variety of mounted objects survive from the first than from the second half of the century, but documentary sources reveal a wide range of materials being used, including agate, alabaster, mother-of-pearl and horn. A few freak survivals, such as a chalcedony bowl of about 1500 at New College, Oxford,[47] the rock-crystal Giant Salt at All Souls and the cover to a fourteenth-century nautilus cup in the same collection[48] also testify to the taste for exotic materials.

Cup, silver-gilt and coconut, early sixteenth century, unmarked; $8\frac{1}{4}$ in. high (Ironmongers' Company).

Parr Pot, silver-gilt and glass, 1546, maker's mark a fleur de lys;
6 in. high (Museum of London).

The survival of Tudor spoons in disproportionately large numbers is attributable more to the sentimental importance that was attached to them than to their relatively low scrap value. Throughout the Middle Ages and the sixteenth century silver spoons were regarded as peculiarly personal objects. They are frequently mentioned specifically in wills, and apostle spoons, whether singly or in sets, were a standard christening gift. The survival intact of so few sets of spoons is due to the fact that it was usual for testators to divide them, often their most valuable single possession, between the beneficiaries.

Their prominence in late medieval and Tudor life also ensured a much wider demand for silver spoons than for other kinds of plate, and accounts for the thriving provincial trade in spoon-making at a time when the market for other kinds of plate was largely concentrated in London. Many spoons

Group of spoons, silver. From left to right:
slip top, 1500, maker's mark a device;
writhen top, 1509, maker's mark a device;
'maidenhead' finial, 1514, maker's mark a device.

survive from the sixteenth and seventeenth centuries with known or unidentified provincial marks, and the records of the Goldsmiths' Company show that much of their business during periodic 'visitations' to inspect provincial goldsmiths' workshops was concerned with breaking spoons of sub-standard alloy and imposing fines on their makers.

The most characteristic features of late medieval spoons are an ovoid bowl, pointed where it meets the stem and of pronounced crescent-shaped profile. The stem is generally of diamond-shaped or hexagonal section, tapering and with a variety of decorative finials. The most popular types, to judge both from existing spoons and inventory descriptions, had acorn or diamond-shaped finials. Throughout the sixteenth century these basic characteristics were retained, although gradually modified in certain

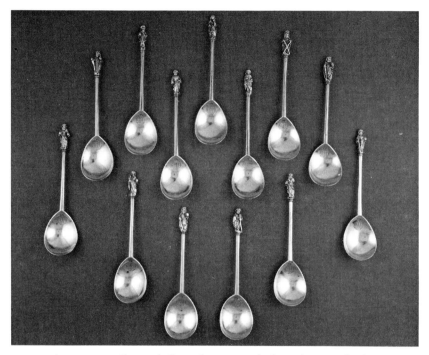

Astor spoons, silver and silver-gilt, 1532, maker's mark a corn sheaf or a sheaf of arrows (British Museum, London).

respects. Bowls became shallower and more rounded, the hexagonal stem became standard and the range of finials seems to have increased. Abstract decorative finials are found in varying degrees of rarity, such as 'seal tops', 'wrythern tops' and 'diamond points', while a wide range of sculptural finials was also produced. The most common of these were apostle spoons, which were made from at least the late fifteenth century onwards. The complete set generally comprised thirteen spoons, with twelve apostles and Christ, or 'the Master', but only two complete sets are known to survive intact from the first half of the century, the set of 1527 in the Huntington Library, California,[49] and the Astor set of 1532 in the British Museum.

The finials of apostle and other decorative spoons were separately cast and then soldered to the spoon, and the extraordinarily high quality of the best of these miniature sculptures is illustrated by the Astor spoons. Generally, however, they were not finished with such care after being taken from the mould, and more often the finials have a coarseness that became more pronounced as the century advanced and apostle spoons became available to a progressively wider market.

Other kinds of decorative finials, such as the 'lion sejant', 'maidenhead' or 'woodwose', give some indication of the variety that was available, but inventories reveal a far wider range than any survivors, including many of a heraldic nature. A will of 1546 describes 'ij sylver sponys withe angells on the knoppys gylted', another of 1536 lists 'sylver spones with myters, the myters beyng gilt'. The inventory of Henry VIII's jewel house, apart from recording no fewer than sixty-eight spoons of gold, also describes many types quite unrepresented by survivals, such as 'xij silver Spones wt Columbynes at the endes', 'xxiiij Spones of Silver gilt wherof xij hathe Sicles at ther endes' or 'Five Spones gilt wt Rooses in the knoppes'.[50]

In their variety and inventiveness spoons are a microcosm of early Tudor plate, but in the unevenness of their survival they are also a reminder of the distorted picture likely to emerge from a history of early sixteenth-century plate based on the evidence of surviving pieces alone. This distortion is certainly modified, but not to any very great extent, by surviving objects from the second half of the century.

Three

THE ELIZABETHAN AGE

It is usual to associate styles in English silver with reigning monarchs, but in practice they generally coincide only very approximately. Queen Elizabeth I came to the throne in 1558, but the style associated with her name did not gain general acceptance until some years later and by the end of the century was already showing clear signs of being superseded by a style that lasted until well into the seventeenth. But it is convenient to treat the second half of the sixteenth century as a unit, mainly because it was equally affected by social and economic factors that led to a significant broadening of the market for domestic silver and metalwork and to a commensurate increase in the range of goods manufactured.

For the social and economic future of the country the single most important event of Henry VIII's reign was not the break with Rome, but the dissolution of the monasteries, and its economic and social effects continued to be felt until well into his younger daughter's reign. The official justification for confiscating the land and treasures of what was collectively by far the wealthiest institution in the country was that the monasteries were corrupt and that they owed their allegiance to the Pope rather than the King, but the effect was to put the virtually bankrupt royal finances back on to a temporarily more stable footing. Moreover, this policy went beyond finances and beyond the Church. Its real purpose was to secure political stability and the future of the House of Tudor by effecting a radical change in the power of the Crown relative to that of both the Church and the old aristocracy. Under Henry VII (1485–1509) and Henry VIII their power was systematically undermined, and their lands and lives made as much subject to the King's favour as was the power and authority of the Church.

Most of the confiscated land was granted, either by gift or sale, to supporters of the King or his ministers and the result of this was enormously to increase the number of landowners in the country. But until the eighteenth century the most important source of wealth was land, and the division of the monastic lands in the mid sixteenth century effectively established what amounted to a new class, which evolved into the new aristocracy and gentry of the seventeenth and eighteenth centuries.

For the poor the effect of these social changes was of a different kind. The creation of a new stratum of relatively and securely wealthy superiors was one factor that led to a gradual decline in living standards throughout the sixteenth century and up to the Civil War (1642–9). Another was Henry VIII's repeated debasement of the coinage from 1526, which was continued until 1551. In a misguided attempt to increase royal revenues, these measures reduced the silver content of the coinage from sterling standard to as little as 25 per cent, and the consequent erosion of confidence in the currency must have played a significant part in the inflation of the sixteenth and early seventeenth centuries that reduced the value of wages in real terms by as much as 50 per cent between 1500 and 1640. Nor was the plight of the ordinary worker helped by the Statute of Artificers of 1563, which imposed ceilings on wages and prescribed fines for employers who exceeded them. But by far the most important contributor to falling general living standards was the increase in the population of England that took place during the sixteenth century and which inevitably led to the rise in the price of agricultural goods exceeding that of manufactured. Some estimates put the increase of agricultural prices between 1550 and 1640 at as much as 500 per cent,[1] while industrial prices rose only half as much.

Devastating though the effect of this must have been on the population as a whole, there can be no doubt of its advantages for the landowning and mercantile sectors of society, and their steadily improving circumstances are clearly reflected in the increasingly elaborate furnishings that inventories of the period describe. While wealthy merchants had been and continued to be clients of goldsmiths and other craftsmen, numerically they were of much less significance than the gentry and prosperous yeomen. William Harrison, writing in the third quarter of the sixteenth century,[2] is often quoted by writers on pewter, but also makes revealing observations on the way this new expanded class adapted to their changing circumstances and shows that increased demand for plate was merely one aspect of a general trend towards more comfortable living:

The furniture of our houses also exceedeth, and is grown in manner even to passing delicacy and herein I do not speak of nobility and gentry only, but likewise of the lowest sort in most places in our south country that hath anything at all to take to. Certes, in noblemen's houses it is not rare to see abundance of arras, rich hangings of tapestry, silver vessel and so much other plate as may furnish sundry cupboards to the sum oftentimes of a thousand or two thousand pounds at the least, whereby the value of this and the rest of their stuff doth grow to be almost inestimable. Likewise in the houses of knights, gentlemen and merchantmen, and some other wealthy citizens, it is not geson [unusual] to behold generally their great provision of tapestry, Turkeywork, pewter, brass, fine linen, and thereto costly cupboards of plate, worth five or six hundred or a thousand pounds to be deemed by estimation. But as herein all these sorts do far exceed their elders and predecessors, and in neatness and curiosity the merchant all other, so in times past the costly furniture stayed there, yet now it is descended yet lower even unto the interior artificers and many farmers, who ... have, for the most part, learned also to garnish their cupboards with plate, their joined beds with tapestry and silk hangings, and their tables with carpets and fine napery, whereby the wealth of our country ... doth infinity appear.[3]

Although allowance must be made for some exaggeration in Harrison's account, especially in his reference to conditions among 'the lowest sort', there can be no doubting the basic genuineness of his observations, particularly since they applied specifically to the south of England. The goldsmiths' trade was concentrated in London because until about 1560 it was effectively the only city where plate could be assayed and hallmarked. The economic importance of the capital relative to the rest of the country also grew enormously during the sixteenth century. Between 1560 and 1600 its population nearly doubled and by 1600 about 5 per cent of the population of the country lived there. But the disproportionate concentration of the nation's wealth within that 5 per cent is clear from the fact that in 1500 it contributed as much towards the Parliamentary subsidy as all other towns put together and by the end of the century much more.[4]

From about 1560, however, there was a resurgence of the goldsmith's craft in the provinces, and in particular in Norwich, Exeter and Chester. Seven towns had been granted the right of striking their 'touch mark' by an act of 1423, but there is no record of any assay offices being set up in consequence. Indeed, in spite of having been mentioned in the act, it was necessary for the goldsmiths of Norwich to petition before their assay office was finally established in 1565. Around the same time plate began to be assayed and hallmarked in Exeter, Chester and York. One circumstance that gave rise to this resurgence was the programme initiated by Archbishop Parker to convert all chalices into 'decent communion cups'. Since under the new liturgy the wine was taken by the congregation rather than being restricted to the priest, most chalices were too small for the job and had to be replaced. The new cups, made to a standard formula with a domed foot, waisted stem and tapering bowl engraved with strapwork, served the dual purpose of having a larger capacity and symbolizing the severing of ties with Rome by being quite different in appearance from 'Popish' chalices. Most churches met the cost of the conversion by using the metal of their chalices and the programme provided the staple business of many London and provincial goldsmiths over about a twelve-year period. Nevertheless, the high quality of some provincial pieces testifies to a tradition of gold-smiths' work that must have been well established before the opening of the assay offices. Indeed, makers such as Richard Hillyard of Exeter (father of the famous miniaturist), William Cobbold of Norwich or William Mutton of Chester produced plate of nearly as fine a quality as could be found in London.

However, London traditionally had a further significance for goldsmiths in that it was the seat of the court and the source of royal patronage. During the reign of Henry VIII this had been of enormous importance, but under Elizabeth economic circumstances were more constrained and patronage less flamboyant. While Henry had competed with other princes, such as Francis I of France and Charles V, the Holy Roman Emperor, to have the most brilliant and splendid court in Europe, Elizabeth's concern was to spend no more than was strictly necessary to maintain appearances.[5] The inventory of the royal Jewel House, compiled in 1574, lists quantities of gold plate and jewel-encrusted silver-gilt, which had already been con-siderably eroded before the end of the century and of which virtually nothing now remains. But although less extravagant than in Henry's time, royal patronage was still important to London goldsmiths, whether sup-plying the royal household's needs for domestic plate – such as the twenty-four 'depe bolles guilt' weighing 616 ounces that were supplied in 1581,[6] or the 159-piece dinner service weighing 3,414 ounces received by the Jewel House in 1583[7] – or for the large number of diplomatic gifts that were presented to ambassadors and foreign princes each year.

A special category of gifts, and one that must have provided much employment for goldsmiths, was the traditional New Year's gifts that were exchanged between the Queen and her most prominent subjects each year. The value of these would vary according to rank, and the Jewel House inventory describes a bewildering variety of objects that entered the royal collection by this means each year, such as 'A Cup of Cristall garnisshid with siluer guilt pearle and stone gevon by the Lord Keper' in 1580,[8] or 'A Sault of golde with a Couer with two personages nakes [naked] with a lion

*Queen Elizabeth Salt, silver-gilt, 1572, maker's mark a bird;
$13\frac{3}{4}$ in. high (Tower of London).*

in the toppe of the couer gevon by the Lady Burley' in 1584[9] and the 'Cvp of Crystaull Fasshyoned lyke A Boate slytely garnisshid with golde with a Cover of golde garnisshid with Frogges with Sparkes of Rvbyes in ther noses', given by the Earl of Sussex in 1587.[10]

Not all these objects were necessarily new at the time, but substantial numbers of them evidently were. A warrant of 1560 instructed the Master of the Jewel House to put some 4,000 ounces of 'olde broken and vnseru-isable' plate into the hands of the Queen's goldsmiths, Affabel Partridge and Robert Brandon, 'whereby they may be able the better to furnysh our service towching newyeris guifts and plate to be provided and new made for rewards to be gevon to Ambassatours and other'.[11] Affabel Partridge was probably the owner of a maker's mark (a bird in a shaped shield) that is found on some of the finest surviving plate of the period, such as the so-called Queen Elizabeth Salt of 1572, and although we have little idea of the nature of the most extravagant gold and jewelled objects described in the inventories, this corpus of plate gives a very good idea of the standard generally expected under Elizabeth I's patronage.

Outside that related to court commissions, sufficient survives of fine decorated domestic plate from the second half of the century to enable us for the first time to trace stylistic developments with some certainty. The influence of continental mannerism on English silver is clearly illustrated by the Wyndham Ewer of 1554 in the British Museum. Its most distinctive features, the grotesque spout and handle, are reminiscent of the designs of Flemish artists such as Balthasar Sylvius, and these influences continued to be a factor in the most fashionable English plate throughout the second half of the century. The Queen Elizabeth Salt, attributed to Partridge, epitomizes this style. The emphasis of its design is decidedly vertical, even allowing for the fact that the scroll supports to the cover are probably later additions, and the goldsmith has given it a sense of presence and importance by height. This is quite different from the measured horizontality of Holbein's designs and surviving display plate of twenty-five years earlier. The gold-smith has incorporated some unusual embossed plaques, but the decorative surround to these consists of embossed fruit and strapwork that, although seldom of this quality, had become a ubiquitous feature of decorated plate by about 1570. Similarly, the use of vases, applied brackets, stamped ornament, and figure finials are all standard features of the style.

Towards the end of the century, however, the influence of continental design became concentrated in a more exclusive assertion of German style. The presence of German goldsmiths in London, always significant during the sixteenth century, evidently became even greater towards its close. The Aliens Returns for Elizabeth's reign show some 150 or so Dutch and German goldsmiths working in London,[12] and a visitor of about 1610 observed 'nor is it long since ... the goldsmiths in London were nearly all Germans'.[13] Not surprisingly, certain objects almost certainly produced by native goldsmiths are on occasion entirely modelled on German prototypes. The Wilbraham Cup of 1585 was undoubtedly made by an English goldsmith, as the decoration on the foot is completely English, but equally the shape is German.

While objects such as this testify to the fact that fine plate was certainly being produced in English workshops, the majority of surviving pieces suggest that there was a marked decline in the standard of craftsmanship for less important commissions which continued during the seventeenth century. This was noted at the time with some concern by the authorities at Goldsmiths' Hall, who observed in the *Order for the Masterpiece* in 1607 that

... [the] true practise of the Art & Mystery of Goldsmithry is not only grown into great decays but also dispersed into many parts, so that now very few workmen are able to finish and perfect a piece of plate singularly ... without the help of many and several hands, which inconvenience is grown by reason that many of the idler sort betake themselves to the sole practice and exercise of one slight and easy part ... some to be only hammermen ... [others] work nothing but bell salts, or only bells, or only casting bottles.

This should perhaps be attributed, at least in part, to the almost exclusive concern of the Goldsmiths' Company for the quality of the alloy, which led to the wardens taking a less critical interest in craftsmanship than officials of the guilds in Germany and other European centres, such as Antwerp and Paris. Some attempt was made to remedy the situation by setting up a 'workhouse' at the Hall, where goldsmiths wishing to register a mark should come and make a testpiece 'commonly called a Masterpiece to be begun and finished by himself and approved by the Wardens and 2 skillful workmen of the Mystery nominated yearly'.[14]

The criticisms of the *Order for the Masterpiece* also allude to another notable feature of Elizabethan silver, the specialization of the craft. This had probably always been the case, but never before the sixteenth century do we have clear evidence of it. Makers' marks and the records of the Goldsmiths' Company reveal well-established dynasties of spoon makers; other makers seem to have concentrated on communion cups or other specific categories of plate. The reason for this was obviously economic and similar concern

Wyndham Ewer, silver-gilt, 1554, maker's mark intersecting triangles;
13¾ in. high (British Museum, London).

Wilbraham Cup, silver-gilt, 1585, maker's mark SB; $11\frac{1}{2}$ in. high (Gilbert Collection, Los Angeles).

is evident in the frequent occurrence of reused castings and ornament that was stamped out with a die rather than being hand-chased.

Among decorative and ceremonial plate, the ewer and basin, cup and

Leigh ewer and basin, silver-gilt, 1574 and 1556, maker's mark on ewer M; diameter of basin $17\frac{1}{2}$ in. (Goldsmiths' Company).

cover and the salt continued to play important roles during this period. The Leigh Ewer of 1574 and its basin of 1556 are typical of the third quarter of the century. Embossed and engraved with strapwork and foliage of moderate quality, the ewer is of a cup-like form that was soon to be completely superseded by one with ovoid body and waisted neck, of the type already represented by the Wyndham Ewer. Although variety was achieved through variations of decoration, Elizabethan ewers were essentially limited to these two forms.

The cup and cover, on the other hand, was subject to a wide variety of treatment, and its form was handled more experimentally during the second half of the century than at almost any other time. Some of these variants are of continental inspiration, such as the Wilbraham Cup or a cup of 1563

Cup and cover, silver-gilt, 1561, maker's mark a cup;
$14\frac{1}{2}$ *in. high.*

in the Inner Temple, with melon-shaped body and tendril stem.[15] Most, however, are designed according to a fairly standard formula, consisting of domed foot, vase-shaped stem and domed cover whose finial echoes the form of the stem. A typical example of this formula is a cup of 1561 formerly in the possession of Watford Church. But within these constraints the Elizabethan goldsmiths seemed able to produce an apparently endless series of variations. This was achieved through modifications to the proportions, the shape of the bowl and the arrangement of ornament, but only occasionally through the actual nature of the decoration, which in most cases continued to be the familiar engraved or embossed fruit and strapwork. The inventiveness of the standing cup in itself says much for its continuing importance during the late sixteenth century.

For much of Elizabeth's reign the standing salt, or 'great salt', retained its ceremonial significance, although there are signs that by the end of the century it had begun to decline in importance. Whereas ceremonial salts of the early sixteenth century had been arguably the most creative form of all, their Elizabethan successors generally fall into two categories, namely the pedestal and the drum. It is difficult to determine which, if either, came first, and by the third quarter of the century they had become vehicles for equally imposing and ambitious schemes of ornament. A wider range of form and material does seem to be evident among salts of the pedestal type, which perhaps indicates that a greater importance was attached to that type, but as with so much plate of the sixteenth century, it is unwise to treat the corpus of surviving pieces as necessarily representative. The pedestal salt was generally of square section, with a domed base that was mirrored in the upper part and a domed cover with tall vase or figure finial. This basic formula, however, was varied by the incorporation of different materials such as rock-crystal or glass into the construction, or the introduction of architectural features into the design. Two of the most dramatic salts of this type are the Gibbon Salt of 1576 in the Goldsmiths' Company Collection,[16] which is designed as a temple with a figure enclosed within rock-crystal at the centre, and the Vyvyan Salt of 1592 in the Victoria and Albert Museum, with colourful panels of *verre églomisé* in the sides.

The basic form of the drum salt was the same as the pedestal, though of circular section, but it generally seems to have been handled somewhat more conventionally. Inventories of the period show that these could reach enormous proportions. The 1574 royal inventory describes several salts in excess of 100 ounces, and the Hardwick Hall inventory of 1601 also includes one that is far larger than any surviving today. Naturally the high bullion

Vyvyan Salt, silver-gilt and verre églomisé, 1592, maker's mark WH; 15¾ in. high
(Victoria and Albert Museum, London).

Drum salt, silver-gilt, 1581, maker's mark RM; 11 in. high
(Gilbert Collection, Los Angeles).

content of these enormous salts made them especially vulnerable to being melted down, and among the largest extant are the Mostyn Salt of 1586, in the Victoria and Albert Museum,[17] and the Reade Salt of 1568, made by William Cobbold of Norwich, which stands fifteen and a quarter inches high.[18] The Queen Elizabeth Salt of 1574, with its allegorical panels, is the most splendid surviving example of the form, and the Reade Salt, although of unusually fine quality, is much more typical of both the form and decoration of drum salts, nearly all of which are embossed with a standard pattern of fruit and strapwork.

It is perhaps significant that the type of decoration associated with great salts such as the Mostyn and Reade is also found on most smaller standing salts of the period. Generally of circular section, though occasionally square, these should probably not be regarded as ordinary domestic salts at all, but rather as ceremonial pieces too, intended for use either in lesser households or at banquets in conjunction with the great salt, but at places of lesser importance on the table.

The occasional survival of smaller and less highly decorated salts, such as an engraved example of 1550 in the Goldsmiths' Company Collection, perhaps gives some idea of a type that would have been more common than the great salt and its smaller equivalent. Of the most basic domestic salts, however, none survives from the sixteenth century, although a small plain circular example of 1603, formerly in the Swaythling Collection,[19] may give some idea of the 'xviij rounde lowe Stocke Saultes' listed in the 1574 royal inventory, even though the latter were rather larger and weighed around ten ounces each.

A third category of decorated salts, well known to collectors and with about two dozen surviving examples from the end of the sixteenth and the beginning of the seventeenth centuries, is the bell salt. Most are modelled to a standard formula and are designed to break down into three parts, with two tapering plinth-shaped salt cellars fitting one on top of the other and surmounted by a dome-shaped caster with pierced ball finial. It could therefore be used either as a three-part functional object, or, when assembled, as a decorative piece. Although the earliest known example is hallmarked for 1589, the form is recorded in the 1574 royal inventory, which lists several salts of 'belle fation with a Cover', and as early as 1552 in the inventory of the Duke of Somerset's plate.[20] But the description in inventories of salts of 'double bell fashion' in itself implies a distinction between those and others of ordinary or single bell shape, and it may be that a plain example of 1586 represents the more standard utilitarian form. Given the

Small salt, silver-gilt, 1550;
5½ in. high (Goldsmiths' Company).

tendency over succeeding centuries for decorated plate to be preserved in preference to plain, the fact that no double bell salts, decorated or otherwise, survive from before the last decade of the century, may simply indicate that earlier examples were usually plain and utilitarian. Certainly by the early seventeenth century, far from being regarded as a novelty, they were sufficiently common for strict regulations to be laid down by the Pewterers' Company ordaining the standard size of 'Great duble bells with pepper

Bell salt, silver-gilt, 1600, maker's mark TS; 8 in. high
(Untermyer Collection, Metropolitan Museum of Art, New York).

boxes and baules, the halfe dozen to weighe 9 lb'.[21] The transformation of a previously ordinary functional form into a decorated type may be taken as further evidence of the decline of the ceremonial role of the salt and a symptom of the growing fashion for more intimate dining in the private 'closet' rather than the relatively public great hall.

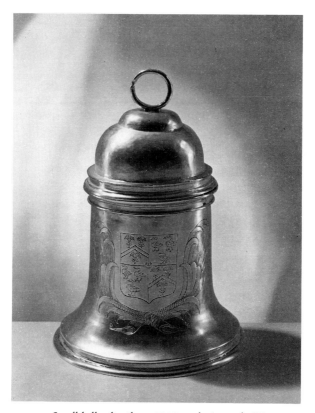

Small bell salt, silver, 1586, maker's mark CB;
$3\frac{1}{2}$ in. high.

Important though developments in ceremonial plate were, the most striking feature of the period seems to have been the increased supply of silver available for plate of a more practical nature as a result of the enormous influx of bullion from the New World. The impact of this was not so much on traditionally important categories of plate as on the expanded range of objects available, especially in the field of domestic plate. Some of these, such as the tankard and the spice box, appear to have been

Wine cup or bowl, silver-gilt, 1583,
maker's mark a snail; $5\frac{1}{4}$ in. high
(Gilbert Collection, Los Angeles).

quite new. Others, like the standing bowl, had clearly existed before but seem now to have become more widely available. The function of these shallow-bowled, stemmed vessels is not entirely clear. One section of the royal inventory, apparently describing such objects, calls them 'spice plates', while another refers to them simply as 'bolles' or bowls.[22] Possibly their use was interchangeable, although a clue may be found in a painting by Anton Claeissens in the Groeningemuseum, Bruges, which shows plain vessels of this type being used to hold fruit and sweetmeats,[23] while others with more elaborate stems are being used as drinking vessels.

As with the early part of the century, the bulk of surviving Elizabethan domestic plate is connected with drinking. These fall into three main groups: tankards, beakers and goblets. Beakers, as we have seen, certainly existed

Beaker, silver and silver-gilt, 1579, maker's mark M,
a line across; $3\frac{3}{4}$ in. high (Untermyer Collection,
Metropolitan Museum of Art, New York).

during the fifteenth century, and the almost complete absence of recorded examples during the first three quarters of the sixteenth century has therefore probably more to do with accidents of survival than with production. They are possibly to be identified in some cases with inventory references to 'bowles', since Sir William Fairfax's inventory of 1590 is quite typical in referring to 'A nest of Bowelles with a cover weighing xlv ounces', however, the inconsistencies of terminology and briefness of inventory descriptions

*Tankard, silver and silver-gilt, 1578, maker's mark TT; $7\frac{5}{8}$ in. high
(British Museum, London).*

Tankard, silver, 1572, maker's mark HS;
$7\frac{1}{2}$ *in. high.*

make it impossible to reach a definite conclusion on this point, and in most cases 'bowls' would seem to be cups on feet.[24] The standard Elizabethan beaker is of tapering cylindrical form, with flared lip and engraved foliage and strapwork on the upper part of the body. They are often surprisingly large and a capacity of between one and two pints was not unusual. Presumably these were intended for beer, as were tankards.

Tankards only became common in silver during the Elizabethan period and a good deal of uncertainty surrounds their early development. The word seldom occurs in contemporary inventories, although other terms such as 'livery pott' and 'hans pott' do and sometimes appear to have been used interchangeably. Although related silver-mounted vessels survive from the first half of the century, few solid silver ones are known before the 1570s. The few 'tankerds and hans pottes' that appear on the royal inventory of 1574 imply that they must still have been something of a novelty and may explain some of the inconsistencies in terminology. Two basic forms are found: a very rare pear-shaped type and the more standard tapering cylindrical variety. The former, as was suggested in the last chapter, may have been derived from pottery or pewter shapes. The latter are generally assumed to have originated in a type of mounted vessel whose body was made from an ox horn, and a tankard of 1561, formerly in the Swaything Collection, was of this type.[25] Most surviving solid silver examples of this form are flat-chased or engraved around the barrel, and embossed on the foot and cover with standard strapwork and fruit, but two tankards, including one of 1572 in a private collection in Scotland, with engraved hoops and staves in imitation of wooden barrels, may be the only surviving representatives of a domestic type that was probably more common at the time.

Attempts have been made to distinguish between the pear-shaped and tapering cylindrical forms, identifying the former as 'livery pots', used for serving, and the latter as tankards, for drinking. The vagaries of contemporary inventories, however, again make it impossible to be certain, and it is probably safer to regard the two forms simply as alternative types serving the same function. In any event, surviving examples do suggest that the cylindrical form gained popularity around the time that the other fell out of fashion.

An important category of secular plate in Elizabethan England was the flagon. The term is misleadingly used nowadays to refer exclusively to large cylindrical and pear-shaped pouring vessels which are obviously related to tankards. Although usually of secular origin, these survive in appreciable numbers, due to the fact that they were sometimes presented to churches for use in the communion service and were subsequently preserved in their care. In fact these are more probably the vessels generally referred to as 'pottes' or 'livery pots'; the term 'flagon' was not usually applied to this type of vessel until the second half of the seventeenth century and was used in the sixteenth to describe a class of pouring vessels,

Pair of tankards, silver-gilt, 1604, maker's mark IB; $8\frac{1}{4}$ in. high
(Gilbert Collection, Los Angeles County Museum of Art).

which could take a number of different forms. Their common feature seems to have been the provision of a carrying chain, but their shape ranged from a pear-shaped vessel resembling the medieval pilgrim bottle to containers in the form of animals with detachable heads. Although common enough in great houses at the time, the large size that they could reach has led to their almost complete destruction and the only survivals today are those presented by successive embassies to Moscow and preserved in the Kremlin Museum. The importance that must have attached to this type of plate is implied in Harrison's account of English dining customs, in which he writes:

Large jug, silver-gilt, 1615, maker's mark RB;
24¼ in. high (Kremlin Museum, Moscow).

As for drink, it is usually filled in pots, goblets, jugs, [or] bowls of silver in noblemen's houses; also in fine Venice glasses of all forms; and, for want of these elsewhere, in pots of earth of sundry colours and moulds, whereof many are garnished with silver, or at the leastwise in pewter, all which notwithstanding are seldom set upon the table, but each one, as necessity urgeth, calleth for a cup of such drink as him listeth to have, so that, when he has tasted of it, he delivereth the cup again to some one of the standers by, who, making it clean by pouring out the drink that remaineth, restoreth it to the cupboard from whence he fetched the same.[26]

Just as late sixteenth-century tankards seldom deviate from the usual pattern, so goblets, which earlier in the century had displayed a bewildering variety of forms, had settled by about 1590 to a fixed formula consisting a small tapering bowl, elongated stem and spreading, slightly raised foot. Decoration is usually restricted to flat-chased foliage and strapwork around the bowl. This relative lack of inventiveness may in part be explained by the interest that was being aroused by the new availability of Venetian glass. This trend was also noted by Harrison, who observed that 'It is a world to see in these our days, wherein gold and silver most aboundeth, how that our gentility, as loathing these metals (because of the plenty) do now generally choose rather the Venice glasses, both for our wine and beer, than any of those metals or stone wherein before time we have been accustomed to drink.'[27]

As in the earlier part of the century, the relatively low bullion content and enduring popularity of mounted vessels during the Elizabethan period has ensured the preservation of plate in this category in much more representative numbers. By the second half of the century the mazer had virtually disappeared from the repertoire of English silversmiths (although it was still made in Scotland), and most mounted vessels were made for pouring or drinking purposes. The most common of these is the 'tigerware jug', a brown stoneware with mottled salt glaze that was produced in the Rhineland and imported to England. These seem first to have arrived in about 1530 and at that stage were generally of a squat form with bulbous body and cylindrical neck. Later in the century they became increasingly elongated. Many were furnished with silver mounts, especially in London and Exeter. However, the decline in standards that is apparent in other areas of the craft is particularly evident in the gradually deteriorating quality of these mounts, and may partly reflect the disrepute into which these vessels gradually fell. Around the middle of the century, when this form of German stoneware must still have had a certain novelty, the quality of their silver mounts tends to be very high. But by about 1575 the rate at which they were imported had grown so much that whatever chic they may have had twenty-five years earlier had been completely lost. It would also appear that towards the end of the century similar pots were being produced in England. In describing the new fashion for costly Venetian drinking glasses,

Goblet, silver-gilt, 1616, maker's mark AB;
$5\frac{1}{2}$ *in. high.*

Harrison observed that most people had to 'content themselves with such as are made at home of fern and burned stone',[28] thereby implying that they were by then within the means of virtually everyone. By the end of the century silver-mounted examples occur only in small numbers in the inventories of the wealthy, and their official fall from grace is signalled by the fact that by 1600 all but one of the stoneware jugs listed in the royal inventory of 1597 had been sent to the Mint.

Jug, silver-gilt and German stoneware ('tigerware'), 1581, maker's mark RB; 10½ in. high (Untermyer Collection, Metropolitan Museum of Art, New York).

This decline in quality is much less evident in the mounts that were made for other imported materials, presumably because they were less common than stoneware. The fine incised saltglaze jugs from Siegburg in Germany were occasionally mounted in England, and a continued, though reduced, use was made of coconut. But most materials that received mounts did so because they were considered exotic. Chinese blue and white porcelain, colourful Isnik pottery, nautilus shells, ostrich eggs and rock-crystal all fell into this category. Among the first of these might be mentioned the collection of silver-mounted Chinese porcelain from Burghley, some of which still remains in the house, and the ewer of 1589 at Hardwick Hall.[29] With these exotic mounted pieces Elizabethans came closest to the continental practice of commissioning or collecting fine goldsmiths' work for the *Schatzkammer*, or princely treasury. The seventeenth-century painting of the Paston Treasure in Norwich Castle Museum shows a large group of mounted vessels that were quite clearly regarded as heirlooms and works of art rather than objects for practical use. The fine quality of the mounts of many of these pieces reflects this rather special attitude.

The rate of survival for ordinary domestic silver from the second half of the century is only marginally, if at all, greater than for the early Tudor period. The Earl of Essex's 1588 inventory values twenty-six platters at almost £210,[30] whereas the 'ix puther platters' in another inventory of 1574 are priced at only 10s. Assuming the platters to have been of similar size, this makes silver at this time approximately 140 times the price of pewter, and the enormous sums of capital that such plate represented account for the negligible survival of ordinary domestic wares. Many of the categories of utilitarian plate that were made for the wealthy are consequently known only by their brief inventory descriptions. We have very little idea of their actual appearance, and the extent of this destruction is apparent from the fact that, with the exception of spoons and communion cups, the vast majority of surviving Elizabethan plate is gilt, whereas most ordinary domestic plate would have been white. In about 1540 Viscount Lisle, Lord Deputy of Calais, possessed 'A bason with a cover', weighing 137 ounces, 'A Shayving basone with an Ewer' and four candlesticks.[31] About thirty years later Archbishop Parker's inventory lists 'One gilte pott called a layer, with a cover' weighing twenty-seven ounces, and 'a flower pott, withe a cover',[32] while the list of Sir William Fairfax's plate compiled in 1590 includes 'A spowte pott' of twenty-nine ounces, 'one silver Standishe' of eighteen ounces and 'a silver Cullander of orrenges'.[33] The list of Queen Elizabeth's 'kytchen plate' includes such tantalizing entries as 'oone Boyling

Jug, silver-gilt and Chinese porcelain, 1589, maker's mark IH; 14 in. high
(National Trust, Hardwick Hall, Derbyshire).

Plate from dinner service, silver and silver-gilt, 1581,
15½ in. diameter.

potte of siluer with a handle or baile of siluer with three feete', 'oone porige potte', 'oone Instrument of siluer to rost puddinges and Apples' and also a number of strainers to 'presse Orainges'.[34]

Given how common domestic eating plate appears to have been among the wealthy, our knowledge of this category of plate is therefore particularly inadequate. Viscount Lisle was not unusual in owning two dozen trenchers (plates), two platters and two dozen dishes, and similar categories of plate appear in other aristocratic inventories, but our only direct clue to their appearance is the late sixteenth-century service referred to in the previous chapter (see p. 40). But dishes such as these represent only one type of Elizabethan dinner plate, and others described in the royal inventory were clearly quite different. Typical entries refer to 'oone standing Trencher guilt with a Salt at thone [the one] Corner', weighing twenty-six ounces, 'sixtene guilt Chardgers' of 1,407 ounces, 'sawcers' and a 'Poringer guilt with two Eares'.[35] Some indication, at least, of the nature of these objects can again be inferred from surviving Tudor pewter, which Harrison informs us was 'sold usually by the garnish, which doth contain twelve platters, twelve dishes, twelve saucers, and those are either of silver fashion or else with broad or narrow brims'.[36] The evidence points to the fact that the appearance of these basic objects did not change a great deal during the course of the century, although Harrison also observes in the same passage that 'dishes and platters in my time begin to be made deep like basins, and are indeed more convenient both for sauce, broth, and keeping the meat warm'.

In other respects the pewter industry underwent a major transformation during the second half of the sixteenth century, and the same commentator describes how 'our pewterers ... are grown in such exquisite cunning that they can in manner imitate by infusion [casting] any form or fashion of cup, dish, salt bowl, or goblet, which is made by goldsmiths' craft, though they be never so curious, exquisite and artificially forged'.[37] Inventories of pewter from the latter part of the century, such as one of 1563, describe quite sophisticated wares, including '1 basson and a yourer [ewer], 12 flower cyps, 4 salts and covers of pewter, 6 pewter pottes, 9 candlesticks'.[38] A late sixteenth-century livery pot in the collection of the Pewterers' Company[39] is of exactly the same form as contemporary silver examples, and other surviving pewter forms can safely be assumed to have had their counterparts among lost classes of plate. Indeed, for the reasons outlined in the previous chapter, more mundane types of plate almost certainly took their lead from pewter prototypes.

The destruction of silver candlesticks from the Elizabethan period has been as complete as that for the earlier part of the century. Inventories tell us very little about the appearance of ordinary examples, for the simple reason that the reader would be expected to know. For example, the 1601 Hardwick Hall inventory describes the main features of interesting objects such as 'sixe Candlestickes wrought with stages [stags] and talbotes white waying twoo hundreth fortie ounces' or 'sixe Candlestickes like gallies white waying Fourscore and too ounces',[40] but other, presumably more standard types are given no description at all, other than their weights.

Candlestick, pewter, late sixteenth century;
8½ in. high (Pewterers' Company).

However, the survival of a very small number of pewter examples, most of which have been excavated, may well provide the best indication of the appearance of ordinary silver candlesticks. Most of these are relatively squat and have a circular domed base and baluster stem. Of another type altogether, one of the most remarkable is the Grainger Candlestick of 1616 in the Victoria and Albert Museum,[41] which is elaborately decorated with cast ornament and which, given Harrison's claim that pewterers could 'imitate by infusion any form or fashion' of goldsmiths' work, may possibly represent one of the decorated forms made in silver.

Throughout the late sixteenth and early seventeenth centuries the most personal item of plate remained the spoon. The basic remarks made on this subject in the previous chapter apply equally to the latter part of the

Candlestick, pewter, late sixteenth century;
$6\frac{1}{2}$ in. high.

century. Form remained remarkably standard, even among provincially made spoons, although changes gradually occurred, especially to the shape of the bowl and width of the stem. Bowls became increasingly rounded and the exaggerated crescent-shaped profile was reduced; the form of stems also gradually evolved into a consistent, slightly flattened tapering hexagonal section. But in all general respects the character of the spoon remained unchanged from the stage of development it had reached by the early

Group of spoons, silver. From left to right:
baluster finial, 1553, maker's mark a crescent enclosing a mullet;
seal top, 1564, maker's mark a campanula; apostle spoon ('the Master'),
provincial, late sixteenth century.

sixteenth century. The range of finials was, if anything, reduced; owners' initials were frequently pricked or engraved on 'seal top' spoons, and the finials of this type became one of the most popular of all, rivalling even the apostle, during the late sixteenth and early seventeenth centuries.

Apostle spoons continued to be popular throughout the sixteenth century and well into the seventeenth, but their decline from fashion in court circles probably began much earlier. The remarkable miniature sculptures of the early sixteenth century are seldom matched by those later in the century, and groups such as the Tichbourne Celebrities of 1592[42] were exceptional. Normally old moulds continued to be used until they were quite worn out, and the quality of castings declined accordingly. One reason for this is presumably that such spoons were being supplied to a clientele that had not previously been able to own plate and was consequently less discriminating, or less anxious to pay for fine craftsmanship, than wealthier patrons. In spite of the high cost of plate in relation to ordinary wages, by the end of the century a modest possession such as a few silver spoons had for the first time come within the grasp of a surprisingly large number of people. Partly because of their personal appeal and partly because they contained only two or three ounces of silver, they would inevitably have been the first plate to be acquired and are almost invariably the items specified on inventories mentioning only one or two pieces. Cristine Burgh of Richmond, formerly prioress of the nunnery of Nunkilbing, for example, left six silver spoons valued at 20s. in her will in 1566, even though the total value of her estate was only £14, and instructed that these be divided between the various beneficiaries.[43]

Although a general decline in standards at the end of the century is undeniable, it was certainly not universal. Despite the lack of control exercised by the Goldsmiths' Company over craftsmanship and despite the presence of an arguably less discriminating element in the market, there is enough evidence of the continued presence of distinguished goldsmiths to show that there were still patrons who demanded high standards. A series of fine covered cups from the last years of the century dispense with the mannerist preference for complex profiles and ornament that had been the convention for the most fashionable plate, and are characterized by simple, well-proportioned outlines with restrained decoration that are without any continental precedent. Flat-chasing, although a relatively simple and stylized technique, was occasionally used at this time with real sophistication. Several engravers of plate, notably Nicaise Roussel, were also working in England during the closing years of the century and producing work to a standard that has seldom been exceeded.[44] Lastly, some of the most remarkable mounted vessels known, especially of exotic or rare materials, date from the last decade of the century. This imbalance between the standards of the craft as a whole and those of the most skilled goldsmiths was dictated by the difference between the expanding market for cheaper wares and the standards that wealthy patrons continued to expect. It is a trend that continued into the following century and became, if anything, even more pronounced.

---------- *Four* ----------

THE EARLY SEVENTEENTH
CENTURY

The seventeenth century, particularly in its middle years, is one of the strangest and least understood periods of English history. It is also one of the most important, from which many of our most basic political institutions have evolved. The opposing sides in the Civil War (1642–9) were divided mainly by political differences, but in part also by ideological ones, and the war itself was no more than the most conspicuous and violent conflict in a century that saw numerous different ideologies and interests compete with varying degrees of success for the reinforcement or overturning of the existing order of society. These radical ideological differences, and the fervour with which they were pursued, did not only affect political allegiances, but were evident in every aspect of life.

The calamitously costly Civil War resulted in a political revolution, but produced little change in the overall burden imposed by government on the financial resources of the country. Charles I's (r. 1625–49) massive and arbitrarily imposed taxation was replaced by the unprecedented cost of maintaining Cromwell's New Model Army. Under the Commonwealth (1649–60) taxation may have been more even-handed, but it was equally heavy. Moreover, the series of forced 'loans' which the King had exacted from institutions such as City livery companies and the universities, and which had been met largely by disposing of plate, was matched after the war by reprisal confiscations of estates belonging to royalist families. During the interregnum a major, if temporary, change in the structure of society took place. Some £5.5 million worth of land was confiscated and sold, while over £1.5 million was raised in fines.[1]

With the only certainties in such an environment being political and financial instability, conditions before the restoration were not conducive to large-scale investment in plate. In fact, a general decline in demand for decorative plate had been apparent for some time. Royal commissions were on a scale much reduced from that of Henry VIII's reign, and even the traditionally reliable demand occasioned by the exchange of New Year's gifts declined as the resources of the Jewel House were plundered for this purpose rather than new commissions being given. This is not to say that patronage ceased altogether. Superb plate continued to be made, both for private and civic purposes, and the records continue to mention important presentations of plate in the traditional manner, such as a gold cup and cover to James I (r. 1603–25) from the City of Coventry on his 1617 progress, or a gold ewer and basin to Oliver Cromwell from the City of London. It is true, also, that royal patronage continued at a certain level, and massive plate in the Kremlin, such as livery pots, water jugs, salts and cups presented by Sir John Merrick's embassy in 1620, was mostly of English manufacture. But the quality of much of this compares unfavourably with the finest surviving early Elizabethan plate.

Curiously, no such decline is evident in other crafts. English architecture was enjoying one of its most creative phases, pewter continued to enjoy a fine reputation, and the little furniture of any importance to survive in an unaltered state can be of remarkable quality. Apart from the Goldsmiths' Company's failure adequately to supervise the craft, therefore, the explanation for these declining standards is probably to be sought in the unequal competition that English goldsmiths faced from continental imports. The debased coinage of Henry VIII's reign had made it difficult for the company to enforce sterling standard in plate with any reliability, but Elizabeth's re-establishment of sterling coinage was followed in 1576 by an act imposing stiff penalties for goldsmiths submitting sub-standard plate for assay, or for wardens subsequently found to have hallmarked such plate.[2] It also illegalized the sale or exchange of any plate failing to meet the required standard. German plate of the period was usually in the region of 87–89 per cent pure and consequently fell under this ban. But its lower silver content also made it cheaper, and the extent of the company's failure to prevent its importation is evident even in Elizabeth's and Charles I's inventories, which list many items of 'Almaine making'. Some of these would certainly have entered the royal collection as gifts, but in 1606 a group of working goldsmiths complained to the company 'of such as sell Noremberdge [Nuremberg] plate which in regard of the fashion [workmanship] is uttered before [esteemed above] the English plate being not withstanding viii penny in the ounce worse in fineness than the English workmen dare to work for fear of incurring the danger of the Statute law'.[3] The records of the company show that this continued to be a problem, and on a number of occasions the wardens tried to impose their authority by ordering the destruction of sub-standard Nuremberg plate.

It is difficult to form a balanced view of the state of the craft in the early seventeenth century, since much of the finest plate must have been destroyed soon after it was made. This was generally not old enough either

Inkstand, silver, 1639, maker's mark AI;
$16\frac{1}{2}$ in. long.

to have acquired the status of heirlooms, or to have been bequeathed to the relative security of the Church, and was consequently more exposed to the risk of being melted down than its older equivalents. Nevertheless, a few survivals, such as a remarkable group of plate decorated with fine filigree ornament and associated with an unknown maker whose mark is a monogram, apparently made up of the letters TYL or TZL, show that at least some very skilled goldsmiths were working in London at the time. Charles I also sought the service of outstanding goldsmiths for special commissions, and the presence of the Utrecht goldsmith Christian van

Vianen in the King's service from about 1633 shows that the taste for sophisticated plate was not as dead in England as most survivals might suggest.

Van Vianen worked in the extraordinarily original 'auricular' style that had been pioneered by his uncle and father, Paul and Adam van Vianen. The style makes use of embossed decoration in high relief and derives its name from the fluid, cartilaginous ornament that is its main characteristic. Virtually all van Vianen's English work, such as the seventeen-piece service of altar plate for St George's Chapel, Windsor, which he completed in 1639, has been lost, although a small number of pieces supplied to Algernon Percy, 10th Earl of Northumberland, still exist.[4]

The anonymous TYL or TZL maker, the small body of whose surviving works are from around the first decade of the century, worked in a quite different style. Typified by a silver-gilt standing cup of 1611 in the Victoria and Albert Museum and a standing salt of about 1610 at Woburn Abbey, this involved the use of sophisticated applied filigree decoration.

Sophisticated plate such as this, however, was exceptional. Survivals of more standard decorated plate and even of the royal plate in the Kremlin which was sold to the Tsar in 1627 testify to an unusual insularity of taste. This is often associated with the decline in standards already evident at the end of the previous century and lends credence to contemporary complaints.

This is particularly apparent in the flat-chased or shallow relief decoration that was favoured for plate such as bell-salts, cups and ewers and basins. Appearing as early as the 1580s, this consisted essentially of the same motifs found in mid-Elizabethan silver, but reduced to a simpler and more schematic formula which was technically less sophisticated. Foliate motifs are treated less naturalistically and with a greater concern for abstract pattern-making. Stock ornament now consisted primarily of two-dimensional strapwork, geometric flowerheads and scallop shells, often on a punched matted ground. There is occasional evidence of familiarity with continental pattern books, such as the grotesque sea-monsters of Adriaen Collaert,[5] but for most purposes these had ceased to be a factor in English plate.

A similar insularity is evident in the shapes of major types of vessels. Instead of following the fashionable German forms of the time, English standing cups of the last quarter of the sixteenth century departed increasingly from continental precedent, becoming simpler and more uniform and generally with bowl and cover with progressively steeper sides. The most characteristic of these was the so-called steeple cup, of which some 150 examples have survived, spanning the period 1599–1630, but whose distinctive feature can be recognized on inventories from as early as the mid sixteenth century. These are of surprisingly repetitive form, with tall waisted foot, baluster stem with applied brackets and ovoid bowl and cover surmounted by a tall steeple-like finial on similar brackets. The only significant development in the form over this period was a tendency for the various elements to be stretched so that they became gradually taller and more slender. Intended for display rather than use, these cups were sometimes made in sets of three and the largest of them could be enormous, sometimes reaching a height of more than thirty inches. Their decoration usually consisted of an embossed calyx of foliage around the base of the bowl and repetitive, rather elementary flat-chased strapwork around the lip, with compatible decoration to the foot and cover. This uniformity was occasionally relieved by a slightly more imaginative decorative scheme, such as embossed foliage and strapwork, geometric ornament or friezes of figures, but while their quality varies, they seldom compare with the finest continental plate.

A similar conventionality conditioned the other main category of decorated plate, namely the ewer and basin. Ewers from the first quarter of the century were almost invariably of the already established ovoid form and with a standard foot and lip; handles were seldom cast and were now generally raised in two parts soldered together to form a scroll of D-section. Decoration is similarly limited and with a conspicuous lack of cast ornament, although the use of water imagery in panels of sea-monsters was obviously more popular than on other types of plate.

In spite of their frequently undistinguished quality, the steeple cup and ewer and basin, together with other substantial items such as flagons, livery pots and salts, continued to represent status plate, and their importance was normally enhanced, as in the previous century, by gilding. Decorated tankards and goblets likewise, although not intended for display, would have had a prominence that made the added expense of gilding appropriate. It is symptomatic of an apparent change in attitudes to plate during the second quarter of the century, however, that there is a marked decline in the popularity of gilt plate. Whereas it had been customary to gild most decorated plate in the sixteenth century, white plate now became an acceptable alternative. This was partly a reflection of Dutch taste, promoted by van Vianen, in which gilt plate had never been so fashionable. But it was also symptomatic of an austerity that is equally evident in an increased incidence of simple shapes and plain surfaces, even for ceremonial plate.

*Steeple cup, silver-gilt, 1618, maker's mark CB; 20¼ in. high
(Gilbert Collection, Los Angeles).*

Ewer, silver-gilt, 1609, maker's mark IM, billet below;
13¾ in. high.

Standing cup and cover, silver, 1661,
maker's mark AF; $17\frac{1}{4}$ in. high.

Wrothe Salt, silver, 1633, maker's mark TC in monogram; 6½ in. high
(Admiral Blake Museum, Bridgwater, Somerset).

The steeple cup, for example, gradually evolved into a squatter form, with flat spreading foot and straighter-sided bowl, while the cover dispensed with the steeple altogether and rose instead to a tall cone. The ceremonial salt, although declining in importance over this period, still had a role to play. Most are of a single form: a cylindrical or waisted drum with brackets fixed to the upper part which were intended to support a dish or be covered by a napkin. The standard ewer and basin during the 1630s, such as those presented to the Corporation of Portsmouth or Winchester College and Trinity College, Cambridge, displays a similarly clumsy austerity: a foot and body of severely functional form plainly based on contemporary communion cups, with large scroll handle made from raised rather than cast components and simple beak-shaped spout.

The decoration of such prominent plate was generally as subdued as its

*Ewer, silver, 1637, maker's mark RM, cinquefoil below; $9\frac{1}{4}$ in. high
(Corporation of Portsmouth).*

form and frequently restricted to armorial engraving or bands of matting.
During the sixteenth century armorial and decorative engraving on plate
had occasionally reached the very highest levels of artistry, but in the
seventeenth it was reduced to a level that was at best uninspired and at
worst barely competent. A native school of engraving had never existed
in England, and the few sixteenth-century engravers of plate to have been
identified were all of continental origin. The parlous state of the craft in the

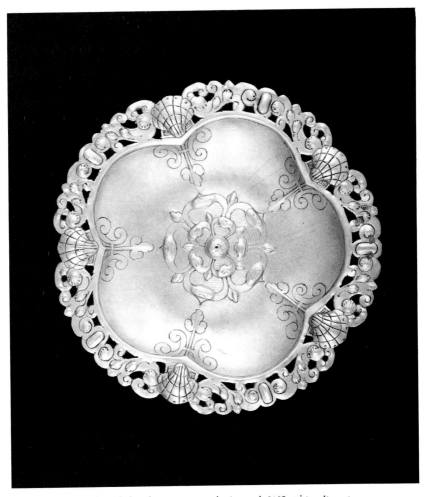

Standing dish, silver, 1627, maker's mark WS; 8½ in. diameter
(Gilbert Collection, Los Angeles).

following century illustrates both the crucially important role played by
foreign craftsmen in England and the great reduction in their numbers
before conditions stabilized under the restored monarchy.

It is difficult to know whether this shift in style and the prevalence of
plain plate was a reflection of taste or a response to the fact that the
necessary skills for sophisticated decoration were in short supply. Probably
it was a mixture of both. While the poverty of form and the inferior quality
of engraving apparent even in some of the most important plate of the

Saucer, silver, 1635, maker's mark FI above a catherine wheel; 3⅝ in. diameter (Victoria and Albert Museum, London).

period suggests the latter, it is also likely that Puritan elements considered plainness to lend a dignity appropriate to display plate, as opposed to the 'vanity' of elaborate ornament. The surviving work of the most outstanding maker of the period, whose mark is a 'hound sejant', shows an extraordinary breadth of taste and, while being of consistently high quality, ranges from the severely plain to the highly ornate. Presumably these widely differing styles satisfied patrons with equally different preferences, and their tastes in decoration probably also reflected much deeper attitudes. It also seems likely that the eventual triumph of the Puritan cause in the Civil War led to the widespread destruction of ornate plate in the same sort of ideological wave as the iconoclastic movement of the mid century. This would have distorted our perception of the relative popularity of plain and ornate plate at the time.

These trends — parallel fashions for plain and decorated plate and a general decline in standards of craftsmanship — are equally evident in ordinary domestic plate. Certain features and types of decoration, however, are particularly characteristic of the period. Utilitarian domestic plate shares with contemporary display pieces a tendency to be of severely functional form and to be of remarkably thin gauge. Much of the most typical decoration, indeed, is intended to compensate for the weakness of this thin metal while at the same time reflecting the same concern for minimizing cost. The standard decoration for standing dishes between about 1620 and

1640, for example, consisted of a debased form of Elizabethan fruit and strapwork chased in low relief and pierced with a fret saw. Although its quality is generally indifferent, the embossing had the effect of imparting a rigidity to the metal, while the piercing made obvious further savings. Embossed fruit and scrolls or purely abstract patterns, often of a rudimentary nature, were common for small items, such as wine tasters and saucers.

Decoration was gradually rationalized under the Commonwealth, when a form of flat-chasing evolved not unlike that in fashion at the beginning of the century. It differs from the latter, however, in having abandoned strapwork and in being less tightly packed. This type of decoration, without parallel elsewhere in Europe, epitomizes the insularity of English plate in the mid century. Although naïve, it has considerable charm and is in complete contrast to the international embossed baroque style which became so popular after the restoration.

The seventeenth century is the first period from which a sizeable quantity of ordinary and plain domestic plate survives. The nucleus of this is made up not only of goblets, tankards and other drinking vessels that are familiar in one form or another from the Elizabethan period, but also of increasing quantities of plate connected with eating. Small domestic salt cellars, saucers (small dishes for sauces, often erroneously dubbed 'sweetmeat dishes' today) and porringers make their first appearance among surviving plate, and also plates, fruit stands and candlesticks. Many of these items can be found from time to time in inventories of the previous century, but during the seventeenth they begin to figure more prominently. For example, in addition to the usual array of standing cups, flagons, ewers and basins and standing salts, the Earl of Northampton's 1614 inventory lists such items as thirteen candlesticks, 'foore fruite dishes partlie gilte ... three little trencher saltes ... half a dozen sawcers ... a porrenger and cover ... a warming panne ... 6 sallett dishes and one pie plate ... a standishe [inkstand] of silver with a cover'[6] and so on. Most of these categories are not represented by actually surviving plate until a little later, but this and other inventories show that they were definitely in regular use by the second decade of the century.

At least two factors help to account for the growth in domestic plate, already under way during the latter part of the previous century. In the first place the price of plate relative to other goods seems to have been declining, almost certainly as a result of the enormous influx of bullion during the second half of the sixteenth century. The Earl of Northampton's silver and silver-gilt was valued at 5s. and 6s. an ounce respectively, and a ewer and basin supplied by Christian van Vianen to the King in 1636 was

Goblet, silver, 1634, maker's mark HS; 7 in. high.

priced at 5s. 6d. per ounce for the metal.[7] Forty years earlier Archbishop Parker's inventory had valued the silver and silver-gilt at 4s. 8d. and 5s. 4d.[8] The price of plate, therefore, can be reckoned to have risen by only about 20 per cent over a period when the general increase in prices had been estimated at around 100 per cent for manufactured goods and 250 per cent for agricultural produce. Therefore those who derived their income from the land were obviously well placed to augment their plate. Secondly, dining customs continued to change over this period; the great hall with its traditional ceremony had for most purposes given way to a more intimate style of dining in the 'closet' or small private dining-room with fewer attendants and no onlookers. The only places where traditional forms of ceremonial plate continued to have a role, other than on state occasions, were those institutions where formal dining in the hall, such as Oxford and Cambridge colleges and City livery companies, was continued.

The range of ordinary drinking vessels in use during the second quarter of the century was also expanding. The largest group was the goblet, which continued to be the usual vessel for wine until finally ousted by drinking glasses at the end of the century. Even in the sixteenth century Harrison had noted that Venetian glass was becoming fashionable, and the replacement of the decorated gilt goblet by a plain, white vessel of similar form is probably an indication of the complete acceptance of glass by the wealthy. The evolution of the goblet over the next thirty years was parallel to that of the standing cup: while gradually gaining in size and capacity, its proportions became squatter, the stem of more rounded, baluster form and the bowl with a flatter base and steeper sides. Their middle-class rather than aristocratic nature is implied by the fact that they are seldom decorated, except when institutionally owned, even with a coat of arms. Ownership is more commonly indicated by pricked initials, such as on the goblet of 1634, originally owned by William Bradford, one of the Pilgrim Fathers who sailed to America on the *Speedwell* in 1620. Although made principally for the middle range of the market, these goblets are generally of comparatively thick gauge and with cast stems. A cheaper form of goblet was also available around in the middle of the century. Known sometimes as dram cups, these were of somewhat smaller capacity and were presumably intended for spirits; they contained no cast parts and were of thinner gauge, generally strengthened by crudely executed flat-chasing.

The form of beakers, or 'beer bowles', continued unaltered in essentials from the sixteenth-century type, although usually smaller, and with no significant modification to the engraved decoration of the Elizabethan model. An apparently novel form of the early seventeenth century, however, was the so-called 'college cup' or 'ox-eye cup'. These plain bulbous vessels, often of surprisingly heavy gauge and with small ring handles, were probably one of the antecedents of the later caudle cup[9]; they appear to have been largely limited to institutional ownership, notably Oxford colleges,

Beaker, silver, c. 1670, probably provincial;
$3\frac{1}{4}$ *in. high.*

although the few that survive make it unwise to place too much significance on this possibly fortuitous fact. While bearing some resemblance to a type of sixteenth-century cup surviving at Corpus Christi Colleges in Oxford and Cambridge (see p. 37), the form is actually derived from Netherlandish tin-glazed pots of the late sixteenth century, which were presumably available to a wider market and which, interestingly enough, are often inscribed with the sacred monogram.

The other important category of drinking vessel was the tankard, which occurs during the first half of the century in three distinct forms: a plain tapering type with flat cover, a more cylindrical variety with similar cover and idiosyncratic skirt base and a very rare, small form with bulbous sides. Only three examples of the last group are recorded, although it was

Small goblet ('dram cup'), silver, 1660, maker's mark
TC in monogram; $2\frac{3}{4}$ in. high.

presumably a fairly common form at the time. The skirt-footed form, however, is paralleled in pewter by a number of surviving flagons, such as one in the collection of the Pewterers' Company which is dated about 1650. The earliest surviving mugs, similar in form but smaller and occasionally with a detachable cover, also date from this period.

The most successful innovation of the mid century, which evolved into one of the typical vessels of the second half of the century, was the caudle cup or porringer. It seems to have appeared in its earliest form around 1650, as a straight-sided, shallow vessel on rim foot, with cast handles and characteristically restrained embossed decoration. Generally it was supplied

Small tankard, silver, 1646, maker's mark TG; 4 in. high
(Gilbert Collection, Los Angeles).

with a cover. Its origins may be traced perhaps to the college cup or, more probably, to earthenware antecedents. That imported Dutch silver might also have played a part in its evolution is suggested by a shallow two-handled bowl and cover of 1636 which is among the plate commissioned by the 10th Earl of Northumberland from Christian van Vianen. [10] In any event, it was used to contain a gruel-like alcoholic drink rather than solid food. While for most purposes it was a practical object, some of the finest in the Commonwealth period and later were gilded and made *en suite* with a footed salver, which suggests that they were intended for display rather than ordinary use.

*Covered mug, silver, 1628, maker's mark CC, a tree between
and pellets above; 5 in. high.*

The terminology relating to these vessels has long been subject to confusion and calls for some explanation. 'Porringer' is applied by historians of pewter and American silver to a shallow vessel with a single, pierced flat handle, which is generally, though erroneously, referred to in the literature of English silver as a 'bleeding bowl'. The picture is further complicated by the fact that certain objects, probably more akin to the shallow French two-handled *'écuelle'* form, are listed as early as 1574 in the royal inventory and described as 'porringers with covers'. Vessels of an

Porringer and salver, silver-gilt, 1656 and 1657, maker's mark IH in monogram;
diameter of salver 12 in.

indistinguishable form are occasionally found as the covers of mid-century skillets, discussed below, and it is possible that some were originally made as skillet covers and retained after the skillet was damaged or worn out. The confusion arises from inconsistencies in contemporary usage, and it would seem that terms such as 'caudle cup', 'posset cup' and 'porringer' were used almost interchangeably, depending perhaps more on the use to which it was put rather than on its form.[11]

The earliest ordinary plate associated with food to survive in more than isolated examples dates from the early seventeenth century. From this period items such as small plain salt cellars, sugar boxes and casters begin to be found. Most of these objects are of such a rudimentary nature that they display no awareness whatever of current decorative styles; it would seem, moreover, that they differed little from earlier silver examples that have now been lost and it is likely that, as in the previous century, they were modelled on standard forms produced for mass consumption by pewterers. Silver dishes (see p. 110), for example, retained the slightly domed centre found in the previous century, although they had by the mid century a broad rim characteristic of most pewter dishes of the period.

Top: *Sugar box, silver, 1650, maker's mark a hound sejeant; 7¾ in. long.*
Bottom: *Pair of salt cellars, silver, 1665, maker's mark IC.*

Other categories of plate occurring for the first time can, however, be traced to base-metal prototypes with more confidence. The earliest extant silver porringers of the shallow, single-handled kind date from around 1630. Sufficient numbers survive in pewter from the sixteenth and early seventeenth centuries, however, to establish that this must have been a standard form, and the silver version, when it does finally occur, follows the other very closely. Similarly, some of the earliest surviving plain

Pair of candlesticks, silver, 1649, maker's mark AM; $6\frac{3}{4}$ in. high
(Museum of Fine Arts, Boston).

domestic candlesticks are a trumpet-shaped pair in the Boston Museum of
Fine Arts, hallmarked for 1649. This form is excessively rare in silver, and
in pewter too, though rather less so in the latter. Its extreme simplicity of
form suggests that it was first made in pewter, since it is well suited to
casting, and indeed pewter examples can certainly be traced further back,
the earliest being a pair at Cotehele, in Cornwall,[12] and another in the
collection of the Pewterers' Company, both of which date from the 1630s.[13]

Pewter has never been a suitable material for cooking, on account of its
softness and low melting point, and most culinary plate is modelled not on
pewter, but on brass. Although, in common with other categories of
domestic plate, this tends to survive only from the mid seventeenth century,
we know that it was used in the houses of the wealthy from much earlier.
The 1601 inventory of Hardwick Hall, for example, lists a considerable
range of kitchen plate, including 'a skellet ... a great pott white to boyle
things in ... a grydyron ... a frying pan ... a Chafer for water ... a bucket
without a Cover ... [and] a Chafing dishe with a perfuming pan'. The form
of a silver skillet, or saucepan, with its characteristic tapering feet, is closely
related to those in brass, the only significant differences being that the latter
generally have a cast iron rather than turned wood handle, while the few

Skillet and cover, silver, 1634, maker's mark VS,
a fleur de lys below; $4\frac{3}{4}$ in. high.

surviving examples in silver are smaller than those in brass and have, or
appear originally to have had, a cover. The relative simplicity of a perfume
burner of 1628 in the Los Angeles County Museum of Art likewise betrays
its probable kinship to a brass model.

Chafing dishes preceded the eighteenth-century dish stand with burner
and contained hot coals to heat the dish or vessel placed on top of it.

*Perfume burner, silver, 1628, maker's mark TI; 8¾ in. high
(William Randolph Hearst Collection, Los Angeles County Museum of Art).*

Known to have been made in silver since the Middle Ages, the earliest to survive in that metal date from nearer the end of the century, but it was evidently a standard enough item for Samuel Pepys to have 'bespoke ... a silver chafing dish for warming plates' in January 1666.[14] Again, it is reasonable to assume that the form of this and earlier examples was rudimentary and based on brass prototypes. Most of these utilitarian domestic objects would have been familiar enough in base metal to patrons and goldsmiths alike. Brass 'skellottes, pannes' and a 'chafer' are listed on Viscount Lisle's inventory of about 1540; Edward Catherall, a brewer and small farmer of Luton, possessed a brass 'chafinge dishe' in 1612,[15] and Sir Thomas Fairfax in about 1625 owned a considerable quantity of brass and silver, including a chafing dish in both metals. Clearly, therefore, such utensils had permeated most levels of society and it would have been

Dish, silver, 1650, maker's mark of Arthur Manwaring;
$13\frac{1}{4}$ *in. diameter.*

natural for goldsmiths to follow their pattern when asked to make one of precious metal.

In spite of the survival of the odd inkstand, spout cup or spice box to flesh out the descriptions found in inventories, however, there are still many objects from the first half of the seventeenth century of which we can form only a vague idea. The 'note of the plate which stood upon the cupboard in [Sir Thomas Fairfax's] chamber' around 1630, for example, lists a number of items about which we can only speculate, such as '2 litle silver cruets ... a plaine silver bottle ... one great spown & two lesse spownes, for preserving with'. The same document lists 'foure silver livery pottes' as distinct from 'three silver hall pottes', although whether the different names implied a different appearance is quite unclear. This is in marked contrast to the picture which emerges of the second half of the century, about which our knowledge is very much fuller.

Five

THE RESTORATION

The return of Charles II in 1660 has traditionally been associated with a complete change in the artistic climate. In many ways his restoration did indeed mark a watershed, both politically and artistically. For there can be no doubt that once Parliament had resolved to restore the monarchy, there was considerable impatience for the King's arrival, and in no area was the general excitement more clearly expressed than in the patronage of artists. Land was restored to those from whom it had been confiscated, lords and bishops were again in the ascendancy and the City prospered.

The installation of Charles II on the throne of England led, in particular, to a significant revival in the goldsmith's trade. For with the restoration of the monarchy the security of the aristocracy was also restored, and in consequence people were again prepared to invest in plate. At the same time the defeat of the Puritan cause returned opulent display to favour, and the wealthy were once more prepared to spend money on elaborate decoration. More specifically, the injection of royal patronage had a very direct impact on the flagging business of London goldsmiths. While the King himself spent around £2,000 a year at this time on the revived custom of exchanging New Year's gifts,[1] the official issue of plate to ambassadors and other high-ranking officials also provided a powerful impetus to the trade. Samuel Pepys described the operation of the system when he acted on behalf of the Earl of Sandwich on 4 January 1661: 'I had been early this morning at White-hall at the Jewell-Office, to choose a piece of gilt plate for my Lord in return of his offering to the King (which it seems is usuall at this time of year, and an Earle gives 20 pieces in gold in a purse to the King); I chose a gilt tankard weighing 31 ounces and a half, and he is allowed 30; so I paid 12s for the ounce and a half over what he is to have.'[2]

But the impact of the restoration, both in political and artistic terms, would have seemed less dramatic to contemporaries than it has been made to seem in retrospect. The King was only invited to return because the climate of opinion in the country had already shifted sufficiently to make the monarchy acceptable once more. Patronage had already been on the increase before the end of the Commonwealth, and the taste for which Charles II's reign (1660–85) is so famous was already evident in some plate from the late 1650s.

It is difficult to gauge the full measure of new business created by the restored monarchy. According to figures which the Goldsmiths' Company was asked to submit to the King's Council in 1664, the amount of plate assayed over the period 1653–62 remained remarkably constant, varying between 28,000 and 35,000 lb. each year.[3] But these figures are almost certainly misleading, and a substantial increase in business for the goldsmiths of London after the Restoration can hardly be in doubt, if only on the grounds of the sheer quantity of plate surviving from after 1660 in relation to that from the preceding period. Moreover, royal plate from this period is seldom marked, and the hallmarking of commissioned plate did not become obligatory until 1697, unless 'set for sale'. A considerable proportion of plate from Charles II's reign was therefore struck with the maker's mark only and would not have been accounted for in the figures submitted by the company.

In terms of taste the most obvious affect of the restoration was not so much to introduce a new style, for this had been creeping into English silver for some years, as to give it a focus and impetus that had been lacking under the previous régime. For while the taste of the court automatically produced a fashion, the foreign craftsmen who were attracted to England in its wake provided the skills that the fashion demanded.

During the second quarter of the century design had become increasingly insular, not least because the presence of immigrant craftsmen became steadily less conspicuous as political uncertainty lasted. With the re-establishment of the monarchy that situation changed. Charles II and his court had spent part of their exile in France, where they had become accustomed to the prevailing taste for comfort and luxury. His return was quickly followed by almost universal acceptance of new styles in English silver and by a new influx of foreign craftsmen. The latter was modest compared with the massive Huguenot immigration later in the century, but their presence was responsible for the introduction of important new styles and techniques and for raising standards that had declined so seriously during the preceding fifty years.

By far the most important stylistic innovation of the period was the introduction of the Dutch floral style. In Holland the fashion for flower paintings and for embossing or engraving plate with precise, studied botanical decoration had gradually developed over the second quarter of the seventeenth century. But in England this kind of exact floral rendering had no precedent and must have seemed quite startling to contemporaries. Some of the very finest examples of this new style are found among the splendid services of church plate that were commissioned soon after the restoration, in particular that of Christ Church, Oxford,[4] and Bishop Auckland, the residence of the Bishop of Durham. Very soon it gained almost universal popularity and by 1665 nearly everything from the grandest royal display plate to the most ordinary domestic porringer, cup or beaker was decorated in the same style. There is no doubt, however, that the results were very varied and the poor quality of much of this chasing illustrates how far most English goldsmiths lagged behind the standard expected of their peers in France, Germany or Holland.

Elements of the auricular style, which had been introduced to England during Charles I's reign (see p. 89) and which had largely failed to take root then, also began to appear in early restoration silver, especially in the work of more sophisticated goldsmiths, such as the 'hound sejant' maker. Some of these new styles would have filtered into the country through the circulation of printed pattern books, including those of Stephano della Bella and Adam van Vianen, the latter of which was published by his son, Christian, in 1650 under the title *Modelles Artificiels*.[5] But the strongest influence was that of alien goldsmiths, who were again working in London in significant numbers.

Skilled continental goldsmiths were in a position to supply the demand for fine decorative plate which could not always be met by native craftsmen. The ill-feeling which this inevitably generated in the trade is reflected by the repeated petitions to the wardens of the Goldsmiths' Company to take action against the 'strangers', although there was in practice little that could be done unless their workshops were within the City jurisdiction. Traditionally free areas such as Westminster and the Liberty of St Martin-le-Grand were exempt from the authority of the guilds, and were consequently a common resort for immigrant craftsmen.

Presumably some of these goldsmiths had been employed by the King during his exile; certainly a number were assisted by royal commissions after they arrived in England and in 1663 the King actually commanded the company to mark the plate of three foreign goldsmiths in his service.[6]

The procurement of all the coronation regalia, royal domestic plate and official plate for ambassadors and diplomatic gifts was the responsibility of the Lord Chamberlain through the royal goldsmith, and the latter's influence with regard to alien goldsmiths was obviously very important. This is particularly well documented in the case of Sir Robert Viner (1631–88),

Beaker, silver, c. 1670, maker's mark RD;
$4\frac{1}{2}$ in. high.

who was appointed royal goldsmith in 1660 and who, in common with an increasing number of putative goldsmiths in the late seventeenth century, was in effect a banker rather than a working craftsman.

Relatively few makers' marks from the second half of the seventeenth century have been identified, and it is only after 1697, when all makers were obliged to register new marks, that a comprehensive list of London goldsmiths is available. However, a significant number of those appearing on the best plate of the period are apparently for foreigners. The most outstanding makers from the period covered by this chapter are Arthur Manwaring and the 'hound sejant' maker (see p. 97), Jacob Bodendick, Wolfgang Howzer and Thomas Jenkins. The first two mentioned had evidently competed for the few choice commissions of the Commonwealth period and were well able to adapt to the new continental style when required. Manwaring's standing cup of 1663 in the Goldsmiths' Company collection (the Feeke Cup)[7] and the 'hound sejant' maker's caudle cup at Wadham College, Oxford,[8] both show a perfect grasp of the auricular style still, if only just, acceptable in Holland, although Manwaring's sense of form is more conventional than the latter's.

We have no way of knowing whether the 'hound sejant' maker was a native or an alien, although from his prominence during the interregnum it is almost certain that he was English. Bodendick and Howzer, on the other hand, are documented as natives of Limburg in Germany and Zurich respectively, and George Bowers, appointed 'embosser in ordinary' to the King in 1661, was described as being 'born in foreign parts'. Howzer's work is particularly notable for its fine embossing, exemplified by the chapel plate which he made through the good offices of Sir Robert Viner for Bishop Cozins of Durham in 1660–61. We can safely assume that he was a plateworker as well as a chaser, however, since his name occurs in the records of the Goldsmiths' Company in connection with certain offences against the hallmarking regulations[9].

Of Bodendick's characteristics as a goldsmith we have a much more rounded view. Although clearly capable of producing plate compatible with English taste, his most notable contribution was the introduction of certain typical north German styles and techniques which were quite unfamiliar in England, in particular cagework and cast auricular tankard handles. The former involved piercing and embossing a thin sheet of silver and sliding it over the plain barrel of a cup. It is highly decorative, and the technique has the advantage that the pierced sleeve plays no structural role, so that it can be made very thinly and raised in much higher relief than the actual body of the cup. The cast tankard handles required more metal than the more usual raised and soldered ones, but had far greater decorative potential (see p. 118). They were also symptomatic of a new interest in the sculptural decoration of silver which became an important feature of some of the lavish furnishings of the period, such as wine cisterns and andirons.

The best English makers were not slow in following the lead of these new continental styles and standards. Some of these, such as Manwaring,

Cagework cup and cover, silver and silver-gilt, c. 1670, unmarked; $7\frac{1}{2}$ in. high
(Untermyer Collection, Metropolitan Museum of Art, New York).

Francis Leake and Francis Garthorne, have been known for some time, but perhaps the most versatile and accomplished was the more recently identified Thomas Jenkins, whose known works span the period 1668–1704. Nearly a hundred items or sets of items bearing his mark have been recorded[10] and it is possible to trace almost the entire development of late seventeenth-century domestic and display plate through his work alone.

This is the first period for which large decorative pieces survive in any numbers. The grandest plate of this category was silver furniture, the fashion for which originated in France. Although such staggering examples of

Pair of tankards, silver, 1671, maker's mark of Thomas Jenkins; 10 in. high
(National Trust, Dunham Massey, Cheshire).

extravagance as Nell Gwyn's silver bed, which contained no less than 2,265 ounces of silver, no longer survive, the sumptuous suite of silver furniture at Knole gives a good idea of their rich effect. These were generally constructed on an oak carcass, to which sheets of embossed silver were pinned, but the quantity of metal used to make such objects was very considerable.

Allied to furniture was the late seventeenth-century fashion for 'chimney piece furniture', which included andirons, bellows and fire irons and the garniture of vases which often decorated the mantelpiece. Fire irons with silver handles are and always were a comparative luxury. Sets survive at Burghley and Ham House, and John Evelyn, when he visited the latter in 1678, described it as 'furnished like a great prince's'. Garnitures of vases, on the other hand, are much more common and are again represented by an exceptional group at Knole. Although usually embossed in the Dutch manner with cherubs and naturalistic foliage, their inspiration was oriental porcelain, which was now becoming quite widely available, and the charac-teristic form of these tall beaker-shaped and bulbous covered vases follows that of the Chinese models fairly closely.

Suite of furniture, silver, 1676–81; length of table 40 in.
(National Trust, Knole, Kent).

Andiron (one of a pair), silver, c. 1680, unmarked; $29\frac{1}{2}$ in. high
(National Trust, Knole, Kent).

*Wine cistern, silver, 1680, maker's mark of Robert Cooper; 27 in. long
(National Trust, Ickworth, Suffolk).*

The embossed floral style was also well suited to wine cisterns and wall
sconces. Unlike the novel garnitures of vases, these had certainly existed
earlier in silver, although none from before the restoration has come to
light. Typical of the expansive character of the late seventeenth-century
cistern are examples of 1677 by Thomas Jenkins in the Victoria and Albert
Museum[11] and of 1680 by Robert Cooper at Ickworth, but most surviving
examples are of the same shallow oval form with four feet and lion's mask
handles.

The sconce, or wall light, first survives in silver from around 1675 and
by 1720 had already faded from fashion, presumably because of the fire
risk that was associated with the new fashion for hanging draperies around
window frames. But its origins lie much further back in brass, and the four
'plate Candlesticks of brass to hang on the wales [walls]' at Hardwick in
1601[12] seem not to have been especially unusual. These were generally
made from embossed dishes, probably imported from Nuremberg and
Dinant, with a candle branch fixed to its lower rim, so that the branch
projected and the dish acted as a reflector. Occasionally they were found
in silver too. Henry VIII is known to have owned some, the 1574 royal
inventory lists 'two Candeleplates of siluer and half guilt',[13] and Charles I

— 121 —

also possessed a set of four at his death in 1649. The National Trust's collection of sconces is quite unparalleled and out of all proportion to its other holdings of silver: in addition to those at Belton and Erdigg, there are no fewer than twenty-four at Knole, including a set of twelve dated 1685.

Grandiose plate such as this, mainly appearing for the first time, was the most prestigious of the day and largely filled a vacuum left by the decline of traditional forms like the standing salt and the ewer and basin. A certain ambiguity surrounds the latter during the late seventeenth century, since it was still made for ceremonial or display purposes but virtually ceased to have a practical role after the fork came into general use. The demise of the standing salt, on the other hand, was more clear-cut. While having an important ceremonial role, the salt had never been intended for display on the sideboard but had been made to stand on the table and to be used. Its use had been directly associated with the custom of dining in the great hall, where large numbers were seated according to a clear hierarchy. With the abandonment of the hall the salt became redundant, and by the time of the restoration it was made only for use on special occasions, such as state banquets, or for university colleges and City livery companies, where the old style of dining was still maintained.

The embossed floral style was not the only popular type of decoration during the late seventeenth century. It was often modified by the introduction of friezes of figures, some of which were clearly derived from the pattern books of Stephano della Bella or Polifilo Zancarli[14] and caudle cups of the third quarter of the century were often decorated with heraldic beasts such as lions and unicorns. Towards the end of the century this figurative and naturalistic style was superseded by a greater use of broad embossed flutes. These stylistic trends, however, were punctuated by one or two isolated decorative developments that were apparently without precursors or successors, but which were the occasion of some of the most charming tributaries of the main stream of English silver.

Fascination with the mystery of the Orient has periodically manifested itself in the decorative arts in a type of imaginative and fanciful decoration known as chinoiserie. The word refers more to the subject matter than to its specific treatment, and one of its most distinctive guises is a form of flat-chased decoration which enjoyed a brief period of popularity from about 1680 to 1685. The main features of this decoration are oriental figures and exotic birds and foliage, frequently set in fanciful landscapes enhanced by bizarre architectural follies. It is found on plate bearing the marks of as many as twenty-five different makers, disappears as suddenly as it appeared,

*Sconce, silver, 1685, maker's mark TS; $9\frac{3}{4}$ in. high
(National Trust, Knole, Kent).*

Tankard, silver, York, 1657, maker's mark of John Plummer; $7\frac{1}{4}$ in. high
(Victoria and Albert Museum, London).

and was presumably carried out by a specialist chaser or workshop to whom plate was sub-contracted for decorating. The style is represented in the National Trust's silver by a pair of mugs by George Garthorne at Polesden Lacey[15] and a monteith bowl at Erdigg (p. 9), while one of the finest examples of all is a remarkable pair of tankards of the same year as the mugs, made for the first Earl Brownlow and formerly at Belton.[16]

The recovery of engraving during the latter part of the seventeenth century did not generally equal that of embossing or chasing, and most engraving on plate is confined to coats of arms within crossed plumes. A

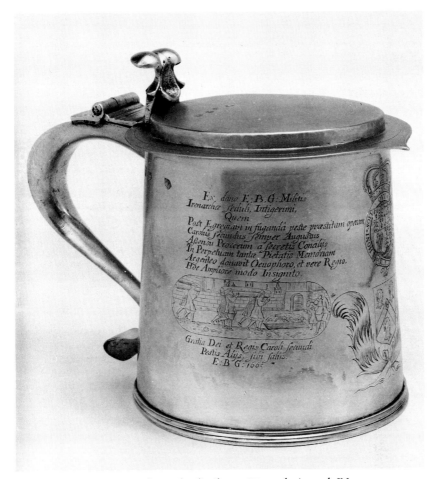

*'Fire of London tankard', silver, 1675, maker's mark IN
above a bird; 7 in. high.*

small number of finely engraved pieces, particularly the botanically engraved tankards by John Plummer of York, testify to the fact that some talented engravers were working in England, but the indifferent engraving of the tankards made for Sir Edmund Berry Godfrey to commemorate the Plague and the Fire of London shows equally that distinguished quality was not always expected, even for important commissions. Most of these engravers are anonymous, and the few that have emerged, such as Simon Gribelin and Blaise Gentot,[17] who were responsible for some of the most spectacular engraving of the turn of the century (such as the former's altar dish of 1706 at Dunham Massey, or the latter's magnificent table top at Chatsworth) suggest that improved standards in engraving were partly the result of injected foreign talent.

Not all display plate, however, was lavishly decorated, and some of the most important pieces of the period were relatively plain or of distinctly

The Croft Cups, silver, 1685, makers' marks SH and of Benjamin Pyne; 14½ in. high (British Museum, London).

conservative appearance. The ewer and basin of 1675 presented by Samuel Pepys to the Clothworkers' Company[18] is particularly finely engraved, but is otherwise perfectly plain. The comparatively austere fashion for broad bands of punched matting also persisted well into the new period. In no way an excuse for technical shortcomings at this stage, it is characteristic of some of the heaviest and most distinguished gilt plate and was chosen as the appropriate style for important presentations, such as porringers made for New Year's gifts and a tankard of 1675 presented to General Monck.[19]

As important as the revolution in decoration, if less dramatic, was the evolution of form. This affected formal and ceremonial as much as practical plate, but was particularly evident in the transformation of the standing cup. Still the most important item of display plate and the traditional form for presentations or bequests, the standing cup and cover underwent a fundamental change of character during this period that is difficult to trace from surviving examples, but led eventually to the establishment of the two-handled cup and cover as one of the most characteristic forms of the early eighteenth century.

Typical standing cups of the early restoration period follow the form established in the second quarter of the century, although tending towards gradually squatter proportions. The Croft Cups of 1685 by Benjamin Pyne

The Calverley toilet service, silver, 1683, maker's mark WF, knot below
(Victoria and Albert Museum, London).

and an anonymous maker with the mark SH, however, combine aspects of the standing cup and the porringer to produce an entirely new form that has the dignity and presence of the former, but proportions closer to the latter. The facts that these cups have been decorated in a restrained manner and were made by different goldsmiths for a family of only modest wealth make it unlikely that they would in fact have been the novelty at the time that their freak survival makes them seem now. The cups were made in accordance with a provision in the will of Ann Archer, who requested that 'my four Children may have thirty pounds a peece to buy them strong peeces of plate, all of one fashion, with the inscription, The Legacy of their dead mother...' It would seem in such circumstances much more likely that a familiar and relatively conventional design would have been chosen, rather than one that was new or experimental.[20]

The two-handled cup may have been a new form, but the role it played had existed before. A more significant innovation was the introduction of the matched silver dressing-table, or toilet, service. The earliest surviving English services date from after the restoration, although they were certainly made earlier in the century. The fashion was probably introduced from France and is indicative both of the growth of interest in elaborate display plate associated with rooms other than the dining room, and of the increasingly complex cosmetic preparations that were fashionable during the late seventeenth and early eighteenth centuries. The extensive range of items that made up these services, together with some of their functions, are described in *Mundus Muliebris*, published in 1690 by John Evelyn and supposedly written by his daughter Mary:

> The dressing-room and implements
> Of toilet plate, gilt and embossed
> And several other things of cost.
> The table mirroir, one glue pot,
> One for pomata, and what not?
> Or washes, unguents and cosmetics;
> A pair of silver candlesticks;
> Snuffers and snuff-dish; boxes more,
> For powders, patches, waters store
> In silver flasks, or bottles, cups
> Cover'd or open, to wash chaps.

Some services from the early eighteenth century are decorated with dignified restraint, but the importance of the restoration services is evident from the fact that most are very elaborately decorated and gilded. Embossed services, such as the Calverley Service in the Victoria and Albert Museum, seem to have been particularly popular, but other fashionable types of decoration included chinoiserie and engraving. One of the finest and most unusual seventeenth century services is one of about 1673 at Knole, which is parcel-gilt and decorated with panels of matting and applied cyphers.[21]

The range of ordinary domestic plate available during the latter part of the seventeenth century seems to have increased significantly. During the nine years over which he kept his diary, Pepys recorded the gradual additions he made to his 'cupboard of plate' as he became more prosperous. Some of these he bought for himself and others he accepted as gifts. By 1663 he possessed cups and covers, tankards, a ewer and basin and flagons. In 1665 he records the payment of £6 14s. 6d. for twelve salt cellars,[22] and by the following year his inventory included chafing dishes, candlesticks, inkstands, plates and a 'silver snuff-dish which I do give myself for my closet'.[23] In 1669 he even accepted a 'noble silver warming-pan' as a gift, although admittedly with some misgivings over whether he should take what was so obviously a bribe.[24]

A particularly popular innovation during the last twenty years of the century was the punch bowl and a related vessel, the monteith (see p. 9).

Porringer, silver, 1674, maker's mark IN, mullet below; $6\frac{1}{8}$ in. high.

The latter was designed for cooling glasses, and its name is explained in a well-known passage from the diary of Anthony Wood in 1683, where he writes that 'This yeare in the summer time came up a vessel or bason notched at the brims to let drinking glasses hang there by the foot so that the body or drinking place might hang in the water to cool them. Such bason was called a "Monteigh" from a fantastical Scot named "Monsieur Monteigh" who, at that time or a little before, wore the botton of his cloake or coat so notched.'[25] Its decline in popularity after about 1720 was probably associated with the tendency for eighteenth-century drinking glasses to be made with progressively smaller feet which would have been less easy to suspend in this way.

A more common vessel still was the caudle cup, or porringer, and the range of styles in which it is found is a reflection of its popularity. But other domestic plate also appears in a wide range of styles. Sugar boxes and salvers were available in every style from the severely plain to the lavishly embossed. Candlesticks also appear to have been available in a range of

Porringer, silver, 1679, maker's mark IH, fleur de lys and pellets below; 9 in. high
(Untermyer Collection, Metropolitan Museum of Art, New York).

styles that suited very different budgets. The most standard type of the late seventeenth century was in the form of a fluted column on square or octagonal base and was raised from sheet. But heavier and more elaborately decorated cast patterns were also available. The latter ranged from baluster stems on plain bases to stems in the form of human figures on scrolling acanthus foliage bases.

The recovery of the market for domestic plate is epitomized by the immense popularity of the tankard. Over four times as many survive from the twenty years after the restoration as from the previous two decades. Some of these were of massive proportions on cast feet and were intended for passing from one person to another, but most take a standard form,

Pair of candlesticks, silver, 1688, maker's mark possibly II;
$9\frac{1}{8}$ *in. high.*

with squat tapering cylindrical body on rim foot and with flat cover. Decoration generally consists either of a simple band of embossed acanthus foliage around the lower part of the body or, more rarely, a broad band of punched matting (see p. 14). The majority, however, are quite plain, decorated only with engraved coats of arms within standard plume mantling.

These tankards correspond closely in form to their pewter equivalents, and the evidence again points to the conclusion that for ordinary domestic patterns the silversmiths were following the styles already established by the pewterers. The uniformity of most silver tankards also recalls the pewterer's methods of production, which required the use of expensive moulds and made frequent design changes uneconomic. Moreover, there

Pair of candlesticks, silver, 1700, maker's mark of Joseph Bird;
$6\frac{1}{8}$ in. high.

was apparently a much greater variety of details such as cast thumbpieces available among pewter tankards than silver ones, while a number of design innovations, notably the domed cover, would appear to have come first in pewter, then to be followed by silver. This is almost certainly significant and is further evidence for the leadership provided by pewterers in this area of the market.

Tankard, silver, 1679, maker's mark IR;
$6\frac{1}{2}$ *in. high.*

A similar affinity between the two metals is recognizable in the patterns used for other mundane practical plate. Most silver plates and dishes during the late seventeenth century, as earlier, are plain and continue to correspond closely to pewter patterns. Other domestic items, ranging from kitchen plate to toilet plate such as shaving jugs and bowls or chamber pots, seem also to be directly modelled on pewter or brass patterns. The types of

— 133 —

Plate, silver, 1669, maker's mark AF;
10 in. diameter.

spoons usual in silver in the seventeenth century, including 'seal tops', 'slip
tops' and 'puritan' spoons during the first half and 'trefid' spoons during
the second, are likewise all found in pewter too. Indeed, the wide variety
of decorative patterns, often of a commemorative nature, found on pewter
trefid spoons is, as with tankards, a reminder of how much larger the market
was for pewter than for silver.

Shaving jug and basin with soap box, silver, 1682, maker's mark WS; length of dish 13¾ in. (Gilbert Collection, Los Angeles).

A less clear account can be given of the evolution of the fork, and survivals from before the closing years of the seventeenth century are rare. Obviously their rise in popularity was linked to the declining use of the ewer and basin, and it may safely be assumed that they were in general use by the end of the century, when they begin to figure quite prominently in inventories. Their stems followed the same patterns as spoons, although they are never found with decorative finials. The earliest forks seem generally to have had two prongs and by the end of the century to have acquired a third. By the middle of the following century, however, it was found that four-pronged forks were considerably safer to use. This presumably partly explains the rarity of seventeenth-century examples, in that this fundamental change in design would have rendered old forks obsolete and more likely to be melted down than old spoons.

No models in pewter or brass were available for the first plate made in connection with tea and coffee. These new beverages made their first appearance in England during the third quarter of the seventeenth century, but were slow to win general acceptance. Coffee houses were suppressed in 1675 and described as 'a great resort of idle and disaffected persons' and tea was enormously expensive. Pepys had tried it in 1660 and pronounced favourably upon it,[26] but he was fortunate in being given such a treat, since the cost of a pound of best quality tea at that time was £3 10s., the

Group of trefid spoons, silver. From left to right:
c. 1663, maker's mark IC; provincial, c. 1685; provincial, c. 1680.

equivalent of a year's wages for a maid. By 1700 it had dropped to £1 a pound and by 1760 to 10s. But even so, when compared with the average price of meat at 3d. a pound, this was still a very considerable luxury. Unlike beer and tankards, therefore, there was an economic affinity between tea and silver in that those who could afford the former would also have been able to afford the latter, and there was consequently no equivalent pattern in pewter for goldsmiths to follow. Until the second quarter of the eighteenth century, when European porcelain teapots first became available,

Coffee pot, silver, 1681, maker's mark GG; $9\frac{3}{4}$ in. high
(Victoria and Albert Museum, London).

tea wares were the exclusive preserve of goldsmiths, and the design of the first silver teapots, which were invariably very small, was either based on that of imported chinese porcelain examples, or followed the shape of coffee pots. Silver tea cups were also modelled on Chinese porcelain tea bowls, which had been imported into Europe since as early as the 1640s.

Coffee, although also expensive, was never an extravagance of the same order as tea. By the time of their suppression there were over 400 coffee houses in London alone, and they were regarded as fashionable meeting places at which to transact business. The earliest known silver coffee pot is in the Victoria and Albert Museum and is hallmarked for 1681. It and others from before the very last years of the century are formed as a plain tapering cylinder with straight spout and conical cover and have a crude inelegance which betrays their derivation from the tin pots used in coffee houses.

Teapot, silver-gilt, c. 1685, maker's mark RH; $5\frac{3}{4}$ in. high
(Victoria and Albert Museum, London).

These were only the beginnings of a category of English silver which was later to become one of the most important aspects of the goldsmith's ordinary business, and which expanded dramatically in the early years of the eighteenth century as the demand for tea and coffee – and chocolate – grew and the fashion developed for taking these beverages at home.

Six

THE HUGUENOT CONTRIBUTION

Just as the restoration of Charles II in 1660 had accelerated the adoption of a radically new style in English decorative arts, so the equally dramatic adoption of a completely new taste shortly before the end of the seventeenth century was linked to affairs of state. The bloodless revolution of 1688 in England resulted in the displacement of James II (r. 1685–8), the last of the Stuart kings, by his daughter, Mary, and son-in-law, Prince William of Orange (r. 1688–1702), as joint rulers. Slightly earlier, in 1685, the reversal of a royal edict in France had led directly to the flight of some 200,000 Protestant citizens, a significant proportion of whom settled eventually in England.[1] While in Holland William had employed French artists and architects for the decoration of his palace at Het Loo, and the transfer of his court to England ensured the adoption of French taste here too. It was fortuitous for the development of the arts in England that the arrival over a few years of some 40–50,000 French refugees made it possible for this new taste to be readily satisfied by craftsmen already familiar with its demands.

The revocation of the Edict of Nantes by Louis XIV in 1685 was the culmination of more than 150 years of various degrees of religious and political persecution of French Calvinists, or Huguenots. As persecution had become more overt the flow of its victims leaving the country increased. During Elizabeth's reign, when persecution in France was particularly rampant, it had been government policy to encourage the settlement of immigrant craftsmen, provided they were sound Protestants, since it was felt that they would improve the level of English trades by introducing new techniques and skills.

Soon after his accession to the French throne, Henry IV (1594–1610) had supposedly settled the question of religious freedom by the 'irrevocable' Edict of Nantes in 1598 which permitted Protestants to worship in their own way within certain specified limits. This and the establishment of the

United Provinces in Holland in 1609 stemmed the flow of Protestant refugees into England during the early seventeenth century, but the provisions of the edict were gradually eroded during the reigns of Louis XIII (r. 1610–43) and XIV (r. 1643–1715), exposing Huguenots to increasing official and unofficial harassment. In 1685 the edict was finally revoked absolutely, effectively outlawing Protestants who refused to recant and resulting in a huge tide of refugees leaving the country.

The impact of the revocation itself was not felt immediately or suddenly in England: many had emigrated as early as the 1670s, as conditions became less tolerable at home, while others had been wary of England as a completely safe refuge until James II's Declaration of Indulgence in 1687. For many Huguenots, therefore, like the goldsmith Paul de Lamerie's parents, the route to England was by way of a period in Holland. By 1700, however, it has been estimated that as many as 23,000 had arrived in London, amounting to about 5 per cent of the population of the city.[2]

Like many refugee communities, the Huguenots in London were anxious to preserve their own cultural identity and reluctant to integrate with the rest of society. They congregated in specific areas of London, especially Soho and Spitalfields, maintained their own educational and religious institutions and continued to speak French. Yet in spite of their initial separatist attitude, by the third decade of the eighteenth century a combination of industry and natural ability had raised a surprising number of Huguenots to prominent positions in society, while the community as a whole had come to dominate certain trades, particularly those of the textile worker and the goldsmith. By the reign of George I (1714–27) the tables had turned and the success of most prominent native goldsmiths largely depended upon their readiness to accept the new standards and styles that had been introduced by the immigrants.

The long history of religious persecution in France meant that there had been French goldsmiths working in London since the sixteenth century. The Aliens Returns for Elizabeth's and James I's reigns show that in addition to the Dutch and German goldsmiths in London, there were about sixty French.[3] These had generally been regarded with some hostility by native craftsmen, and the volume of complaints levelled against them was to a large extent a measure of the numbers of refugees arriving in London at the time.

One of the first immigrants in the new wave to be admitted to the Goldsmiths' Company was Pierre Harache, who received his letters of denization in June 1682 and was admitted to the company in the following month on the payment of £2 6s. 8d. He presented a certificate indicating that he had 'lately come from France for to avoid persecution and live quietly, is not only a Protestant, but by his Majesty's bounty is made a free denizon, that he may settle here freely with his family'.[4] But the refugee community had already begun to make a considerable impact; in 1683 many of the most prominent English goldsmiths, including George Garthorne and Anthony Nelme, signed a petition to the wardens of the Company, pleading that

... divers aliens and forreigners are come into this kingdome and reside in and about this City, and that some of them ... do ... keep houses, and shops, and exercise and practise ye said Trade and Mistery of ye Goldsmiths, by which evill example other Aliens of ye same Mistery are encouraged ... to come and enjoy ... the same priviledges and immunities equall with Us, which (considering the great numbers of our Natives already exercising ye said Mistery and ye deadnesse of Trade) will certainly bring us and our familyes to great Poverty and want, and put us upon the extremity of seeking other waiyes for a Livelyhood, unlesse some speedy remedy be taken.[5]

The truth of the matter is not that there were too many goldsmiths or too little trade, but that the Huguenots were prepared to produce finer work at more competitive rates than native goldsmiths. A further petition of 1711 grudgingly acknowledged part of this when it complained of 'the admittance of the necessitous strangers, whose desperate fortunes oblige them to worke at miserable rates', and furthermore, that the new styles for which their work had created a demand had now 'forced [English goldsmiths] to bestow much more time and labour in working up their plate than hath been the practise in former times'.[6]

The petition of 1683 seems to have had some effect, and few of Harache's compatriots appear to have been admitted to the company until well into the 1690s. That the Huguenot community continued to flourish despite such concerted opposition is a telling vindication of their talents, their capacity to adapt and the demand for their products. Certainly their greater technical skills were quickly recognized, and some leading native goldsmiths, such as William Lukin, evidently employed Huguenots extensively for major commissions. But the close community in which they chose to live must also have fostered a spirit of mutual help that would not necessarily have existed among native craftsmen. The natural ties of the minority group were strengthened by a tendency to marry within the community and by similarly motivated commercial loyalties. A typical example is that of the goldsmith David Willaume, who was the brother-in-law of Louis Mettayer; his daughter married David Tanqueray, the latter two both being goldsmiths, and his sister-in-law married the engraver Simon Gribelin. Throughout the first quarter of the eighteenth century Huguenot goldsmiths almost invariably chose their apprentices and associates from the families of fellow Huguenots, and the work of Simon Gribelin, for example, is usually found on plate with a Huguenot's mark. The community must also have benefited considerably from the presence of their compatriot, Daniel Marot (1663–1752), whose designs were frequently drawn upon in the early work of Paul de Lamerie and other Huguenot goldsmiths and who, as architect to William III, must have been in a position to influence commissions.

A further reason for their success must be that, contrary to the state of things implied in the 1685 petition, trade was evidently very good during the closing decade of the century. It has been estimated that between 1688 and 1701 – a period of comparative peace and expanding commerce – the wealth of England increased by as much as 20 per cent,[7] and a significant percentage of this must have been put into that traditional form of capital, plate. The preamble to the hallmarking act of 1697 makes it clear that the demand for new plate was being met by the melting down of large quantities of coinage or coin-clipping (trimming silver from the edges of coins) and that this was causing serious disruption to the economy.

The act sought to remedy the problem by imposing a higher standard of purity for wrought plate, while retaining sterling standard for the coinage. The new standard for plate was to be eight pennyweight in the pound finer than sterling, or 95.8 per cent pure as opposed to 92.5 per cent. It also imposed a new set of hallmarks to distinguish plate of the higher standard: 'The worker's mark [is] to be expressed by the first two letters of his surname, the marks of the mystery or craft of the Goldsmiths, which, instead of the Leopard's Head and the Lion, shall for this plate be the figure of a woman, commonly called Britannia and the figure of a lion's head erased, and a distinct variable mark to be used by the warden of the said mystery, to denote the year in which such plate is made.'[8] From the historian's point of view the act is of great significance, since the registration of new makers' marks lifts the anonymity from the vast majority of London goldsmiths, and with the exception of those contained in a single missing register from the 1760s, it is possible to identify nearly every London goldsmith's mark from 1697 onwards.

However, it failed in its main purpose. The withdrawal of coinage from circulation and 'the wicked and pernicious crime of clipping' continued unabated, and in 1719 it was repealed by a new act. Under this legislation sterling standard was reinstated for wrought plate, although Britannia standard was retained as a legitimate alternative – as it remains – and it was laid down that the makers' marks for sterling plate should in future comprise the initial letters of the maker's Christian name and surname. The strain that demand for new plate put on the currency was now to be remedied by a duty of 6d. an ounce, payable when the plate was hallmarked. This effectively increased the basic price of silver, apart from the charge for fashion, by about 10 per cent. But although bitterly opposed by goldsmiths, the new duty seems in fact to have made little difference to demand. This may perhaps partly be explained by the fraudulent evasion of the duty by some goldsmiths through a practice known as 'duty dodging', which is explained in the following chapter.

The revolution in taste introduced by the Huguenot goldsmiths was as dramatic as that of forty years earlier and set new standards in technical as well as stylistic terms. The techniques particularly associated with the Huguenots were not new, but were practised by them with a skill that greatly expanded their decorative potential. These were primarily 'cut-card' ornament, casting and raising. Engraving might also be mentioned, although engravers were generally specialist craftsmen working for goldsmiths, rather than goldsmiths themselves.

'Cut-card' work (see pp. 6, 11) had been introduced around the middle of the previous century, probably from France. But whereas English goldsmiths had tended to use it only for elementary decoration, the Huguenots handled it with great sophistication. It involved the creation of relief decoration by the application of strips of silver, cut into the desired pattern and applied to the body of the object. It required considerable skill with the use of solder at carefully regulated temperatures, but resulted in a precision and a sharpness of line that could not be achieved by embossing. The restrained relief of this type of decoration could be enhanced by superimposing further layers of cut-card or cast mouldings.

Although decorative castings had always been available, they had largely been restricted during the second half of the century to elements such as mounts, finials, thumbpieces and decorative handles to tankards. Most late seventeenth-century handles tend either to be raised from sheet and soldered together, or thinly cast with an evident concern for the extra cost in metal that this involved. Huguenot goldsmiths instead usually cast handles in halves, which were hollow and seamed down the middle and which enabled forms of a more generous and sculptural character to be produced with a less extravagant use of metal than might appear. Cast mouldings were also

— 143 —

Bowl and stand, silver, 1702, maker's mark of Benjamin Pyne (bowl) and Richard Syng (stand); diameter of bowl 4 in.

used much more extensively than on most native English plate, for details such as borders, spouts and decorative masks and panels.

The Huguenots' contribution to style was as important as their technical innovations. During the last decade of the seventeenth century, a style had evolved among English goldsmiths that made limited use of cast elements and was chiefly characterized by fairly thin gauge metal decorated with broad bands of embossed flutes and gadrooned borders. The contrast

Bowl and cover, silver-gilt, c. 1695, maker's mark of Pierre Harache;
5 in. diameter.

between this and the Huguenot style is illustrated by comparison of a covered bowl of 1702 by Benjamin Pyne, one of the leading English goldsmiths, with one of about 1695 by Pierre Harache. The former is of satisfactory, but not especially elegant, proportions, while the entire decorative effect is dependent upon the play of light in the flutes. The latter is more subtle and makes extensive use of sculptural castings and elaborate cut-card decoration. It is also raised from heavier gauge metal than would have been possible had the decoration been embossed.

The evolution of English silver over the first twenty-five years of the eighteenth century can largely be seen as the interaction of these two styles. On the one hand, the Huguenots were introducing English goldsmiths to an already fully developed style which inevitably took time to assimilate; on the other, the Huguenots were themselves confronted with demands from their patrons, not all of which were familiar and to which they had to adapt. For most purposes the technical skills of the leading English makers, especially Benjamin Pyne and Anthony Nelme, were the equal of the best Huguenots, and the differences in style that continued to prevail into the eighteenth century are probably due partly to conservative elements in the taste of patrons.

Teapot, silver, 1725, maker's mark of Thomas Farren.

The demands of clients also led Huguenot goldsmiths to play a leading role in the simultaneous evolution of a quite different style, commonly known as the Queen Anne style. Particularly favoured for smaller domestic objects such as sauceboats, teapots and coffee pots, this was characterized by carefully balanced proportions but was of an almost austere plainness that was considered, even by patrons who commissioned elaborately decorated ornamental plate, appropriate to utilitarian objects. It was in this area, perhaps more than in any other, that the synthesis of the English and Huguenot contributions is most evident and where the work of native and immigrant goldsmiths is most similar.

The assimilation of technique and form is illustrated by a further comparison, this time between two ewers by the same two makers, which represent the characteristic ewer forms favoured respectively by Huguenot and native English makers. Benjamin Pyne's silver-gilt ewer of 1699 is based upon the English form established about twenty years earlier: although of attractive and balanced proportions, it is essentially a cup-like vessel to which spout and handle have been added. In relation to the bold design and sculptural character of Pierre Harache's helmet-shaped ewer of 1700 it is almost severe. However, its decoration shows an awareness and command of the Huguenot vocabulary that was unusual for all but the very best English makers.

Ewer, silver-gilt, 1699, maker's mark of Benjamin Pyne;
11 in. high.

Ewer, silver, 1700, maker's mark of Pierre Harache;
$12\frac{1}{4}$ in. high.

Comparable to the Harache ewer, but with a more restrained scroll handle, is one by David Willaume of 1715 at Attingham Park (p. 11).

The Huguenots' ability to adapt to and reinterpret existing forms is seen most clearly in their response to the peculiarly English demand for two-handled cups and covers, through which can be traced the entire development of the Huguenot style. The typical English two-handled cup of the

Cup and cover, silver, 1709, maker's mark of David Willaume; 11 in. high (British Museum, London).

late seventeenth century was still closely allied to the caudle cup or porringer. Of squat proportions, it is generally articulated with bands of embossed ornament to the lower part of the body and the cover. Most early Huguenot cups are decorated only with applied cut-card decoration and engraving. Yet in spite of their severity they have a dignity and presence that eludes those of most native English makers. Their overall proportions are similar to those of their English counterparts (with width over handles approximately equalling height), but they tend to have a marginally less squat body and more boldly cast handles.

Comparison of a cup of 1709 by David Willaume with one of 1731 at Dunham Massey by Peter Archambo defines the evolution of the style

Cup and cover, silver-gilt, 1731, maker's mark of Peter Archambo; 10 in. high (National Trust, Dunham Massey, Cheshire).

over the first quarter of the century: essentially the vocabulary is the same, but the proportions of the later cup have been extended, the mouldings lightened and the general effect made less formal by the double scroll to the handle. Decorative engraving or flat-chasing inspired by French *Régence* pattern books was also used from about 1720, especially by Paul de Lamerie, and significantly lightened the style.

Many of the typical Huguenot forms can be illustrated by reference to one patron, a significant proportion of whose massive holdings of silver still remain in the house for which he commissioned it, Dunham Massey in Cheshire.[9] George Booth, 2nd Earl of Warrington (1675–1758), was one of the most extravagant patrons of English eighteenth-century goldsmiths,

Dessert dish, silver, 1724, maker's mark of Paul de Lamerie; $13\frac{1}{4}$ in. long (National Trust, Ickworth, Suffolk).

and by the end of his life he had amassed a total of no less than 26,589 ounces of plate. He was quite obsessive about his silver and in 1750 compiled a remarkable inventory in his own hand, entitled 'A particular of my plate and its weight', in which he listed each piece individually, together with its precise weight. While he patronized a number of makers over nearly fifty years of rapidly changing fashion, he sought only the services of Huguenot makers and seems consistently to have demanded the style that had been in fashion when he had first started to commission plate. Thus, despite the long period over which he was accumulating his silver, the style which persists at Dunham until the end of his life is not significantly different from that in fashion around 1720. It is an astonishingly homogeneous group which makes virtually no concession to rococo taste. While he clearly insisted on the finest quality, most of his plate is of a comparatively austere character, depending for its effect largely on form rather than ornament. As such it is in striking contrast to the National Trust's other important collection of early and mid eighteenth-century silver, the magnificent plate commissioned by his contemporaries, John and George Hervey, first and second Earls of Bristol (d. 1750 and 1775), for Ickworth.

Apart from the chapel plate, the silver at Dunham falls into three groups: that made for the dining-room, that for the bedroom and that for use about the house. Pride of place in the dining-room during the early eighteenth century was given to the two-handled cup, which had by now completely replaced the traditional standing cup and cover. Although used for ceremonial purposes in the livery companies of London, in the private house it was primarily a display piece that might stand as a centrepiece on the table or in pairs on the sideboard. A pair of silver-gilt cups of 1731 by Peter Archambo remain at Dunham, although his inventory lists a further seven, the earliest of which he had acquired by about 1710.

The ewer and basin had by now also ceased to have any practical role and was intended purely as imposing decoration for the sideboard. Accordingly the basin now became a shallow dish and was treated increasingly as a plain surface for heraldic decoration. It is significant that Warrington's extraordinary inventory of plate, which is mainly of a functional nature, contains no ewer and dish of this type, nor any representative of the other important item of sideboard plate fashionable at the time, namely the 'pilgrim', or wine bottle. These massive vessels were ultimately derived from a form of bottle carried by medieval travellers, and their distant ancestry is reflected in the chain suspended between two handles attached to either shoulder of the flask. Sixteenth-century flagons of similar form, made in London and Paris, are preserved in the Kremlin and the Louvre,[10] and a few survivals are known from the 1660s onwards. The splendid late seventeenth- and early eighteenth-century examples, made by English and Huguenot makers alike, were probably the final flowering of a more or less continual tradition, most traces of which have been lost through recycling.

Other massive items of dining-room plate, however, were of a more practical nature, and one of the most sculptural pieces at Dunham Massey is a wine cistern of 1701 by Philip Rollos, for which a matching fountain was supplied in 1728 by Peter Archambo.[11] The wine cistern had two distinct functions. Another, larger, example of 1729 by Archambo at

*Pilgrim bottle, silver-gilt, 1699, maker's mark of
John Bodington; 16¾ in. high.*

Dunham is described in the inventory as 'a large Cisterne for bottles',
whereas the 1701 piece, with its fountain, is termed 'a Cistern to wash
glasses in'. This particular form of plate was gradually rendered redundant
by the development of more extensive services of flatware and sets of
glasses so that it was no longer necessary to rinse these during the meal.
But most other large-scale display plate of traditional kind declined in

popularity from the second quarter of the eighteenth century until almost the beginning of the nineteenth. Ewers and dishes continued to be made, but less frequently; wine cisterns for bottles were generally replaced by smaller vessels and pilgrim bottles passed out of fashion altogether. This was almost certainly as a result of the 6d. duty imposed in the 1719 act,

Wine cistern, silver, 1701, maker's mark of Philip Rollos; 25½ in. long
(National Trust, Dunham Massey, Cheshire).

and although there seems to have been no significant decline in the total weight assayed during the ensuing period, most patrons are likely to have thought twice about paying an extra £25 on a 1,000-ounce piece of plate. Certainly the wine cistern continued to have a role in other materials, and many from the mid and late eighteenth century are of carved mahogany with a metal liner.

The introduction of the wine cooler, or ice pail, designed to hold a single bottle, was clearly independent of this, as two of the earliest, a magnificent pair in gold presented to the Duke of Marlborough, date from about 1700.[12]

Few from the early eighteenth century survive, however, and they can hardly have been common at the time, since the compiler of an inventory of the Duchess of Marlborough's plate in 1712 apparently did not recognize the form and described them as 'very large ewers'. Known examples are almost exclusively by Huguenot makers and are generally two-handled and

*Pair of wine coolers, silver, c. 1710–15, maker's name of Philip Rollos
(National Trust, Ickworth, Suffolk).*

of circular or octagonal section. Among the most splendid of the first quarter of the century are the pair of about 1710 by Philip Rollos at Ickworth.

Almost more significant than the changes that affected display plate were the additions being made to the range of plate associated with the service of food. Most of these seem initially to have been the preserve of Huguenot makers too, and at least two of the novelties that appeared during the first quarter of the century can be attributed again to French influence, presumably brought to the attention of English patrons by the immigrant craftsmen. Soup tureens may have some ancestry in covered bowls, a few of which survive from the mid seventeenth century, but the word itself is of French derivation and the Huguenot interpretation of the form was quite new. There were three at Dunham during Warrington's time. It is not

One of a pair of wine coolers, gold, c. 1700, unmarked; $10\frac{1}{2}$ in. high
(British Museum, London).

known when he acquired them, since their present whereabouts, and hence
the date of their hallmarks, are not known, but the very fact that a patron
as conservative as he would allow them in his house is probably reason
enough for supposing that they were already accepted by about 1715. One
of the earliest surviving, by Paul de Lamerie, is hallmarked for 1723 and is

Soup tureen, silver, 1723, maker's mark of Paul de Lamerie; 11 in. long
(Woburn Abbey, Bedfordshire).

in the Bedford collection at Woburn Abbey. It is decorated with applied cut-card and has a large ring handle on the cover.

The sauceboat was apparently also introduced from France. Louis XIV's household accounts record the order in 1700 of four sauceboats, 'a deux anses et deux becs',[13] but the double-lipped sauceboat does not actually appear in English silver until the reign of George I, and indeed the first examples have a distinctly French appearance that was gradually eroded as the form became accepted and anglicized.

Other forms introduced by Huguenot goldsmiths included the cruet frame and a novel type of double spice box, but they also reinterpreted and refined existing ones. During the second half of the seventeenth century the form of the domestic salt cellar had generally followed that established by pewterers, and was often raised and embossed from thin sheet. By contrast, Huguenot forms tend to be more elaborately constructed and of heavier gauge metal, the additional cost presumably being justified on the grounds that they would wear better. During the seventeenth and eighteenth centuries most plate was ordered to replace existing but worn-out or old-fashioned pieces, and it was usual to pay for it, at least in part, by

Pair of double-lipped sauceboats, silver, 1724,
maker's mark of Peter Archambo.

turning in old plate. Consequently, if the customer had more old plate than he needed, it was in one sense unimportant whether the new be made to a heavy or a light pattern. A typical entry from the diaries of the Earl of Bristol is that for 7 November 1696: 'Paid Mr. Edw. Waldegrave, a goldsmith of Russel Street, for 11 dishes, 1 dozen of plates, a coffee-pot, and a porrige ladle, weighing 802 ounces, at five shillings $3\frac{1}{4}$d per ounce, and for the graving £211 7s 0d, £7 3s 0d in money, the rest in old plate my dear fathers.'[14]

The range of new plate in the dining-room is illustrated by the Earl of Warrington's inventory, which lists novel items such as egg-frames, 'bottle-plates' (coasters) and 'bottle tickets' (wine labels). Of course, since he compiled his inventory in 1750, he did not necessarily possess all these objects within the period of this chapter, though most of them were certainly available during or a little after the first quarter of the century. Perhaps the most fundamental innovation of early eighteenth-century dining plate, again reflected in the Earl's inventory, was the matched table service. Sets of spoons, it is true, had been known for centuries, but only in the late seventeenth do sets of spoons and forks become standard equipment, and

Pair of salt-cellars, silver, 1731, maker's mark of Peter Archambo;
2 in. high (National Trust, Dunham Massey, Cheshire).

early in the following century complete sets of spoons and forks, duplicated in a smaller size for dessert and occasionally with teaspoons and steel-bladed knives, appear in significant numbers for the first time. The earliest 'pattern' or shape was the so-called 'dog-nose', which evolved from the trefid form and which had the same characteristic 'rat-tail' moulding to the back of the bowl. From about 1710 a new type, generally known today as the 'Hanoverian' pattern, appears and is characterized by a rounded up-turned end to the stem.

While many of the novel forms of the early eighteenth century appear to have been introduced from France and were made at first almost exclusively by Huguenots, other kinds of plate, traditionally more familiar in England, continued to form a staple part of the repertoire of native goldsmiths. Punch bowls and monteiths, in particular, seem to have been

Spoon and fork ('dog nose pattern'), silver, 1697,
maker's mark of Lawrence Jones.

Knife, fork and spoon ('Hanoverian pattern'), silver-gilt, 1712, maker's mark of Thomas Spackman (knife with maker's mark of William Twell).

made almost exclusively by English goldsmiths, mainly in the traditional English embossed style, although assimilating certain new techniques, such as the use of cast handles and borders.

Traditional techniques continued to be used for tankards, mugs and beer jugs during this period, which were also largely ignored by Huguenot makers and underwent relatively little change in design. The former, in

Punch Bowl, silver, 1717, maker's mark of Benjamin Pyne;
$11\frac{1}{2}$*in. diameter.*

particular, differed little from their seventeenth-century equivalents. The only significant modification was the domed cover, and this almost certainly followed a model already established in pewter. However, on the rare occasions when Huguenots did turn their attention to these forms, their skill at raising heavy-gauge metal into attractive forms and their ability to enhance form with cast sculptural details tended to result in extremely accomplished objects. Among these should certainly be included the tankard of 1701 by David Willaume at Polesden Lacey.

The range of plate associated with the bedroom was not greatly expanded during the eighteenth century. Most of the objects had existed before, and although items such as shaving bowls and jugs do not survive in any

Beer jug, silver, 1708, maker's mark of Benjamin Pyne;
$12\frac{1}{4}$ in. high.

Tankard, silver, 1701, maker's mark of David Willaume; 8 in. high
(National Trust, Polesden Lacey, Surrey).

numbers from before the eighteenth century, they are known from inventories to have existed at least from the fifteenth. The Earl of Warrington's inventory lists a group of items under the heading 'My Chamber plate', all of which were practical objects which, in pottery, pewter or brass, would have had a place in most bedchambers at the beginning of the eighteenth century. They include a 'trimming bason' and ewer, a 'washball (or soap) box', a hand basin, a chamber pot, a pair of candlesticks, snuffers and tray and a 'hand (or chamber) candlestick'. More unusual was the final item on the list, 'a bason to wash my mouth'. In their essentials, the shaving jug and basin, the soap box and chamber pot had changed very little from the

Shaving jug and basin, silver, 1747, maker's mark of Daniel Piers; height of jug 7 in. (National Trust, Dunham Massey, Cheshire).

seventeenth century. As with tankards in the previous century, these objects were more familiar, to patrons and goldsmiths alike, in base metal, and chamber pots tend usually to follow the form of those in pewter. Similarly, the design of the shaving jugs and basins at Dunham, the earliest of which were supplied in 1716 by the Huguenot goldsmith Isaac Liger, are modelled on the form of contemporary French examples in brass.

The most prestigious plate associated with the bed chamber continued to be the toilet service. Although items of toilet plate were made for gentlemen, such as shaving plate, 'oatmeal boxes and plates' and 'hand powder boxes', the full service was the perquisite of the lady of the house and was as much a reflection of her status as the display plate in the dining-room was of her husband's. The finest of them are therefore composed of a large number of pieces, often with very elaborate decoration. Most were presented on the occasion of marriage. The essential items were unchanged from the seventeenth century and consisted of a mirror, comb and cosmetic boxes, a jewel casket and a pair of candlesticks. This was supplemented by a variety of smaller boxes and brushes and occasionally a small ewer and basin. But in the early eighteenth century there was a tendency for toilet services to acquire more and more pieces that reflected the increasingly elaborate cosmetic preparations of the time. The largest known of these services is one of 1708 by Benjamin Pyne, engraved with the arms of the

*Toilet service, silver, 1754, maker's mark of Magdalen Feline
(National Trust, Dunham Massey, Cheshire).*

Dukes of Norfolk and comprising no fewer than thirty-four pieces.[15] The service of 1754 at Dunham Massey, made for Warrington's daughter to a design that would not have looked out of place thirty years earlier, was not much smaller, with twenty-eight pieces.

Among plate about the house which was not associated with a particular room, the most important groups are lighting equipment, salvers, inkstands and, perhaps most important of all, tea and coffee plate.

Candlesticks had an undiminished importance in the eighteenth century, and the Earl of Warrington's inventory lists no fewer than forty-five pairs of domestic candlesticks, in addition to candelabra, chandeliers and sconces. During the last twenty years of the seventeenth century an alternative to the raised column candlestick gradually gained a place in the market, in the form of a small cast type, generally on octagonal base and with baluster stem. Leading English makers such as Ralph Leeke and Benjamin Pyne had been making these from as early as the 1680s, but their rapid rise in popularity around the turn of the century was undoubtedly due to the Huguenot predilection for casting. Usually these were made in three pieces,

Inkstand, silver, 1716, maker's mark of Isaac Liger; $11\frac{3}{4}$ in. long
(National Trust, Dunham Massey, Cheshire).

with stem and socket cast in identical halves, the foot separately made and the three parts soldered together. They had several advantages over sticks raised from sheet. In relation to their size they used more metal, but they tended to be smaller than other varieties and savings were made by the stems being hollow; they were not necessarily quicker to make than raised sticks, because of the laborious chasing and polishing necessary after casting, but their considerably greater solidity made them stronger and more resistant to heavy wear. Pockets of conservatism continued to be met, but by the second decade of the century the earlier type had a real market only in provincial areas such as Exeter.

Before the invention of the self-consuming candle wick in the late eighteenth century, snuffers were essential for trimming the wick to

Two candlesticks, silver. Left, 1708, 7¾ in. high;
right, 1730, 6¾ in. high; both with maker's mark of Isaac Liger
(National Trust, Dunham Massey, Cheshire).

prevent guttering. Snuffers, usually of scissor form with a box-like device at the end, were produced, either with a small oblong tray or with a vertical stand en suite with the candlesticks (see p. 170). They were made by specialists and usually bear a different maker's mark from that on the stand.

The extent to which techniques conditioned design is more obvious in the radical difference between the usual Huguenot and English approaches

Sconce, silver, 1700,
maker's mark of Joseph Ward;
$11\frac{7}{8}$ *in. high.*

to wall sconces. There were twenty-four at Dunham in the eighteenth
century, but although none survives there today a number are still at
Belton, built by Sir John Brownlow of Humby in 1685, including examples
of both types. Those by English makers are of the type already fashionable
in Charles II's reign, and have a shaped backplate embossed with foliage
or putti and with variously matted or burnished surfaces designed to play
with the reflected light. The typical Huguenot form, on the other hand,

— 169 —

Snuffers and stand, silver, 1724, maker's mark of
Matthew Cooper; 7 in. high.

has a cast backplate of a more formal and architectural design. It depends heavily on the type of ornament introduced by Daniel Marot and is conceived as an integral part of the decoration of the room: these back plates are much narrower than those of the native English type because they are intended to be placed on either side of a mirror, in order to reflect the maximum possible light. A rarer form of Huguenot sconce, not designed for this position, consisted of a simple gadrooned border to an oval mirrored backplate and is represented, for example, by a set of four at Chatsworth.

By far the greatest area of growth for goldsmiths during the early eighteenth century was in the field of tea and coffee plate, and it is significant that with notable exceptions such as Anthony Nelme and Benjamin Pyne,

Teapot and stand with burner, silver, 1709,
maker's mark of Anthony Nelme.

most plate made in connection with its service seems in the first instance to be by Huguenot makers. Tea had become available in England only during the latter part of the previous century, and its prohibitively high cost had restricted it to a tiny stratum of society. But between 1706 and 1750 its price fell dramatically and this change was reflected in an even greater rise in consumption, as imports rose over the same period from 54,600 lb. to 2,325,000 lb.[16]

During the period of this chapter tea was still a beverage for the wealthy, and its very cost made it natural that it should be served out of silver and prepared at table by the lady of the house and that its consumption should be associated with an element of ceremony. Again on account of its cost, teapots were generally small, but in other respects their design was subject to experimentation. During the first decade of the century they tend to be pear-shaped and either of circular or octagonal section, while the shape generally favoured around 1720 was wider around the upper part than the base and with flush cover (see p. 146). Other items associated with its preparation also evolved early in the eighteenth century and reflected the seriousness with which this new beverage was taken. Some of the earliest teapots were equipped with stands and burners, but these were soon

Pair of tea caddies, silver-gilt, 1754, maker's mark of Magdalen Feline; $4\frac{5}{8}$ in. high (National Trust, Dunham Massey, Cheshire).

replaced by kettles which could be used to refill the pot. Kettles were usually of similar design to the teapots, but larger and with a swing handle.

Equally essential to the complete 'equipage' were milk jugs, sugar bowls and tea caddies. The latter were sometimes supplied in pairs, for green tea or bohea tea, and occasionally with a third caddy or bowl *en suite* for blending the tea. It is a further indication of the preciousness of tea that these caddies were often equipped with a lock, presumably to prevent the contents from being pilfered by the servants. In the early days the service also contained silver cups, though their impracticality due to silver's conductivity soon led to their abandonment in favour of imported Chinese porcelain cups. The Dunham Massey inventory lists still further items associated with tea, all of which became increasingly usual during the first quarter of the century: '24. Tea Spoons, 2. pair of Sugar Tongs, 1. Strainer Spoon, 3. gilt Boats to hold the Tea Spoons.'

Tea table, silver and mahogany, 1741,
maker's mark of David Willaume II; 24 in. diameter
(National Trust, Dunham Massey, Cheshire).

The tea service would sometimes be completed with an oblong tray or salver, and there still remains at Dunham Massey a 'Tea Table' which consists of a circular salver made to fit on to a mahogany table which is cut with notches to accommodate the salver's feet. The size of the kettle often qualified it for a separate silver stand, the grandest of which were

Three casters, silver, 1707, maker's mark of David Willaume;
7½ in. and 6¼ in. high.

designed to stand free on the floor and were of tripod form with tall baluster stem. Few of these survive today, but they were presumably more common in the greatest houses at the time and on account of their high bullion content were subsequently converted into other things when no longer fashionable. The Earl of Warrington, for example, possessed a tea kettle and lamp which weighed around 115 ounces, but had a stand which at 262 ounces was more than twice as heavy.

Coffee pots also went through a variety of experimental forms before a consensus as to the appropriate basic form was reached. But partly because coffee was generally taken with breakfast rather than as an after-dinner drink, they never acquired the same paraphernalia of associated vessels. Coffee pots were made by Huguenot and English makers alike; however, the Huguenot makers tended to prefer a distinctly French pear-shaped form with side-mounted baluster wood handles, while English makers used the C- or S-scroll handle, which eventually prevailed and which was initially

Two chocolate pots, silver. Left, 1705, maker's mark of William Deny, 10 in. high; right, 1701, maker's mark of William Lukin, $8\frac{1}{2}$ in. high.

fitted at right angles to the spout and subsequently moved to the position opposite it. The most popular form throughout the first quarter of the century was the tapering cylinder with domed cover, which was clearly a modification of the primitive form with conical cover in use in the late seventeenth century (see page 137). The other popular beverage of the early eighteenth century was chocolate, and chocolate pots generally followed the form of coffee pots, differing only in the hinged or pivoted finial, designed so that the contents could be stirred. On rare occasions chocolate pots survive with original stirrers, such as one of 1738 in the Ashmolean Museum, supplied by Paul Crespin to the Tollemache family for £14 4s. 6d.

The changes that English silver underwent during the thirty or forty years that have formed the subject of this chapter was a process of interaction and compromise between the French and native English styles. The style that emerged was one that remained unmistakably English, but which benefited immeasurably from the assimilation of French techniques and standards. This was something of a golden age for English silver, and the high demand for plate was in response both to its price and to a relative lack of competition from other prestigious materials. During the early eighteenth century, when pewter was facing growing competition from brass, salt-glazed stoneware, and tin-glazed pottery, the materials that would compete with silver were not yet widely available, and although glass had for some time been the favoured material for wine drinking, the much more serious challenge of porcelain was still some way off.

Moreover, bullion at the beginning of the century was relatively cheap. At about 5s. 6d. an ounce for sterling it was little more than it had been during Elizabeth I's reign. Even at about 6s. for the higher Britannia standard, when set against a price rise in manufactured goods of something over 500 per cent, it was in real terms considerably cheaper than in the latter part of the sixteenth century. Although the Huguenots were accused in the petition of 1711 of working 'at miserable rates', the style they introduced had the great advantage of being as well suited to relatively plain forms as to elaborate decoration; because its main effect depended on proportion rather than embossing, they could almost certainly afford to produce plate at a low rate per ounce when called for. Conversely they did not hesitate to impose a high charge for fashion when the design required it, and Paul de Lamerie charged George Treby no less than 5s. an ounce over and above the cost of the metal in 1724 for the fashion of his famous toilet service in the Ashmolean Museum. But at the other extreme, the Earl of Bristol acquired a silver stew pan and a chamber pot in 1716 at an inclusive cost of no more than 6s. 6d. an ounce, which, given that Britannia standard was in force then, must have allowed only a few pence an ounce for fashion.[17] Yet we may be quite sure, given the patron, that the quality of the craftsmanship would have had no shortcomings.

—— *Seven* ——

THE ROCOCO PERIOD

The period roughly corresponding to the reign of George II (1727–60) was one of consolidation rather than innovation for the goldsmith's trade. In one sense it was perhaps the most memorable of all in the history of English silver, for it was the period of the extraordinarily inventive and energetic style known as the rococo. Some of the most original silver ever made in England was produced during this period, by craftsmen such as Paul de Lamerie, Paul Crespin, and Nicholas Sprimont. But it was also a period from which enormous quantities of ordinary domestic plate survive, and the output of the majority of English mid-Georgian silversmiths, while absorbing the principles of the new style, reflected high fashion only in a much diluted form.

Between about 1720 and 1770 the population of England rose from about 5.3 million to 6.4 million, and the economic potential of such an increase is more than reflected in production and export figures, which rose by about 60 per cent and 100 per cent respectively.[1] But under Walpole's administration (1721–42) fiscal policies which favoured excise rather than land taxes had the effect of benefiting major landowners relative to other sectors of society. In so far as the market for silver might have been affected by the nation's increased wealth, therefore, the clientele probably did not grow very significantly over this period, although there is no doubt that the very wealthy spent a great deal on plate.

It is possible also that the 6d. duty imposed by the 1720 hallmarking act dampened what might have been a more rapidly growing market over this period. Certainly there was a marked increase in the consumption of plate when the duty was lifted by a new act in 1757, which instead imposed a fee of £2 on all those 'trading in, selling or vending gold and silver plate'.[2] The effect of this new legislation can be seen in the significant increase in the total weight of plate that passed through the Assay Office annually.

The main motive behind the act, however, was not to stimulate the goldsmiths' trade but a practical recognition of the fact that numerous goldsmiths (including some of the most famous and prosperous) had for years been evading the duty on large pieces by a fraudulent practice known as 'duty dodging'. In this cunning act of deception the goldsmith would cut around the marks of some small piece of silver and insert the resultant patch of hallmarked silver into a larger new piece. Two-handled cups are frequent offenders, since the join between the body of the cup and the marked plate could easily be concealed under the point at which the foot meets the body. Flat silver such as salvers and dishes are more seldom duty dodgers as there is no convenient way in which to conceal the seam of the hallmarked patch of silver.

In addition to the detrimental effect of official policy on the trade, goldsmiths had to face a more serious challenge in the form of new and attractive materials that were becoming available for the manufacture of domestic wares. Exotic porcelains and luxury glassware had, of course, long been available, but only in such limited quantities as to present no serious threat to the ordinary goldsmith's trade. In the eighteenth century, however, that position changed radically. Attractive clear lead glass began to be produced on a commercial scale in England at the end of the seventeenth century. The discovery of true porcelain by the Saxon chemist Johann Friedrich Böttger around 1710 did not at first have any serious repercussions in Europe, since manufacture was limited to supplying the appetite of Augustus I of Saxony (1670–1733). But by the 1730s surplus Meissen porcelain became available on the market, and by the 1740s hard and soft paste porcelain was being produced in a number of factories in France and Germany.

The lure of this new material is nowhere better illustrated than by the defection of Nicholas Sprimont from the ranks of goldsmiths. A native of Liège, in Belgium, Sprimont had arrived in London around 1744 but by 1748 had abandoned the craft in order to become manager of the newly founded Chelsea porcelain factory. His motives for this unusual change of career are not known. His surviving silver, however, does show a marked sense of plasticity and it is possible that he was attracted by the modelling potential of porcelain; equally, he may have felt that the future lay entirely with porcelain rather than silver and, in a gesture that would have been brilliant had it been right, decided to be among the first in the field in England.

To contemporaries the gesture may have seemed more visionary than in retrospect. The mania for porcelain that gripped some courts on the continent, notably those of Saxony and France, was felt in England too. Fine porcelain was generally much less expensive than plate, and its potential for decorative modelling and colouring weighed significantly against its fragility and made a real impact on the market for silver. Dr Johnson admittedly overstated the case when he remarked in 1777 that 'the finer pieces [of Derby porcelain] are so dear that perhaps silver vessels of the same capacity may be sometimes bought for the same price', but even so, the price of porcelain was arguably comparable once the recoverable, or invested, value of the metal had been discounted. In 1770, for example, a Chelsea porcelain dessert service for twenty-four cost £31,[3] while twenty-four standard silver plates weighing approximately 500 ounces would have cost between £25 and £35 to make, exclusive of the cost of the metal.[4] A more telling comparison still is between the cost of ornate display plate and ornamental Sèvres porcelain. In 1740 George Wickes, goldsmith to the Prince of Wales, supplied his patron with a silver-gilt cup and cover at 15s. an ounce, making a total of £61 13s. Again, discounting the cost of the metal, this would have represented an 'unrecoverable' cost of about £39. The cost of the great showpieces of the Sèvres factory, the *Vase à elephants* and the *Vaseau à mat* in the late 1750s, were about 1,000 livres and 1,200 livres respectively, which translated in mid eighteenth-century terms to about £45 and £50.[5] Moreover, the old role of plate as the most convenient form of holding surplus capital was gradually being undermined by the development of the stock market as a more productive means of using money, and there was every sign of the new material sweeping the English aristocratic market. There was also a substantial demand for dinner services of Chinese export porcelain, and in about 1763 an entire service was ordered from the Chelsea factory as a gift from George III (r. 1760–1820) and his Queen, Charlotte, to the latter's brother, Duke Adolphus Frederick IV of Mecklenburg-Strelitz, at a cost of around £1,200.[6]

In some ways the alarm was a false one. Not all patrons were prepared immediately to abandon their well-tried allegiance to plate; it remained until almost the twentieth century the appropriate material in which to make a prestigious presentation, and débâcles such as the famous South Sea Bubble of 1720 did nothing to strengthen convictions that stocks were a suitable form in which to hold all one's capital. Nevertheless, the sense of unease which these legislatory and market factors must have instilled in the silver trade must have had at least some connection with the changes which took place in the craft during the eighteenth century and which undoubtedly strengthened it against possible competition.

The eighteenth century is the first period for which we have any very clear idea of the organization of the goldsmith's trade and workshop. General accounts such as Campbell's *The London Tradesman* (1747), and the survival of the trade ledgers of George Wickes,[7] one of the most important goldsmiths of the second quarter of the century, give entirely new insights. They reveal a trade which, far from being composed of small workshops producing purely handmade objects, was highly organized and specialized and in which sub-contracting played a major role.

Goldsmiths had always been specialists to some extent, but from the beginning of the eighteenth century this seems to have become a more standard phenomenon and can be traced through successive generations of goldsmiths. The chain is described by Arthur Grimwade:

> By the end of the seventeenth century we can detect trends of specialization in various types of articles which by the middle of the rococo period was an established fact. A study of apprenticeships provides interesting evidence of this. We find for example a line of caster makers starting with Charles Adam, maker of casters in the first fifteen years or so of the century, to whom Thomas Bamford was apprenticed in 1703. Bamford, whose mark also appears exclusively on such pieces, was in turn the master of Samuel Wood (apprenticed to him 1721) and the latter in his turn instructed the young Jabez Daniel from 1739 in the same type of article. Candlestick makers follow in a line from David Green in the early years of the century, through James Gould, apprenticed in 1723/4 and John Cafe in 1730. The latter was master of William Cafe (his younger brother) in 1741 and of Thomas Hannam in 1745. The maker's marks of all [these] are found almost exclusively on cast candlesticks except for those of Hannam who also made waiters. The making of salt-cellars shows the same line of specialists from Alexander Roode, whose mark appears in the early months of 1697, and who became master in 1700 of James Roode, probably a cousin, to whom Edward Wood was later apprenticed in 1715. Wood in his turn became master of David Hennell in 1728, from whom the family concern of salt-cellar makers developed through the second half of the century to expand in the nineteenth into a wider sphere of production.[8]

Specialization of a whole workshop was one way in which costs could be saved and efficiency increased. Another was through the division of labour. Although Adam Smith's *Wealth of Nations*, in which the principle was advocated through the famous example of the pin factory, was published in 1776, he was in fact describing a procedure that was already established practice in the larger workshops of the mid century. Campbell describes many of the different processes carried on in the goldsmith's workshop and the specialist workers who would have been employed, either as permanent employees or as 'outworkers'. These included burnishers, gilders, chasers, refiners and goldbeaters. His book is of particular interest for its inclusion of a table listing the capital costs of setting up workshops equipped for the various branches of trade which he describes, ranging from between £20 and £100 for setting up as a chaser, to between £500 and £3,000 for a gold-smith. The wide range presumably reflects the scale and diversity of operations and the amount of space, capital and equipment that would be needed.

The system is vividly illustrated by the Wickes ledgers, which reveal a detailed, almost intimate view of the business, its partners, employees and associates. Wickes employed upwards of sixty plate workers; workers (usually women) were employed solely for planishing, and other specialist workers included polishers, chasers, hammerers and turners. From 1746 he was in partnership with Edward Wakelin, who would appear to have been responsible for greatly expanding the retail side of the business, and after 1766 the 'Workman's ledger' lists a number of specialist sub-contractors who supplied the business with particular types of plate, such as Ebenezer Coker for candlesticks and waiters, Thomas Pitts for epergnes and Isaac Callard for flatware.

The survival of the ledgers is probably unique, but it may be assumed that other important workshops, such as those of Paul de Lamerie and Peter Archambo, were organized in a similar way. De Lamerie clearly ran one of the most successful goldsmiths' businesses of the second quarter of the century, with an enormous output of always good and occasionally exceptional plate. But it is a major shortcoming in our knowledge of English eighteenth-century silver that we have no information for de Lamerie equivalent to the Wickes ledgers. Certain personal details, such as his baptismal and marriage records, are known, and a legal case from the 1750s in which he was involved establishes that he acted as a retailer of jewellery as well as plate. But while a few surviving bills and a large quantity of plate with armorial engraving enable us to piece together an impressive list of his clients, we have little information about the conduct of his business to support what is implied by the plate itself. His most ambitious works from between about 1738 and 1746, such as the silver-gilt ewer and dish made for the Goldsmiths' Company in 1742,[9] have a sculptural quality lacking at other stages of his career, which suggests that over that period he must have been employing a first-rate modeller, whose identity remains obscure. Specialist craftsmen, such as chasers and engravers, were evidently employed in the workshop, and their work also played an important part in giving de Lamerie's plate its distinctive quality at different periods, but again, virtually nothing about them is known.

In addition to revealing other of Wickes's peripheral activities, such as hiring out plate for special functions, or even buying, as he did in 1752, thirty-four pewter dish covers for a client at £21 8s., the ledgers contain a wealth of information on the cost of plate during the mid eighteenth century. While some items, presumably those made for stock or bought in from sub-contractors, are invoiced with a single price, inclusive of both metal and work, entries for important commissions distinguish between the cost of the metal and the cost of fashion at so much per ounce. The range of prices is revealing. For 'plain fashion' Wickes charged about 5s. 6d. per ounce, that is about 6d. above the current bullion price, but in 1757 he charged the Earl of Lincoln no less than 14s. 6d. per ounce for a pair of candlesticks. These must have been exceptionally grand and were probably gilded as well, in which case their cost would compare with de Lamerie's charges for the Goldsmiths' Company's ewer and dish, which, in addition to the price of the metal, amounted to nearly 6s. an ounce and 4s. an ounce for the gilding.

Fashionable decorated plate had always been more expensive than plain domestic wares, often demanding expenditure of at least as much again as the price of the metal. This could never subsequently be recovered and could consequently not be considered by any except the very rich. But during the second quarter of the eighteenth century the difference in price between utilitarian and fashionable pieces was probably even greater than at other times, on account of the stress placed on novelty and variety of design. While it had been acceptable in the early years of the century for leading patrons such as the Earl of Bristol at Ickworth or the Hon. George Treby (some of whose plate is in the Ashmolean and British Museums) to have commissioned display plate in essentially the same dignified and formal *Régence* style, their mid-century successors required something different, and that in turn placed a heavy burden on new designs and new castings. It was part of the genius of Paul de Lamerie that he managed so frequently to give the impression of complete novelty by means of simply using existing castings in novel combinations.

The rococo emerged in France after the gradual relaxing of the baroque style of Louis XIV's court during the ensuing *Régence* period (1715–23). But the mature style did not emerge until the publication of Juste-Aurèle Meissonnier's revolutionary designs of the second half of the 1720s. These playful, irreverent and highly inventive designs largely achieved their ends by reinterpreting the existing repertoire of ornament, and the novelty of the style consists in the handling of familiar scrolls, cartouches and foliage motifs in a new way, introducing asymmetry, the play of light and dark and a delightful, unpredictable sense of movement. In its most fully developed instances form and ornament are so unified that it is impossible analytically to separate the two. In England this fully developed sculptural approach is found occasionally in the work of silversmiths such as Paul de Lamerie, James Shruder and Nicholas Sprimont, but usually the style is restricted to the application of ornament in varying degrees of elaboration to a fairly simple form.

For ordinary domestic plate, however, the most significant changes concerned form rather than ornament. In place of the austere lines of the early 1720s, undulating curves and scroll mouldings, handles and feet became the order of the day. Such forms have a natural affinity with the malleable nature of the material. Whereas form had previously been regulated by a convention that emphasized and kept visually distinct the different parts of construction, there is a tendency during the rococo period to treat the entire object much more fluidly and to allow the various parts visually to merge with one another, rather than emphasizing the different parts. The typical form for such objects as coffee pots, sauceboats and tureens involves bodies of gently curving outline, meeting a rising central foot or cast scroll feet. In place of the C-scroll handle of the early part of the century, silver handles, which were generally cast at this stage, developed into an increasingly exuberant multi-scroll. This was the basic formula, to which could be added as much cast or chased detail as would have been agreed between goldsmith and patron.

Comparison of a plain chocolate pot of 1738 by Paul Crespin with one of Paul de Lamerie's masterpieces, the pot of the same year made for a fellow Huguenot, John Lequesne, Alderman of London, shows the large range of effects that could be accommodated within the limits of this extraordinarily broad and tolerant style: one a pleasing, well-proportioned shape, no more; the other an exuberant work of sculpture that transcends its nature as a functional object while in no way diminishing its practicality. But the imaginative sculptural nature of de Lamerie's coffee pot was not to everyone's taste. Most of the brilliant rococo creations in silver were the result of a special rapport between patron and goldsmith, such as that between de Lamerie and John Lequesne or the 5th Earl of Mountrath (see p. 191), but some important patrons had no love for what would have been seen as the excesses of the style and for reasons of taste rather than cost preferred plate of a plainer character. The 2nd Earl of Warrington is perhaps the most obvious case of a patron quite untouched by the rococo, but

Chocolate pot and stirrer, silver and wood, 1738,
maker's mark of Paul Crespin; $9\frac{1}{2}$ in. high
(Ashmolean Museum, Oxford).

another is Horatio Walpole, uncle of Horace Walpole of Strawberry Hill, who in 1739 commissioned David Willaume to make a remarkably plain gold cup and cover from a gold chain which he was presented with as ambassador to The Hague.

While the sources of the style were essentially French, and the first rococo silver in England was by Huguenot makers, other factors also contributed to the germination of French decorative styles in England. Printed books of ornament, like those of Meissonier and Nicholas Pineau, were certainly in use in England and some of the leading French goldsmiths were patronized by the English nobility. The great *surtout de table* and soup tureens of Meissonier were designed and made in Paris for the Duke of Kingston in 1726,[10] and in 1735 the 3rd Earl of Berkeley chose to place his order for a large dinner service with the Parisian goldsmith Jacques Roettiers rather than a London workshop. Moreover, in addition to the response of native English artists to the new style, other non-French influences can be

Coffee pot, silver, 1738, maker's mark of Paul de Lamerie,
made for John Lequesne; $11\frac{1}{4}$ in. high.

Cup and cover, gold, 1739, maker's mark of David Willaume II,
made for Horatio Walpole; $12\frac{1}{2}$ in. high.

recognized in English rococo silver. Paul de Lamerie, in particular, made use of German pattern books as well, and Charles Kandler's work seems to show an awareness of Meissen porcelain that suggests the possibility of a connection with his namesake, Johann Joachim Kändler, who was chief modeller of the Meissen factory.

— 186 —

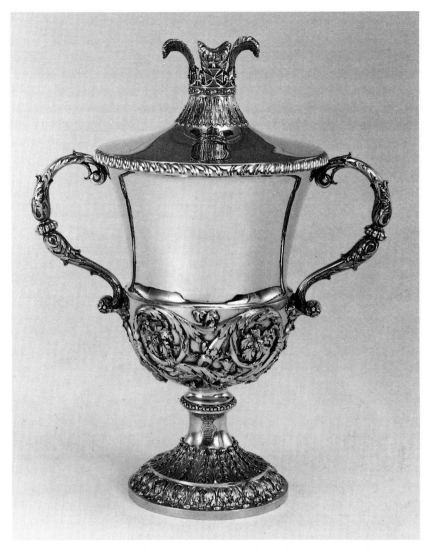

Cup and cover, gold, c. 1736, supplied by George Wickes (unmarked),
designed by William Kent; 11 in. high.

The challenge of new materials, compounded after the middle of the century by attractive and relatively inexpensive creamware, affected all areas of the craft and not just the market for decorative and ornamental plate. In some areas, indeed, judging from surviving silver, it must have seemed little short of disastrous. Hitherto each period had witnessed a gradual expansion of the range and types of plate available. During the second and third quarters of the eighteenth century, however, although certain new items were introduced, a significant decline in demand for other familiar objects also became evident. Items such as goblets and beakers, which had been quite standard during the late seventeenth and early eighteenth centuries, almost disappeared from the repertoire. Teapots, fashionable earlier in the century, were largely replaced between about 1730 and 1760 by china ones, and a similar fate would seem to have befallen silver punch bowls. Sconces fell from fashion altogether in England, and major items such as wine cisterns and toilet services now became quite exceptional. It is only by setting the dramatic and conspicuous development of more popular objects against these apparently recessionary trends that it is possible to form a proper picture of the state of the craft over this period.

The two-handled cup and cover continued to hold a special position until at least the end of the century, both as the standard form of decorative plate for the sideboard or table and as an appropriate item for presentation. Some of the finest were offered as race prizes; others were made for more personal reasons. A fine cup and cover was the obvious choice for Walpole when presented with his gold chain, as it was when Colonel Pelham, private secretary to Frederick, Prince of Wales (1707–51), wanted Wickes to convert a number of gold snuff boxes into a single piece of plate.

Precisely because of this special role, the two-handled cup and cover of the mid century, like that of the Huguenot period, is a microcosm of current fashion and the one object in which virtually all the different facets of contemporary style found expression. The basic design was not especially innovative during this period; it remained close to the formula established around 1720 and a fundamental revision of form did not take place until Robert Adam's designs of the 1760s. Within the constraints of a fairly established form, however, it was subject to an astonishing variety of cast, embossed or engraved ornament. Walpole's gold cup represents the plainest type of all, while one at Anglesey Abbey, made by Peter Taylor in 1746, is at the opposite extreme. Although having a basic symmetry of form, the decoration is completely asymmetrical, designed to convey a wild sense of movement rather than dignified repose and to be the setting for a virtuoso display of techniques. For while the cup itself is raised, most of the ornament is embossed and then enhanced by cast handles and finial and further cast and applied ornament. Others, such as a group of cups of the late 1730s and early 1740s by Paul de Lamerie, take the idea further still by

Cup and cover, silver-gilt, 1746, maker's mark of Peter Taylor; 17 in. high
(National Trust, Anglesey Abbey, Cambridgeshire).

integrating form and ornament to the extent that the two become visually inseparable.

Such distinctive individual styles were exceptional, and more standard designs, surprisingly uniform in detail, were produced in most of the leading workshops. Indeed, the incidence of a variety of makers' marks on a series

— 189 —

of cups dating from 1738–42, all made to the identical design and with identical castings, is almost certainly the result of the sub-contracting so evident in the Wickes ledgers. The earliest of the group appear to be by de Lamerie, and the use of the same handles on cups to other designs with his mark suggest that the model was his, while others with the makers' marks of Benjamin Godfrey, John Le Sage and Thomas Farren may in fact all have been supplied to these goldsmiths by de Lamerie's workshop.[11]

The forces of conservatism, on the other hand, were most notably championed by William Kent (1684–1748), a group of whose designs for plate were published in 1744 by John Vardy. These include a number of pieces for the Prince of Wales and his circle, such as the gold cup made by Wickes for Colonel Pelham. The design has a classic quality that is neither baroque nor rococo, but which evidently had an enduring appeal, since copies of the cup were made by various makers until well into the 1760s. Georges Wickes, much of whose work shows a distinctly conservative attitude towards rococo fashion, also supplied the Prince of Wales with a centrepiece to one of Kent's designs.[12] But while comparatively few objects from this period can be associated with particular designers, there can be no doubt of the strength of the market for plate of a more restrained nature than was demanded by current fashion.

The fashion for other traditionally important varieties of display plate, such as ewers and dishes, wine cisterns and fountains and pilgrim bottles, showed a marked decline during the rococo period. It is true that the ewer and dish was by now functionally redundant, but as display pieces, the broad surface of the dish and the form of the ewer were ideal vehicles for the rococo style, while the fact that it was no longer expected to be put to practical use liberated it from the constraints of practicality. Wickes's ewer and dish of 1735, ordered by the Corporation of the City of Bristol,[13] and de Lamerie's of 1741 and 1742, made for the Earl of Mountrath and the Goldsmiths' Company, are among the most brilliantly inventive plate of the period. Similarly, although highly unusual during the mid century, wine cisterns, such as Charles Kandler's of 1734 (now in the Hermitage Museum, Leningrad), which was modelled by the sculptor Michael Rysbrach, could be magnificent and original works of art.

Part of the explanation for their decline in popularity should almost certainly be sought in the 6d. duty which would have added considerably to the cost of such weighty items. Part also may have been the dramatic appearance of newly made cups and covers which tended to displace more traditional kinds of display plate. But equally significant may have been a

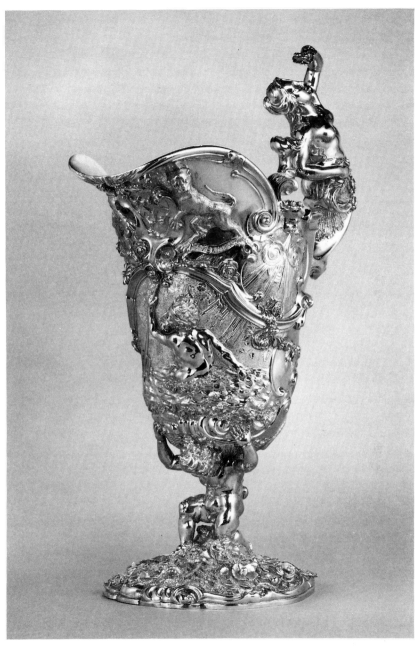

Ewer, silver, 1742, maker's mark of Paul de Lamerie, made for the 5th Earl of Mountrath; 18⅜ in. high (Gilbert Collection, Los Angeles County Museum of Art).

general shift in emphasis in the dining room from the sideboard to the dining table itself.

The most obvious symptom of this shift in emphasis was the development of the silver centrepiece. Originally this was designed in France as a tureen on an elaborate sculptural base surrounded by cruets and casters, but this

Epergne, silver, 1751, maker's mark of
Edward Wakelin; 13 in. high.

type, made by de Lamerie, Crespin and Sprimont,[14] fell from fashion after the 1740s and was succeeded by the type known as the 'epergne'. Part practical, part decorative, these sprawling objects grew in both size and complexity during the middle two quarters of the century. The origins of the name are in fact obscure and, despite appearances, would seem to have no connection with the French language. The form of the earliest examples, however, is French and is derived from those of Parisian makers, such as Claude Ballin. These generally consist of a silver frame supporting a central bowl, flanked by casters and with dishes and candle branches. Kent's design for the Prince of Wales was of this type, but by the middle of the century casters were no longer part of the epergne. Now associated mainly with the service of dessert, it consisted of a series of dishes or baskets, for which candle branches could occasionally be substituted.

The rapid evolution of the typical epergne of the 1750s and 1760s is one of the most remarkable episodes in English silver and epitomizes the inventive spirit of the rococo. During the early 1750s production was largely in the hands of Parker and Wakelin, the successors to Wickes's business; their epergnes were generally quite low and took the form of a

Epergne, silver, 1763, maker's mark of Thomas Pitts; 26 in. high
(Gilbert Collection, Los Angeles).

central basket or dish flanked by four smaller dishes rising from branches above scroll feet. The central basket was for fruit, while the smaller baskets or dishes were intended for sweetmeats or pickles. Over the succeeding decade the number and variety of dishes and baskets grew, the form became higher and the components lighter. The most important factor in determining the size and elaboration of these epergnes was cost. Parker and Wakelin continued to be the principal retailers (although largely supplied by Thomas Pitts) throughout the 1760s, and their ledgers reveal a natural enough correspondence between the number of components and the total cost. Among the 'optional extras' available, perhaps the most inventive was the Chinese pagoda canopy which fitted into the main frame of the epergne and totally transformed its character. The main arena for chinoiserie during

Soup tureen, silver, 1750, maker's mark of Paul Crespin; 14 in. long
(National Trust, Erdigg, Clwyd).

the mid century was tea silver, and this was largely inspired by sources such as Pillemont's engravings and Chambers's designs. But in the case of epergnes, this element was probably inspired by Thomas Chippendale's *The Gentleman & Cabinet Maker's Directory*, which was first published in 1754 and had passed through two further editions by 1762.

In terms of volume, the most important developments of all in mid eighteenth-century plate were those related to the dinner service, which largely took the place of earlier massive display pieces as the principal item of 'capital' plate. Large services had certainly existed earlier, such as that given by Charles II to the Duchess of Portsmouth, which weighed no less than 6,700 ounces,[15] but the innovations in dining plate of the period around 1720 rendered most earlier services obsolete. Items such as soup tureens, sauceboats and cruet frames were all novelties which rapidly gained acceptance and were thereafter regarded as necessities.

In spite of the increasing availability of porcelain as a fashionable alternative to plate, silver still had great prestige. The Wickes and Wakelin

Two plates, silver, 1735, maker's mark of John Eckfourd II;
$10\frac{3}{4}$ in. and $9\frac{1}{4}$ in. diameter.

ledgers give some idea of the strength of demand for new services, which were often made from old-fashioned or worn plate supplied to the goldsmith by the customer. The most magnificent surviving service is probably that delivered by Wickes to the Earl of Kildare in 1747 at a cost of nearly £5,000.[16] It comprised over 170 pieces, including two soup tureens, two cruet frames, four condiment urns, two sugar bowls, ten sauce boats, eight candlesticks, ninety plates, thirty dishes with twenty-two covers, eleven salvers, two bread baskets, various other miscellaneous pieces, a centrepiece and quantities of flatware. Less extensive but nearly as impressive is that made in the same year for the Earl of Thanet by Paul de Lamerie.[17] Apart from private patrons, a further important source of demand continued to be the official issue of plate to ambassadors and other servants of the crown, for example the dinner service supplied to Sir John Cust on his election as Speaker of the House of Commons in 1761, part of which can still be seen at Belton and which includes a wine cistern by Thomas Heming.

Although few complete services survive intact, numerous of their com-

Pair of sauce boats, silver, 1745, maker's mark of Nicholas Sprimont.

ponents do and it is possible to trace a fairly full picture of the range and character of services available. Uniformity of design within the service was considered important, and while exceptions existed, most customers seem to have favoured shaped circular dinner plates and an oval, or shaped oval form for serving dishes and other vessels. Elaborate decoration was usually restricted to the most prominent items, such as soup tureens and centre-pieces, most other components being relatively plain, with decorated borders and engraved armorials. The main decorative feature was shape, which in the mid eighteenth century laid emphasis on gently curving outlines and cast feet and handles, which are usually of a simple scroll form.

In more exceptional, elaborately decorated services, a constant search for novelty and variety was a priority, but even in these services a number of basic trends and formulas characteristic of certain makers can be recognized. Some makers seem to have concentrated on particular basic forms for the soup tureen, which they continued to use over a considerable period, varying the effect principally by the decoration. Charles Kandler, for example, who supplied the magnificent pair of tureens of 1752[18] at Ickworth, favoured a bulbous-shaped oval body that was related to Meissen porcelain forms. Paul de Lamerie, on the other hand, repeated the same flattened oval body throughout the 1730s and 1740s, which he varied by the use of different cast and applied ornament.

Pair of sauceboats, silver, 1739, maker's mark of Paul de Lamerie.

A similar pattern of variety within relatively fixed formulas can be seen in the development of sauce boats, casters and salt cellars. Again, certain basic forms tend to be associated with certain workshops, even though decoration might make this less obvious. For example, while some makers produced sauce boats on a central spreading foot, de Lamerie's almost invariably have an oval body on three or four paw feet. Similarly, salt cellars from his workshop usually have a shallow bowl-like receptacle with bulbous sides and four feet, although variety of ornament again disguises the uniformity of shape. Nicholas Sprimont's work is often characterized by the use of basketwork and fluid scrolls that can be recognized on much of his small surviving corpus of work.

The rationale for such 'house styles' was as much a matter of economics as taste. For while a successful goldsmith in charge of a large workshop might be expected to take a personal interest in major commissions, he was for most ordinary purposes concerned with managing and supervising the work of his employees and apprentices, rather than practising as a craftsman.

Clearly, from an economic point of view, it made sense to allow his plateworkers to continue producing forms at which they were proficient, rather than trying to make them work up new lines, especially when the old were still apparently acceptable to his clientele.

Associated with the dinner service, and sometimes supplied as an integral

Bread basket, silver, 1729, maker's mark of George Wickes; 12 in. long.

part of it, was the basket. Baskets in silver certainly existed in earlier periods, as both inventories and the occasional survival show. But it was only in the second quarter of the eighteenth century that they became popular. In some ways their rise to popularity was in itself a product of the rococo aesthetic. Some of the earliest baskets of the period are pierced and chased to imitate wickerwork, and there is something inherently rococo in the very idea of precious metal being fashioned in imitation of another, quite valueless material. During the late 1730s and 1740s a number of goldsmiths, notably Paul de Lamerie, Paul Crespin and James Shruder, discovered the full potential of silver baskets for expressing the rococo at its most exuberant, through elaborate asymmetrical piercing, engraving and casting. Both the beginning and the end of this evolution can be illustrated through baskets owned by the National Trust, the former by one of 1731 by Paul de Lamerie at Ickworth,[19] and the latter by one of 1750 by John Jacobs at Wallington. Baskets were generally intended for bread or fruit, although one of the four formerly at Dunham Massey is referred to in the Earl of Warrington's inventory as a 'Basket for Knives, Spoons & Forks'.

Plate about the house was subject to less change in this period than that in the dining room. Ordinary and practical plate associated with the bedroom, including shaving jugs and bowls, soap boxes and sponge boxes, mainly retained the forms already established twenty years earlier and was seldom very elaborately decorated. Similarly, plate made in connection with

Bread basket, silver, 1750, maker's mark of John Jacobs; $17\frac{1}{2}$ in. long (National Trust, Wallington, Northumberland).

alcohol seems to have responded to the rococo only to a limited degree. Wine was the fashionable drink of the eighteenth century and this was reflected in the great inventiveness and variety of wine glasses. With glass being not only more fashionable for wine, but cheaper also, goldsmiths had little chance of attracting patrons and during the first half of the eighteenth century silver goblets fell almost entirely from use. But demand for silver mugs and tankards was also much less than it had been in the late seventeenth century, and such as there were generally made little concession to the rococo beyond following the modest baluster form that had been adopted by pewterers, or being engraved with armorials within a rococo cartouche. These developments were part of a more complicated set of circumstances than simply glass becoming more popular than silver; they were related also to improvements in the production of the beverages themselves. Christopher Hill suggests that 'when pewter gave way to glass it helped the sparkling Burton ales to compete with the cloudy London porter',[20] but equally it might be said that the development of an attractive clear ale helped to encourage the production of glass to the detriment of both silver and pewter.

The consolidation of the craft noted at the beginning of this chapter is particularly evident in tea and coffee plate. During the mid eighteenth century tea was still considered a luxury. Although it was gradually declining in price, Thomas Turner, a merchant of East Hoathley in Sussex, recorded in his diary[21] that on 1 August 1759 he paid 9s. 3d. for a pound of green tea, the most expensive type. This compares interestingly with the mere sixteen pence he spent the previous month on four pounds of lobster. But despite its high price, tea became increasingly obtainable during the second quarter of the century and this is reflected in a corresponding demand for appropriate plate.

The so-called bullet, or compressed spherical, shape remained standard for teapots and kettles during the second quarter of the century. Cream jugs were usually of pear form on scroll feet, while tea caddies and sugar bowls tended to be based on variations of the forms already established by the end of the previous period. The latter were often supplied in boxed sets, but the matched tea service actually became significantly less usual than it had been earlier in the century. This apparently curious fact is symptomatic of the threat that porcelain was beginning to pose to the goldsmith's trade. The early part of the century had been characterized by a steadily growing demand for silver teapots, but by the middle years this had fallen off as the market began to develop a marked preference for porcelain. This is nowhere better illustrated than by the recently salvaged cargo of the Dutch East India Company's ship, the *Geldermalsen*, which sank in 1752 and whose cargo — one of the regular shipments of the company — contained no fewer than 500 teapots.[22] Other items in its cargo, all of which were competing to some degree for the same market, included dinner services and several thousand tea bowls.

With the exception of kettles, most tea silver of the mid century is

Kettle and stand with salver, silver, 1749, maker's mark of Thomas Gilpin.

Cream jug, silver-gilt, 1733, maker's mark of Peter Archambo.

relatively plain, conforming in shape to the rococo preference for curvaceous lines and with decoration being restricted to typical engraved or embossed scrolls and foliage. Certain forms and types of decoration are associated with particular workshops. De Lamerie, for example, evidently made many more kettles than other sorts of tea ware, Pezé Pilleau specialized in a type of jug decorated only with a subtle design of facets, and Samuel Taylor made a speciality of vase-shaped caddies embossed with scrolls and foliage. But even items which were not seriously threatened by porcelain were

*Faceted jug, silver, 1730, maker's mark of Pezé Pilleau; 6½ in. high
(Untermyer Collection, Metropolitan Museum of Art, New York).*

nevertheless influenced, both in form and decoration, by the prevailing
interest in the Orient.

In some cases, such as covered sugar bowls, the influence is very literal
and the form a direct copy of Chinese ceramic bowls. More usually, however,
this is expressed in the embossed or engraved chinoiserie decoration typical
on tea silver, especially during the third quarter of the century. The term
chinoiserie refers, as in the seventeenth century, more to an attitude towards
the Orient than to ornament of a particular style or appearance. From the

TOP: *Three tea caddies, silver-gilt, 1754, maker's mark of Eliza Godfrey; 5¼ in. and 5½ in. high.*

BOTTOM: *Tea caddy, silver, 1773, maker's mark of Louisa Courtauld and George Cowles; 3½ in. high (Victoria and Albert Museum, London).*

Chocolate pot, silver, c. 1740, maker's mark of
Charles Kandler; 11 in. high.

1740s to the late 1760s this attitude affected the decoration of tea caddies, which ranged from square boxes engraved with bands and pseudo-Chinese characters in imitation of tea bales shipped from China, to the embossed chinoiserie fantasies of de Lamerie and Crespin.

Chocolate pots in silver also declined in popularity during this period, but more because chocolate itself became less fashionable than because it was served from other materials. Coffee pots, however, were produced in

Salver, silver, 1747, maker's mark of Paul de Lamerie; 10 in. diameter
(National Trust, Shugborough, Staffordshire).

large numbers and with a range of form and decoration that was dictated as much by cost as by taste. The most standard form was a tapering cylinder with incurved base and spout placed opposite the handle. This was superseded around 1760 by an elongated pear form. Occasionally pots of the French type, with pear-shaped body on scroll feet, were also produced, especially by de Lamerie and Kandler. However, within these basic formulas a wide range of prices was available, depending upon the degree of embossed, engraved or cast ornament that was chosen.

Salvers continued to be in demand and it is probably their association with tea services that accounts for their proliferation and variety during this period. The Earl of Warrington's inventory lists many salvers or

Salver, silver, 1741, maker's mark of James Shruder; 20½ in. diameter
(National Trust, Dunham Massey, Cheshire).

'waiters', a number of which are among the plate still at Dunham. Some of
these are described as having specific functions, such as '6 small waiters and
2 larger, to give Drink in [sic]', 'a Waiter for Cards' and 'an oblong waiter
to give Chocolate on'. In addition to being functional, salvers had the
attraction of providing a large surface suitable for heraldic engraving, which
on other varieties of fashionable plate was often incompatible with the
demands for profuse embossed decoration. That they were also made for
display is clear from the fact that the Goldsmiths' Company ordered four
gilt salvers from Thomas Farren in 1742, at the same time as de Lamerie's
ewer and basin and for the same purpose: to replace the buffet of plate that
had been melted down between 1637 and 1667. Although most, such as

— 207 —

Pair of candlesticks, silver, 1742, maker's mark of
George Wickes; 10 in. high.

those at Dunham Massey, have a fairly simply shaped outline, some were
enhanced with extremely sophisticated cast and pierced rococo ornament
around the border.

A much fuller response to the rococo can be followed through the
development of candlesticks and inkstands from about 1730 to 1760.
Candlesticks evolved from two separate types, the plain octagonal and
baluster stemmed formula established in England by the turn of the century,
and the more highly decorated form produced in France. The former was
adapted to the rococo fashion by the accretion of applied or chased
ornament to an otherwise fixed form, and was used even for some of
Wickes's and de Lamerie's most important commissions during the 1740s

Pair of candlesticks, silver, 1739, maker's mark of Peter Archambo; $9\frac{1}{2}$ in. high
(National Trust, Dunham Massey, Cheshire).

and early 1750s. The latter, although rarer, is generally handled with a
greater awareness of the plastic potential of the form. Paul Crespin and
James Shruder were among the leading exponents of French taste and based
their models on silver and ormolu fashions there. Beyond these themes,
some of the most original plate of the rococo period was that in the
form of the various caryatid figure candlesticks of the mid-century. The
antecedents of this type were the figure candlesticks of makers such as
Anthony Nelme, casts of whose kneeling blackamoor figure model were
occasionally used during the mid eighteenth century. But in the rococo
period the sculptural possibilities of cast stems were much more fully
realized. In particular they found expression in the various caryatid figure

— 209 —

candlesticks of which Paul de Lamerie made a certain number during the late 1740s and early 1750s, and of which the pair of 1758 by Simon Le Sage at Ickworth is a fine example. The finest examples of these sculptural forms, however, are almost certainly the unmarked pair in the Victoria and Albert Museum representing Daphne and Apollo and based on drawings by George Michael Moser.[23]

This chapter opened with the observation that the mid eighteenth century was, in terms of the organization of the craft, a period of consolidation rather than innovation. But in terms of design it was one of profound change, the most surprising feature of which was not that fashionable plate was nearly all made in a novel and animated style, but that the basic principles of that style percolated through even to the most ordinary domestic objects. The reason for this lies in the expanded choice of domestic wares available during the first half of the century. In the past, silver had been the undisputed queen of crafts. For decorated plate the goldsmiths had followed their own path, which occasionally made reference to or took inspiration from other materials; for ordinary domestic wares, which were not subject to the same demands of fashion, they tended to follow the precedent set by pewterers, braziers or potters. During the second quarter of the century, however, the elegant appearance and sophisticated decoration of porcelain posed an increasingly serious challenge to the supremacy of silver. The challenge was largely met in silver by the production of forms which emulated the curvaceousness of porcelain vessels in such a way as to emphasize the malleability rather than the rigidity of the material.

The state of affairs at the end of the period, however, by no means represented a clear victory for porcelain, and silver continued to maintain a distinct advantage over the former by virtue of its special and continued ability to represent status. But it also had an aesthetic advantage through its capacity to retain a greater degree of minutely finished engraved, cast or chased detail than porcelain. This is particularly evident in the difference between the two versions of a salt cellar produced by Nicholas Sprimont, first in silver and subsequently in Chelsea porcelain,[24] for the former has a precisely detailed finish that has been quite lost in the modelling and glazing of the latter. It is this sense of precision that distinguishes the finest silver of the period and which was exploited in the plate made to the designs of Robert Adam during the 1760s and 1770s.

Candelabrum, silver, 1758, Simon Le Sage; 18 in. high
(National Trust, Ickworth, Suffolk).

--------- *Eight* ---------

NEO-CLASSICISM AND
INDUSTRIALIZATION

The industrial revolution was more insidious than explosive and, like the technological revolution of today, was virtually an established fact before most people realized that it was happening. The radical changes that took place in the applied arts during the quarter century from about 1765 were the result of three only partially related developments. Broadly speaking, these were in the areas of management, methods of production and design and the interaction of these three is the subject of this chapter.

Two of these areas – management and production – had in fact already undergone significant changes by the middle of the eighteenth century and well before the decline of the rococo style. Specialization had played a major part in the reorganization of the leading London workshops, and it cannot have gone unnoticed that this practice not only improved quality but reduced costs, giving specialist producers a competitive edge over those with wider output. But aspects of industrialization had already been creeping into the craft well before the middle of the century, the main effects of which were again to increase efficiency and reduce costs. As early as 1747 R. Campbell, in *The London Tradesman*, wrote that the goldsmiths' 'business required much more Time and Labour formerly than at present; they were obliged to beat their Metal from the Ingot into what Thinness they wanted; but now there are invented Flatting-Mills, which reduce their metal to what Thinness they require, at very small Expense'. The economic implications of this are obvious enough: speed of production was greatly increased by enabling the first time-consuming stage of producing a workable silver sheet to be eliminated; thinner metal of consistent gauge enabled items to be produced more quickly, which were also lighter and consequently cheaper and available to a wider market.

These changes had a powerful effect on the production of silver. But after the middle of the century major intellectual changes also took place which were equally significant, leading architects and designers to think along lines that were radically different from those of the rococo style. The rococo and neo-classical styles were mutually antipathetical, for while the latter was essentially an intellectual movement, the former was, if anything, determinedly anti-intellectual. Its eventual failure had been inevitable from the start, for of all styles it was the most obviously whimsical and unstructured, and its sense of discipline was so loose that only in the hands of a great master did it avoid tending towards the banal. By its very nature it demanded originality and an ability to look constantly in new directions. In the end it had run the gamut of all possible variations, and because novelty was so central to it, it had to reach the stage where it seemed bankrupt and frivolous.

Its deliberately irreverent attitude towards the classical tradition made an equally radical reaction against it inevitable, and just as the style had originated in France, reaction against it started there too. In 1754 Charles-Nicholas Cochin launched an attack in the *Mercure de France* decrying the absurdity of modelling, for example, 'children small as vine leaves and others so robust as to render their posture on leaves scarcely capable of supporting the weight of a little bird'.[1]

Not only the reaction, but also its approximate direction, was inevitable. It had to be towards a style that was more rational. By the third quarter of the eighteenth century a new mood of intellectual rigour was making itself felt in England, and names such as David Hume, Samuel Johnson and Benjamin Franklin are enough to indicate the direction that the intellectual world was taking. This sense of rigour and discipline was applied as much to art as to any other pursuit, and the way in which it was applied to art was expounded by Joshua Reynolds in his *Sixth Discourse*, delivered to the students of the Royal Academy in 1774. 'Invention is one of the great marks of genius ... [but] it is by being conversant with the inventions of others, that we learn to invent ... The greatest natural genius cannot subsist on his own stock: he who resolves never to ransack any mind but his own, will soon be reduced, from mere barrenness, to the poorest of all imitations; he will be obliged to imitate himself, and to repeat what he has before often repeated.'[2] Reynolds therefore advocated that his students familiarize themselves as much as possible with ancient art and architecture, and in doing so he was aware, as were all his contemporaries, of the enormous advances that had recently been made in the knowledge of these subjects.

It is difficult fully to appreciate the impact made by the discoveries of Pompeii and Herculaneum during the excavations of the 1740s and 1750s,

Three vases, silver, 1771, maker's mark of Louisa Courtauld and George Cowles;
$7\frac{3}{4}$ in. and $7\frac{1}{8}$ in. high (Museum of Fine Arts, Boston).

for they gave for the first time a glimpse of ordinary ancient Roman domestic architecture and artefacts. These sites and those at Rome and elsewhere in Italy were visited by the English aristocracy and assiduously studied by scholars, and the importance attached to them is reflected in the series of expensive illustrated publications that were widely subscribed over the next twenty years. Far from being of purely academic interest, these discoveries were treated almost from the start with a clear idea of their application. Robert Adam was in no doubt that 'the buildings of Ancients ... serve as models which we should imitate', and d'Hancarville, in the preface to his catalogue of Sir William Hamilton's collection of Greek vases (published 1766–7), is even more direct: 'We think also, that we make an agreeable present to our manufacturers of earthenware and china, and to those who make vases in silver, copper, glass, marble, etc. Having employed much more time in working them than in reflection, and in being besides in great want of models, they will be very glad to find here more than two hundred forms, the greatest part of which, are absolutely new to them; then, as in a plentiful stream, they may draw ideas which their ability and taste will know how to improve to their advantage, and to that of the public.'[3] That this plentiful stream was readily drawn upon is illustrated by Josiah Wedgwood's famous black basalt 'First Day's Vase' of 1769 and a less well-known set

Cup and cover, silver-gilt, 1764, maker's mark of Daniel Smith and Robert Sharp,
designed by Robert Adam; 19 in. high
(National Trust, Anglesey Abbey, Cambridgeshire).

of three silver vases made in 1771 by Louisa Courtauld and George Cowles.
The latter were made for Nathaniel Curzon, 1st Baron Scarsdale of Kedleston
Hall, and are now in the Boston Museum of Fine Arts.

In addition to his architectural achievements Robert Adam was also a
gifted designer who was responsible for entire schemes of decoration. His
design of 1762 for furnishing the sideboard at Kedleston is of particular

interest in that it combines new furniture and plate with seventeenth-century pieces from the family collection, such as the two wine fountains and cisterns. New plate made under his direction is among the most sophisticated and brilliantly finished of all English silver. A silver-gilt cup of 1764 by Daniel Smith and Robert Sharp at Anglesey Abbey is one of

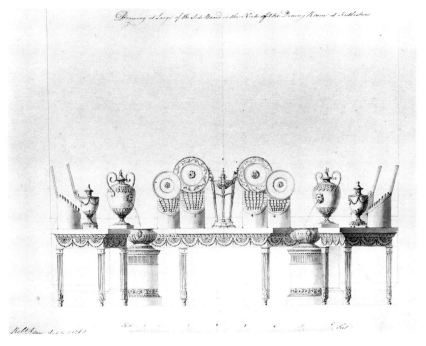

Robert Adam, design for the sideboard and plate at Kedleston Hall (1762).

several made to drawings by Adam and contains all the features of the style which he created. Although he, too, advocated imitation of antiquities, no silver from the classical period had yet come to light, and Adam's procedure was therefore to use such classical forms and ornament as were known and combine them in a suitable composition. The ingredients here are the classical vase shape, which occurs throughout the period, and a variety of ornament, all of which has classical precedent. What distinguishes his style, however, is the precision and control with which the design has been handled. It has a fine sense of line and a carefully managed balance between its horizontal and vertical elements which is emphasized by the finely chiselled details. Indeed, much of the character of the cup is due to this very fine finish which emphasizes the rigid character of the metal, rather than its malleability. The rococo principle by which one element of the design merges with another has been completely rejected, and each component of the design has been kept uncomprisingly separate from its neighbour, so that a perfect distinction is maintained between form and ornament.

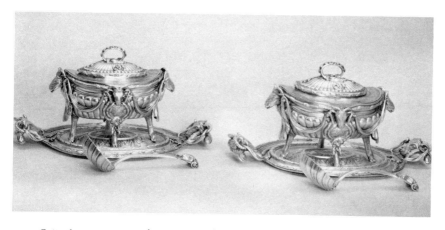

Pair of sauce tureens, silver, 1769 and 1770, maker's mark of Thomas Heming
(Gilbert Collection, Los Angeles).

In France a different attitude towards classicism gained currency. There criticism of the rococo focused, as we have seen, on the absurdity of its decoration rather than its sense of plasticity, and leading goldsmiths tended to favour the use of a range of classical ornament applied to forms that still retained a fluid curvaceous quality rejected by the Adam style. Adam's style did not win universal approval in England, and for those to whom it was not acceptable France remained a powerful cultural magnet. Charles Frederick Kandler (see p. 231), Parker and Wakelin, and Thomas Heming, who was royal goldsmith from 1760 to 1782, were the leading exponents of this alternative style, and a pair of sauce tureens of 1769 and 1770 with Heming's mark illustrate its main features. While its ornament is equally dependent upon antique sources, its lines are less austere and the decoration used more loosely, without the minute precision that marks the Adam style. It makes a more robust and masculine use of classical precedent, but it is also a less violent reversal of the rococo and was for many easier to accept. On a totally different scale, Heming's wine cistern of 1770 at Belton[4] illustrates the same principles of design.

Plate such as this was generally made to special order and was within the reach of only the wealthy. But neither version of the neo-classical style achieved immediate popular acceptance, and the Adam cup in particular was well ahead of its time. Indeed, a toilet service by the same makers and a pair of candelabra by John Scofield, all supplied in 1783 to the Earl of Lonsdale, show that the style was still in vogue for the finest and most

Box from a toilet service, silver-gilt, 1783, maker's mark of Daniel Smith and Robert Sharp; 7⅝ in. long.

costly plate as much as twenty years later. For less sophisticated plate, a period of transition resulting in a range of domestic objects that were neither in one style nor the other was inevitable. A coffee pot of 1776 by Charles Wright in the Victoria and Albert Museum is more typical of the response of the trade in general to changing demands. It shows a certain grasp of the new ornamental vocabulary with its swags and ribbons, but adheres to a shape already established fifteen years earlier and retains a spout that is still typically rococo. Throughout the 1760s and even into the following decade the vast majority of English silver continued to be made in this transitional manner.

This stylistic ambivalence was often a reflection of the conservative tastes of customers, but equally it was a matter of basic economics, for there was

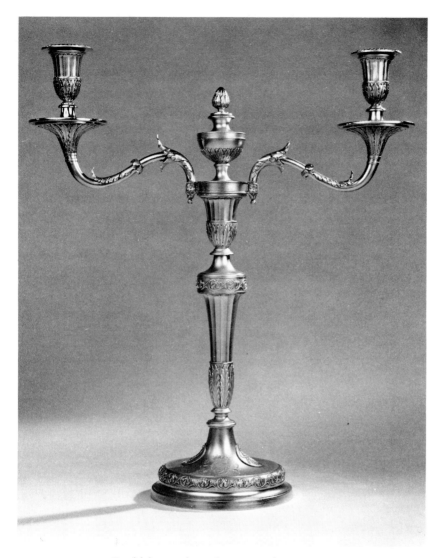

Candelabrum, silver-gilt, 1783, maker's mark of
John Scofield; $16\frac{1}{2}$ in. high.

clearly little incentive for goldsmiths to incur the expense of making new
cast ornament or sinking new dies while existing ones were still acceptable.
However, despite the inevitable period of transition, the new style seems
to have been assimilated by the craft as a whole more quickly than earlier
ones. The floral style of the later seventeenth century, the sculptural forms

— 219 —

*Coffee pot, silver, 1776, maker's mark of Charles Wright; $13\frac{1}{2}$ in. high
(Victoria and Albert Museum, London).*

of the Huguenot style and the inventiveness of the rococo had been manifested in ordinary domestic plate at best by a modification of form and at worst by a crude and misunderstood imitation of current decoration. But during the last quarter of the eighteenth century both an understanding of the principles and a competent handling of the decoration of neo-classicism

One of a pair of wine coasters, Sheffield plate, c. 1780.

are evident in inexpensive Sheffield plate as much as in the grandest commissions.

The explanation of this phenomenon lies in the fact that the craft was subject to a more complex set of influences in the late eighteenth century than in previous periods. In the past, changes of fashion had tended to be imposed on a conservative trade by the demands of fashion-conscious patrons, but now pressure came as much from manufacturers as from their customers. The former were influenced by economic considerations arising from developing mechanized methods of production, while the constituency of the latter was significantly enlarged by an effective reduction in the cost of solid silver and by the invention of Sheffield plate. The fashions favoured by its makers in turn influenced the silversmiths of London and led them to adopt similar methods of production.

Sheffield plate was the first true substitute for solid silver, and after its initial development around the middle of the century it rapidly captured a large market, both in England and North America. Like many important

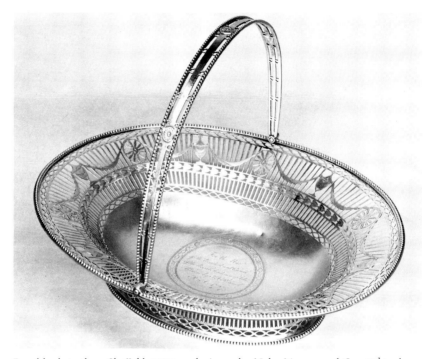

Bread basket, silver, Sheffield, 1779, maker's mark of John Younge and Co.; 12¾ in. long (Royal Academy of Arts, London).

inventions, its principle was discovered accidentally. Thomas Boulsover, a Sheffield cutler, noticed in about 1745 that copper and silver fused together under heat. As a result of further experiments he discovered also that both metals expand equally when rolled under pressure, and that a large sheet of workable copper plated with silver could be produced from fused and rolled copper and silver ingots.[5]

The commercial application of the principle was taken up by another Sheffield cutler, Joseph Hancock, and according to the account of Charles Dixon, also a Sheffield maker, 'the first articles made by Mr Hancock were saucepans plated inside ... The makers then manufactured salt cellars, which had generally blue glass in them to hold the salt. Candlesticks were then made, and one, the Corinthian, was very neat, care being taken to preserve the Order in its construction.'[6] It was not until the 1770s, however, that plating on both sides of the copper was introduced. This enabled a wider range of items to be produced and made it possible for Sheffield plate manufacturers to provide a viable alternative to solid silver. The same writer observed that it 'opened a wide field for the display of genius. They then began the manufacturing of dishes and covers, tureens, bread baskets, butter boats, teapots, sugar basins, cream jugs etc., etc.' By the last quarter of the century a number of firms were producing plate on a large scale, including Thomas Law and Henry and Thomas Tudor in Sheffield and Matthew Boulton in Birmingham.

The London silversmiths were not slow to realize that the new material, because of its lower price, effectively opened their doors to a completely new clientele, and many soon advertised themselves as retailers of Sheffield plate in addition to continuing as manufacturing silversmiths. But although most did not view it as a serious challenge to solid silver, there can be no doubt that Sheffield plate, together with the new clientele that it attracted, was one of the most important factors in determining the character of late eighteenth-century English silver. The curious interaction of these two largely separate markets for solid silver and Sheffield plate has been discussed by Robert Rowe as follows:

In the period under review most silver objects could also be made up in Sheffield plate, thereby reaching a new class of customer whose standards inevitably contributed to current aesthetic values. The collective taste of the country therefore had a broader basis than ever before. In general solid plate was the prototype for the substitute, but not always so. Sometimes the designs that originated with the makers of plated wares had to be followed by the London silversmiths because they set a fashion. This cross-fertilization of ideas between different sections of the community was very noticeable by the 1780s in the simplicity and lack of ostentation of some of the best silverware ... The difference between an object made for the rich and another aimed at the growing number of comfortably well-off tradesmen was one of ornament or material but not of basic design.[7]

However, although available to an expanded market, it is easy to exaggerate the difference in price between Sheffield plate and solid silver, or the range of the market at which it was aimed. Surviving printed pattern books issued by the firm of T. Bradbury and Sons between 1770 and 1790 give[8] a valuable insight into the difference in price between solid silver and its plated counterpart. Manuscript annotations against many of the designs indicate, for example, that a pierced cake basket with swing handle and pierced slits cost £8 3s., while a pair of typical candlesticks, hollow and 'loaded' with pitch, cost £2 19s. In 1760 Horace Walpole visited Sheffield and wrote that he 'bought a pair of [plated] candlesticks for two guineas'.[9] Equivalent objects in solid silver would probably have cost in the region of £30 and £12 respectively. When measured against the cost of similar candlesticks in brass, which would have been between 6s. and 12s.,[10] or the average earnings of a well-paid factory worker, which would probably not have exceeded 10s. a week, it is clear that Sheffield plate was still a commodity limited to the middle classes and above.

The surprising narrowness of the differential in price was largely because of changes in the law and because of the fashion for light, pierced silverware which prevailed from the 1780s. The repeal of the 6d. per ounce duty on assayed plate in 1757[11] effectively reduced the cost of the metal by about 10 per cent, while the fashion in the 1780s for lighter silver than that of twenty years earlier also reduced the cost of the finished article. These factors combined to produce an extraordinary increase in demand for silver during the late eighteenth century. A good indication of the total weight of silver assayed annually during this period is given by surviving records of the 'diet' – the accumulated weight of tiny scrapings taken from pieces submitted for assay. In 1753 these amounted to eighty ounces. In 1763, after the repeal of the duty, the figure had risen to 189 ounces and in 1773 to 194 ounces ten pennyweight, some two-and-a-half times the mid-century level. On the basis of these figures it has been estimated that after 1760 the weight of silver assayed in London amounted annually to some 100,000 pounds.[12]

Part of the explanation for this increased production lies in the industrial methods that were gradually being adopted, both in London and Sheffield, and which themselves help to account for the rapid assimilation of the fashion for light silver during the late 1770s and 1780s. The thinner gauge of metal, prepared mechanically on the flatting mill, tended to suggest certain shapes which would have been less natural to a silversmith starting with a silver ingot. Whereas spherical or bullet-shaped teapots had been natural forms for hand-raised silver, the supply of metal in thin, prepared sheets made seamed cylindrical or oval bodies an obvious alternative. Similarly, the fashion for vase-shaped coffee pots, although consistent with the move towards classically inspired forms, happened also to be better suited to the new methods of production.

A similar reciprocity between the demands of fashion and the constraints of mechanical production affected the decoration in vogue. Asymmetrical pierced decoration had been among the most technically demanding forms of ornament during the rococo period, and attempts at imitation were made during the early days of Sheffield plate. Difficulties were at first encountered in that the underlying copper was exposed when the pattern was pierced through. But this problem was solved with the invention of the mechanical 'fly-punch', which pushed through the metal with such force that it had the effect of dragging the silver through with it and wrapping it around the exposed copper. It was soon noticed that the same machine could be used for piercing solid silver too. Pierced decoration would formerly either have to have been cut with a fret-saw or punched out by hand, both of which were labour intensive and did not allow for the same degree of precision that could be achieved with the fly punch. From a manufacturer's point of view the attraction of the new machine was that much of the work could now be done mechanically, and a regular pattern could be cut in a fraction of the time taken by hand; from an aesthetic point of view the advantage was in the precise symmetry of the mechanical piercing.

A cross-fertilization in the reverse direction is evident in another form of characteristic late eighteenth-century decoration, known as 'bright-cut engraving'. Decorative engraving was relatively unfashionable during the second half of the eighteenth century, and engraving of a non-heraldic nature was unusual. Bright-cutting, on the other hand, is a form of engraving whereby a specially shaped graving tool is used to cut a faceted groove in the metal, rather than simply a line, such that it catches the light and produces a sparkling effect not unlike that of cut crystal. The fashion for this delicate form of engraving lasted only about ten or fifteen years, possibly because it was found that its sharp facets were soon lost through over-cleaning. But although perhaps intended in the first instance as a means of upholding the values of hand-crafted methods, the effect was soon cunningly imitated in Sheffield plate by striking the surface with a faceted die to produce a similar pattern without cutting through to the copper.

The enormous increase in silver production during the late eighteenth century was made up not only of larger quantities passing through the assay offices, but of an expanded range of goods too. This is apparent in the vast quantity of surviving plate and in the manufacturers' pattern books for silver and Sheffield plate that were produced to stimulate orders. The fashion for pierced decoration is evident in a wide variety of objects such as wine coasters, salt cellars, pepper pots, sugar bowls, cruet frames and cake baskets. Many of these were made by semi-industrialized means; the

Epergne, silver, 1778, maker's mark of Thomas Pitts; 14½ in. high
(Victoria and Albert Museum, London).

thin gauge allowed considerable savings to be made in the amount of metal used and also made piercing easier, while the piercing itself made for further economies in metal. In many of these the decorative aspect of the piercing was enhanced by the use of blue glass liners, which also enabled such decoration to be used extensively on hollow-ware.

The extent to which piercing gave a light, almost whimsical quality to plate is carried to its extreme in the epergne. The rather formal grandeur that had characterized the earliest of these centrepieces had been completely overturned by the elaborate fantasies of the rococo period, and during the 1780s an attempt was made to inject classical detail while retaining much the same form. The leading specialist maker of epergnes was William Pitts, who had inherited the business from his father, Thomas, and although most with his mark are of basically similar design, a closer comparison shows that he was evidently prepared to make considerable variations in type or quality of decoration in order to meet a high or lower price. Although the basic design is usually similar, significant variations are found between different examples, which can only be explained by the limit that had been set on their cost. Some employ mechanical fly-punching for the piercing of all the baskets, while keeping cast ornament to a minimum and making pendant swags of die-stamped sheet. Others have many cast branches and swags, make extensive use of engraving and bright-cutting and, most

— 226 —

Cream jug, silver, 1780, maker's mark of Andrew Fogelberg and Stephen Gilbert;
$5\frac{3}{8}$ in. high (Victoria and Albert Museum, London).

significantly, have a far more elaborate pattern of piercing that is hand-cut
with a fret-saw rather than die-stamped.

Other categories of plate, by the nature of their function, were not suited
to pierced decoration but were still designed to express elegance through
lightness. Teapots were usually of cylindrical or oval form, with tapering,
attenuated spouts and decoration usually restricted to bright-cut swags and
applied beaded or reeded mouldings to the borders. Coffee pots and cream

Two tea urns, silver, 1790, maker's mark of Henry Chawner;
$14\frac{1}{2}$ *in. and 22 in. high.*

jugs, while generally vase-shaped, expressed lightness through slender proportions and attenuated loop handles. Tea urns had been introduced earlier, but became popular only during this period and were generally also of tall vase-form. During the third quarter of the century they began to supersede the tea-kettle and were considered a more elegant means of

Entrée dish, silver, 1785, maker's mark of Daniel Smith and Robert Sharp; $10\frac{1}{2}$ in. long.

keeping hot water at hand, since they were equipped with a tap that saved picking up the kettle and pouring. Early examples had a spirit lamp underneath to heat the water, but in 1774 John Wadham patented a means of heating from within by inserting a hot iron into a tube contained inside the body of the urn.[13] By this time the standard tea and coffee service would generally have comprised a teapot, coffee pot, cream jug, sugar basin, tea urn and perhaps additional items such as a caddy or slop basic.

Similar trends are evident in another important category of plate, the dinner service. Most soup tureens and sauce tureens also followed the fashion for vase forms with loop handles, and were in most cases subject to fairly restrained decoration, such as gadrooned borders, heraldic engraving and perhaps applied swags of foliage. The shallowness of entrée dishes made the vase form inappropriate, and during the late eighteenth century these are usually oblong, oval or occasionally octagonal. Covers tended to mirror the form of the body and had a detachable handle so that they could be turned over and used as extra dishes.

There were, however, few forms to which the ubiquitous vase could not be adapted. The single bottle wine cooler had finally become a common part of the repertoire during the 1770s, whether in Sheffield plate or in solid silver, and was almost invariably modelled on the vase; casters, salt cellars and pepper pots, and even candlesticks took their inspiration from the same basic motif.

Throughout this period and well into the nineteenth century London's position as the leading centre of silver production in England remained unthreatened. But it did not go unchallenged, and the main strength of the Sheffield and Birmingham manufacturers lay in the advantage they took of industrialized methods of production. Many London silversmiths viewed the new technology with a complacent suspicion and believed that it was impossible for machine-made goods to equal the quality of the finest hand-made ones. In one sense this was true, and Sheffield plate or die-stamped silver is at its least successful when imitating the complex castings typical of high rococo or elaborate neo-classical silver, simply because it would have been uneconomic to spend a long time in chasing up such objects after their initial assembly. On the other hand, it was at its most appealing and cost effective when limited to objects of simple form that needed little hand-finishing. In goods of this type, for which there was a very sizeable market, the advocates of traditional hand-crafted techniques faced a more serious challenge than they might have cared to admit, initially from Birmingham and Sheffield, but not much later from enterprising London makers too.

The most important and well-documented figure in the history of the industrialization of silver manufacture is Matthew Boulton (1728–1809).[14] Boulton died at the age of eighty-one and his achievement is succinctly described in his epitaph in Handsworth Church in Birmingham: 'By the skillful exertion of a mind turned to Philosophy and Mechanics, the appli-cation of a Taste correct and refined and an ardent spirit of Enterprise, he improved, embellished and extended the Arts and Manufacturers of his Country, leaving his establishment of Soho a noble monument to his Genius, Industry and Success ...' He inherited a moderately successful button-making company from his father in 1759, but his ambition looked to greater things and his ultimate aim had long been, as he confessed to Lord Shelburne in 1771, to become 'a great silversmith'.[15] What prevented him from achieving that goal was the fact that there was no assay office in Birmingham and any silver that he might have made would have had to be sent the seventy-five miles to Chester, or to London, to be marked. For some years

Wine cooler, silver, 1775, maker's mark of Charles Frederick Kandler; $7\frac{1}{2}$ in. high (Victoria and Albert Museum, London).

Boulton was one of the most vocal lobbyists for a bill granting hallmarking powers to Birmingham and Sheffield, and its final passage through Parliament in May 1773 removed the last obstacles preventing him from seriously entering the silver manufacturing trade.

Boulton had in fact been producing silver on a small scale before 1773, but most of his energies had been devoted to other fields, in particular the production of ormolu and Sheffield plate. While the former had put him in touch with wealthy and influential patrons on whom he had hoped to depend as customers for his silver, it was his experience in the production of Sheffield plate that prepared him for his silver-producing career. His purpose-built factory at Soho outside Birmingham, a neo-classical building designed by Sidney Wyatt, was completed in or soon after 1765 and employed over 400 workers. His application of the principle of division of labour was unusually advanced for its time, and a certain Professor G. C. Lichtenberg described with amazement his visit to the factory in 1775 – the year before the publication of *The Wealth of Nations* – where he noted that 'each workman has only a very limited range, so that he does not need constantly to change his position and tools, and by this means an incredible amount of time is saved. Thus, for example, each button fashioned in box-wood, ivory, or anything else, passes through at least ten hands.'[16] The success of this principle is spoken for by the growth of staff and turnover at Soho, for by 1772 the number of employees had risen to 800 and whereas in 1763 his annual turnover was around £7,000, by 1767 – just four years later – it had risen to over £30,000.[17]

During the 1760s Boulton had lengthy discussions with Thomas Bouls-over on the subject of fused plate, as a result of which he took out a patent and had an effective monopoly of plated goods produced in that town, going into production in earnest around 1765. But although one of the principle producers in the country, his real interest lay in solid silver rather than Sheffield plate. He was attracted by its prestige and the commercial possibilities that it offered, and his optimism is clear from the fact that in 1773, the year in which the assay offices in Birmingham and Sheffield were opened, he and his partner John Fothergill presented nearly 10,000 ounces of silver for marking.[18] The reasons for his optimism were not only that he had high hopes of his aristocratic contacts or that he was counting on Robert Adam and James Wyatt to supply him with designs. He was also confident that his mechanized methods of production would enable him to produce goods of fine quality at lower prices than the traditional craft methods of his London competitors allowed.

His manager at Soho, James Keir, wrote that 'it was always on Mr Boulton's mind to convert such trades as were usually carried on by individuals into Great Manufactures by the help of machinery, which might enable the articles to be made with greater precision and cheaper, than those commonly sold'.[19] Boulton himself wrote in his notebook in 1769 that 'all our ornaments may be stamped or may be pressed in the fly press'.[20] Improvements were constantly being made. In 1773 he invested in John Huntsman's new process for making steel dies that enabled a sharper finish to be produced and eliminated the need for hand-chasing stamped ornament.

Candelabrum ('lion' design), silver, 1771 (the branches 1787), maker's mark of Thomas Heming; 19 in. high.

But savings in labour had to be set against the costs of capital investment. The whole process is put revealingly in perspective by an analysis carried out in 1773 by John Scale, one of Boulton's managers, of the cost of a Soho 'lion' candlestick as against a cast London-made example of identical appearance. Scale calculated the cost of work at 3s. 3d. per ounce, as opposed to 2s. 6d. per ounce for the cast London one. On the other hand, stamping the entire candlestick in some twelve sections meant that only thirty-eight ounces of silver were needed for a Soho pair, whereas the cast type weighed an average 108 ounces. Therefore the final cost for a pair of Soho candlesticks came out at £17 2s. as opposed to £44 11s. for the identical article made in London.[21] A further effect of this reduced price was to narrow the gap between the cost of the silver and plated versions of the same design, and in 1771 Sir Alexander Gilmour paid £35 9s. for two pairs in silver, while Lady Hertford paid £15 17s. for the same design in plate the following year.[22]

The evidence is telling, but to an extent misleading, since the cost of making new steel dies gave Boulton's factory an inflexibility when faced with idiosyncratic demands that put his London competitors at an advantage. New models for sand casting could be made at a fraction of the cost of Boulton's dies. He was perfectly familiar with the problem. In a letter of 1776 to a client's agent he writes in apologetic terms: 'please to acquaint her ladyship our reason for not sending a drawing of the candlestick she wanted Triangular ... To make it triangular we must be obliged to sink new Dyes which is very expensive work, and besides takes a long time in execution, so that if we were to make new Dyes we apprehend she would not chuse to wait so long and therefore thought best to decline it.'[23]

Boulton's attitude towards the silver trade had an element of duplicity that largely accounts for his ultimate failure. His aim was to cater for the luxury market, and while he realized the limitations of his methods he also allowed himself to get into difficulties on occasion by attempting projects that were impractical. In 1776 he unwisely wrote to his patroness Mrs Elizabeth Montagu (1720–1800) offering that 'if there is any other taste which you have seen and that you think prettier, we should be obliged to you for a hint of it and we shall make designs accordingly'.[24] The result was a tureen that was largely produced by craft techniques, precisely what the economics of his business required him to avoid. His interest was with ornamental plate and he repeatedly avoided orders for plain utilitarian objects, arguing, as he did to a customer in 1775, that 'we do not profess ourselves makers of the commonest Articles in Silver, such as quite plain spoons, Tankards, Muggs, etc., which are sold very low in London and

Jug, silver and silver-gilt, Birmingham, 1776, maker's mark of Matthew Boulton and John Fothergill; $13\frac{1}{2}$ in. high (Museum of Fine Arts, Boston).

other places, indeed we do not intend rivaling with them in the common way, having in general sufficient orders for ornamented plate'.[25] Yet although Boulton was able to undercut the cost of traditional makers of decorated silverware, his efforts ought to have been directed to large-scale production of more modest objects in which, with the appropriate machinery, he would have been able to make far greater inroads into the market.

Part of the reason for Boulton's failure to fulfil his ambition to become a 'great silversmith' was that he failed to appreciate the financial implications of the material. Although the market for modest silver was rapidly expanding, that for the finest ornamental plate was still limited to the wealthy. Such patrons still looked upon plate as a proper form in which to hold capital, even though perhaps no longer the only form. For these people the fact that a pair of candlesticks could be made of thirty-eight ounces looking exactly like a pair of 108 ounces was not a particularly compelling argument, since the 108 ounces was recoverable money anyway. What was important was that prominent plate look and be solid, and while Boulton's certainly looked the part, the very fact that they undercut the amount of precious metal needed was evidently perceived by many as a false economy.

From the point of view of the history of silver Boulton's work has a special interest, in that many of the products of the Soho factory have a very distinctive style. Boulton was not an artist or a designer himself, but he was acutely aware of the use that could be made of available sources and was anxious to produce shapes and ornamental ingredients that most appealed to his customers. He purchased copies of all the important architectural treatises and catalogues of the day, such as d'Hancarville's catalogue of Sir William Hamilton's vases,[26] and in a letter to Mrs Montagu he frankly admitted that 'as [the fashion] of the present day distinguishes itself by adapting the most elegant ornaments of the most refined Grecian artists, I am satisfied in conforming thereto'.[27] The resultant style, although containing no motifs unique to the Soho factory and although making frequent use of interchanged elements, maintains a sense of form and a balance of plain and decorated surfaces that is both subtle and individual.

In terms of more general economic history, Boulton's importance is as a revolutionary marketer, one of the first industrialists rigorously to apply Adam Smith's economic principles, and as one who challenged, rather than reversed, the traditional supremacy of craft techniques. In commercial terms a far more effective challenge to the London silversmiths came from the leading Sheffield firms, who produced, in particular, thin die-stamped

Pair of Candlesticks, silver, London marks for 1776 and maker's mark of
Robert Jones and John Scofield overstriking Sheffield marks; 10¾ in. high.

candlesticks on a large scale and managed to penetrate the London market
to the extent that many were bought by London retailers and restruck
with London makers' marks and hallmarks. Suspicious though many of
the London makers were of developments in Sheffield and Birmingham, the
implications of mechanized processes on the market were unavoidable, and

even the most prestigious firms had to acknowledge that machine-made plate posed a real challenge. Wakelin and Taylor, for example, who in 1776 succeeded the Parker and Wakelin partnership, bought in plate from a number of specialist makers, including candlesticks from John Carter who was himself supplied from Sheffield. These can still be recognized today by the clearly visible Sheffield hallmarks which were overstruck with London marks before being offered for sale. They are usually formed from thin sheet silver, stamped with restrained classical ornament and filled with pitch for strength. Matthew Boulton also supplied London makers, and calculated that machine-made parts cost approximately half the amount of hand-made equivalents.

But mechanized processes were also penetrating the London trade from within, and one of the most successful silver producers of the late eighteenth century was Hester Bateman. Although Bateman's work is often thought of as one of the last great moments in the tradition of English craftsmanship, quite the reverse was the case. She was, in fact, one of the first London manufacturers to run a thoroughly mechanized workshop which set the pattern for most nineteenth-century producers. Hester Bateman took over her husband's small workshop on his death in 1760, and expanded it over the next thirty years into one of the most prolific concerns in London. The growth of the workshop has been studied by John Culme[28] through the records of its insurance policies. He has observed that most plate bearing her mark shows evidence of mechanized processes, such as

the use of the new, machine-milled beading for the borders which had become available during the same period. That Mrs Bateman and her associates had quick production in mind, even on a modest scale, cannot be doubted: their wine labels, unlike those of any of their contemporaries, frequently had the titles actually struck into the metal rather than engraved. The Batemans' larger pieces, such as cake baskets, were probably first made during 1778/79. As with most of the firm's output until the second decade of the nineteenth century, these were fashioned from thin sheet [which would have been available from specialist suppliers].

Expansion continued, and by at least 1791 it would seem that the firm had acquired its own steam engine and flatting mill and was in a position to supply other workshops with prepared silver sheet. The investment that such machinery required was considerable: the inventory taken of a Sheffield plate manufacturer in 1775 totalled £568, of which £247 was made up by steel dies alone, and Hester Bateman's insurance inventory of 1802 totalled £3,200, the largest item of which was the steam engine, which was insured for £800.

*Cruet frame, silver wood and glass, 1788, maker's mark of Hester Bateman; 9 in. high
(Victoria and Albert Museum, London).*

This impressive growth is evident today in the large quantity of plate
to survive with Hester Bateman's mark. But the inevitable consequence of
what was effectively the beginnings of mass-production is also evident in
the quality of much of it. While some is very well made, this was probably
bought in from other workshops to fulfil special orders; the majority is of
remarkably thin gauge and carefully designed with an eye to minimizing

Cruet frame, silver-gilt, wood and glass, 1784, maker's mark of John Scofield, made for William Beckford; 10 in. high (National Trust for Scotland, Brodick Castle).

production processes and hand-finishing, while at the same time complying with the basic requirements of current fashion.

In this respect there was a marked difference between her work — and presumably her prices — and that of some of her leading contemporaries, such as John Scofield, Smith and Sharp or Wakelin and Taylor. But that it was not a basic difference of style, and that Bateman's products were able to compete as a viable alternative to their more expensively made and finished equivalents, is largely because of the special characteristics of the late eighteenth-century neo-classical style. With the advent of a new style after the turn of the century this was no longer possible.

Nine

THE EARLY NINETEENTH CENTURY

By the beginning of the nineteenth century a major phase in the transformation of the silver trade was complete. Hester Bateman's steam engine was symptomatic of a shift in the balance between traditional and mechanized methods of production, and in that sense was the conclusion of a process that had been gaining momentum since the middle of the previous century. Over the next twenty years a number of manufacturers saw the wisdom of investing in this capability, and in so doing accepted the economic principles on which the success of Birmingham and Sheffield producers such as Matthew Boulton and John Younge and Sons was founded.

An important factor to which manufacturers were responding was undoubtedly the enormous growth in the market for domestic silver, a growth which they sought both to tap and to promote by cheaper and more efficient means of production. In Birmingham, for example, the figures reveal an astonishing growth in turnover at the Assay Office. For in 1774 about 17,000 ounces of silver were assayed; by 1779 this had risen to 61,000 and by 1825 to more than 112,000 ounces.[1] But the ramifications of such business decisions went far beyond affecting levels of output and profitability, and had much more to do with determining the character of nineteenth-century domestic plate and significantly affecting the nature of the trade itself. The high cost of machinery and dies could only be recovered by high turnover, which inevitably led both to repetitive models and to larger factories than had been usual before. Soon after the turn of the century a picture consequently emerged in which production was dominated by large firms, both retailers and manufacturers, and the majority of domestic silver was produced by mechanized means.

The application of industrial processes, however, by no means led to a uniform decline of quality, because the finest plate continued throughout the nineteenth century to depend heavily on traditional as well as mechanized methods. But it was certainly the main reason during the early part of the century for an extraordinary polarity between ordinary plate and the best. While the former tended to be of an adequate, if indifferent, quality, the latter was among the most imposing and well-made display plate ever to have been produced. Although made with the maximum application of machinery, these objects were principally the product of highly organized teams of specialists, which involved designers, modellers and large numbers of other craftsmen. Such teamwork, of course, accounts for the impressive quality of the finest plate, but it perhaps also accounts for the distinct uniformity of taste and absence of individuality which characterizes the main stream of display plate from the first two decades of the century.

But if the uniformity was due principally to large units of production, the taste itself was the result of a number of different factors, not least of which was the appearance of a number of proselytizing publications which sought to influence the design of architecture, furniture and plate by means of arguments which centred, almost to the point of being moralizing, around notions of appropriateness and propriety. Early nineteenth-century display plate, in a style popularly associated with the Regency (1811–20) but in fact in vogue well before 1810, has a character that was deemed to be appropriate to the patriotism and prosperity of the period. It is massive, formal, seriously archaeological in its decoration, and almost invariably gilded. Its successful promotion was largely connected with the fortunes of a single firm, Rundell, Bridge and Rundell, who effectively dominated the market for display plate from the early years of the century until about 1830. But the precise nature of the style which Rundells embraced is usually associated with the publication in 1806 of Charles Heathcote Tatham's *Designs for Ornamental Plate*. Tatham's book, one of the most proselytizing of all, was partly a response to a general dissatisfaction with the kind of classicism that had been associated with Adam and his preface comments that 'It has been much lamented by Persons high in Rank, and eminent for taste, that modern Plate has much fallen off both in design and execution from that formerly produced in this Country. Indeed, the truth of this remark is obvious, for instead of *Massiveness*, the principal characteristic of good Plate, light and insignificant forms have prevailed, to the utter exclusion of all Ornament whatever.' Like Adam, Tatham had gone to Rome to study ancient architecture, but the style that emerges from his designs is closer to that of Piranesi (1720–88) and much more directly imitative of its sources than Adam's. Whereas the latter had used ancient art as a source of inspiration rather than a model to be copied directly, Tatham argued in the same preface that 'the works of the Ancients ... teach us what objects we are to select for imitation and the method in which they may be combined for effect'.

Almost more than any other style that has been considered in this book, this was directed exclusively at the very rich, mainly because of the amount of metal that its display pieces called for. In 1809, for example, Rundell, Bridge and Rundell supplied a pair of gilt candlesticks weighing 917 ounces to the Prince of Wales at a cost of £1,365, and in 1812 three large sideboard dishes at £291 17s. 4d. each, with a further charge of £96 for gilding.[2] A good-quality soup tureen of the late eighteenth century would normally weigh around 100 ounces, whereas a corresponding example in the Regency style might weigh twice as much. Similarly, a pair of late eighteenth-century wine coolers would seldom weigh more than 200 ounces, whereas the Warwick vase, a reduced copy of the ancient Roman marble vase then at Warwick Castle and one of the most popular Regency forms, could weigh easily as much as 500 ounces a pair. Quite apart from the cost of work-manship, therefore, the style inevitably involved the client in considerably greater commitment on account of the metal alone.

The meteoric rise of Rundells from a relatively unimportant firm of jewellers to the holders of the royal warrant for jewellery and goldsmith's work is one of the most remarkable commercial success stories of its time. Philip Rundell had joined the retailer William Pickett in 1767, and by 1777 had become a partner in the firm. Eight years later the senior partner retired and Rundell invited John Bridge, who had been employed in the firm as a goldsmith since 1777, to become a partner. It was allegedly through Bridge's connections and a fortuitous meeting with the King that the royal warrant was transferred to the firm in 1797, but the inevitable increase of business generated by the warrant made a further injection of capital necessary, and in 1803 Rundell and Bridge became Rundell, Bridge and Rundell by the addition of Philip Rundell's cousin, Edmund, to the partnership.

The number of commissions received, however, was such that it was impossible for their existing workshop to meet the demand, and rather than refuse business, the partners decided to employ additional firms for this purpose. By about 1802 they had come to an arrangement with two leading manufacturers, Paul Storr and Benjamin Smith, whereby the majority of the firm's commissions would be supplied by these workshops, and it is for this reason that most of the more substantial plate bearing either Storr's or Smith's mark is additionally stamped with the Latin signature 'Rundell

Bridge et Rundell Aurifices Regis et Principis Walliae Fecerunt' (Made by Rundell, Bridge and Rundell, goldsmiths to the King and the Prince of Wales). The exact nature of the arrangement is not entirely clear, though it would seem that the Storr and Smith establishments became actual subsidiaries of Rundells, rather than merely acting in the capacity of sub-contractors. By at least 1817 Storr was a partner of the firm, and, apparently as part of the same arrangement, the partners of Storr's own firm, Storr & Co., were named on an insurance policy of the same year as Paul Storr, both Rundells, John Bridge and William Theed,[3] who was at the time head of the Rundells design team.

Some indication of the quantity of business that the firm was handling at the height of its success is given by the fact that Storr's and Smith's combined work force apparently amounted around 1807 to as many as 1,000 hands.[4] In such large operations the role of the goldsmiths whose marks appear on the plate was essentially that of managers; they were expected to produce plate precisely in accordance with the drawings and models that were supplied to them, and between 1802 and 1814, when Smith severed his connections with Rundells, there is no detectable difference between plate bearing one maker's mark or the other's. Even the same moulds appear to have been used for plate emanating from either workshop.

One of the factors that contributed to the firm's success was the enormous increase in demand for formal display plate that was partly associated with Britain's expanding role in the world. Since the sixteenth century ambassadors and officers of state had regularly been issued with plate as a means of providing the status appropriate to a representative of the Crown. Although officially intended as loans for the duration of the appointment and accordingly engraved with the royal arms, these issues, such as Speaker Brownlow's plate at Belton, were in practice frequently retained afterwards as a perquisite. But the maintenance of permanent embassies overseas after the beginning of the nineteenth century and the need to equip them with suitably imposing plate created a new avenue of demand. At the same time the desire to reflect similar standards at home, and the custom of celebrating important military victories by presentations of plate, were all symptoms of a growing national pride to which Rundells were well placed to respond. The Marquess of Londonderry's plate at Brighton Pavilion and the silver-gilt dinner service at Attingham Park were both made originally for ambassadorial purposes, the first for Londonderry's use at the Congress of Vienna (1814–15) and the second for the 3rd Lord Berwick, who was ambassador to Sardinia, Savoy and Naples. The grandest collection of presentation plate in connection with military campaigns is the Wellington plate at Apsley House, which includes a silver-gilt shield made by Benjamin Smith to a design of Thomas Stothard in 1822 and a dinner service presented to the Duke in 1816 by the Portuguese government. But more indicative of the

*Pair of salvers, silver-gilt, maker's mark of Benjamin and James Smith,
12 in. diameter (National Trust, Attingham Park, Shropshire).*

general attitude of patriotism are the sixty-six silver vases, inscribed 'Britons Strike Home', which were designed by John Flaxman and presented between 1804 and 1809 to distinguished officers in an effort to 'animate the efforts of our defenders by sea and land'. All were supplied by Rundells and paid for out of the resources of the Lloyds Patriotic Fund, which was established in 1803 by the London insurance underwriters.

Important though the role of craftsmen was in ensuring the fine quality of Rundells plate, the partners were quick to realize that design was the key to their success and it is quite clear in which department responsibility for the artistic character of most of their ceremonial plate lay. The firm spent over £1,000 a year on designs and, apart from Tatham, retained the

Candelabrum centrepiece, silver-gilt, 1814, maker's mark of Paul Storr;
12½ in. high (National Trust, Attingham Park, Shropshire).

services of a number of leading academic artists to supply drawings, including William Theed, Edward Hodges Bailey and John Flaxman. Influential though the Piranesiesque classicism of Tatham was, other antique styles, such as the Egyptian style and the Greek style, also played a significant part in shaping the character of early nineteenth-century display plate.

Tea service, silver-gilt, 1805, 1807, 1809, maker's mark of
Benjamin and James Smith; height of teapot 9 in.

Another major source of inspiration, even at the height of Francophobia during the war, was current French design, and a number of Rundells' most imposing models are closely related to plate produced during the latter part of the previous century, in particular by Robert-Joseph Auguste. This style was evidently absorbed partly through second-hand plate which passed through their hands, partly through published designs and partly from the presence in their design team of a shadowy figure by the name of Jean Jacques Boileau.[5] Little is known of Boileau, but it would seem that he was working for Rundells from about 1802 and his drawings, an album of which is in the Victoria and Albert Museum, show a remarkable affinity to those of the late eighteenth-century French designer Jean-Guillaume Moitte.

There can be no doubt, however, that the most influential figure associated with the firm was John Flaxman (1755–1826), who, although best known for his precise and cool neo-classical sculpture and drawings, was in fact an extraordinarily versatile artist who was in the van of both the naturalistic and neo-gothic styles that flourished in the second quarter of the century. He was head of their design team from 1817 until his death, but had been supplying the firm with designs for a number of years prior to that. Their greatest collaboration was arguably the Shield of Achilles,

Soup-tureen, silver, 1806, maker's mark of Paul Storr; $17\frac{1}{2}$ in. long
(Gilbert Collection, Los Angeles County Museum of Art).

one example of which was bought by the 2nd Earl of Lonsdale and is now in the possession of the National Trust at Anglesey Abbey. A total of four copies of the shield were made in silver-gilt in 1821 and 1822, the others being purchased by George IV, the Duke of York and the Duke of Northumberland. They were made under the artist's supervision and probably in collaboration with the chaser William Pitts, although Flaxman seems to have started work on the project as early as 1810. Its design is based on a passage in the *Iliad* which describes a shield made by the lame god

The Shield of Achilles, silver-gilt, 1822, maker's mark of Philip Rundell,
designed by John Flaxman; $36\frac{1}{4}$ in. diameter
(National Trust, Anglesey Abbey, Cambridgeshire).

Hephaestus for Achilles, and is conceived as Apollo in his chariot surrounded by a frieze which is 'a mirror of the world of gods and men, of banqueting and people fighting, of countrymen and vintners, and many others, including the king himself'. It is a measure both of the capital resources of the firm and of their confidence in the market which they had largely created that the shield was produced entirely as a speculation. Flaxman was himself paid over £825 for his designs and models, and each of the four copies was said to have taken two craftsmen a full year to make. The price of the finished shields was set at £2,000.[6]

Unique though the strength of Rundells' position in the market was, however, they were not without their rivals. In the early years of the century their main competition had come from Wakelin and Garrard, the successors to the business originally founded by George Wickes, but a more serious challenge to their position was presented by Benjamin Smith's defection in 1814. Their most important competitors after this date were probably Braithwaite and Fisher, much of whose more monumental plate

*Inkstand, silver-gilt, 1804, maker's mark of
Benjamin and James Smith.*

was supplied by Edward Barnard & Co. and Green, Ward & Green. The latter evidently entered into a relationship with Benjamin Smith after he left Rundells, and the extent of their strength is indicated by the fact that much of the Wellington plate at Apsley House is inscribed with their signature. This includes the Wellington Shield of 1822 and a massive candelabrum, nearly five feet high, of 1816, both of which were presented to the Duke by the Merchants and Bankers of the City of London.

The 'antique' styles in which all these firms specialized fell basically into the categories of Roman, Greek and Egyptian, but these were not the only styles in fashion during the second decade of the century, and others which were exploited both by Rundells and some of their competitors owed their vogue to factors other than national pride and theories of 'proper' ornament. The nineteenth century is often known as the century of revivals, but a complementary phenomenon was its interest in antiquarianism. It is true that periods of antiquitarianism had existed before, the most obvious of which was of course the Renaissance. But interest then had focused specifically and exclusively on artefacts and literature of the ancient Greek and Roman worlds. In the late eighteenth and early nineteenth century this was replaced by a more general interest in 'old things', which was reflected in the founding of institutions such as the Society of Antiquaries, in the gradual emergence of dealers in 'curiosities' and in the growing interest that attached to auction sales of such material. Although collections of curiosities had occasionally been formed in the past, such as that of Elias Ashmole in Oxford, these had seldom included old plate except in the form of mounted artefacts or natural curiosities. With the exception of family heirlooms or bequests to colleges, livery companies or the Church, it had always been accepted that plate should be in the current style and a significant part of the business of goldsmiths had consisted in regularly refashioning outmoded or worn plate in the newest style.

Rundells have been credited with a marketing innovation that was symptomatic of this change in attitudes: having bought a quantity of surplus old royal plate in 1808, they offered it to some of their leading clients instead of melting it down to be remade as would have been the usual practice.[7] The interest that was thus aroused in imposing antique plate accordingly created a demand for styles that could not readily be supplied by old pieces and which was consequently met by new plate in antique taste. One of Rundells' customers for the royal plate was the collector William Beckford (1759–1844), who purchased two pairs of William and Mary sconces and wrote in 1808 that 'the old pieces from the Royal silver are divine'. He needed more, however, and had no hesitation in ordering the goldsmiths to make up the set with a number of exact copies.[8]

It was in the response of other manufacturers to this new demand that Rundells met with some of their liveliest competition. One of the leaders of the historicist field would appear to have been William Pitts, who was responsible for a number of dishes embossed in seventeenth-century style, made both to Rundells' order and for other retailers. But the most interesting figures of the latter part of the first quarter of the century were the retailer Kensington Lewis and his goldsmith Edward Farrell. Lewis was evidently a colourful figure who posed as something of an authority on antique plate and was equally at home whether dealing in old plate or new.[9] In 1816 he made at least two major antique purchases at Christie's sale of the Duke of Norfolk's plate, and the plate made for him by Farrell ranges in character from close copies of genuine seventeenth-century pieces, which Lewis presumably had in stock, to unmistakably, if eccentrically, contemporary designs.

Monteith bowl, silver-gilt, 1820, maker's mark of Edward Farrell;
16 in. diameter (Gilbert Collection, Los Angeles).

Lewis's greatest coup, and that on which his commercial success largely
depended until 1827, was in attracting the patronage of the Duke of York.
The Duke was perhaps the greatest collector of silver of the period, and
between about 1816 and his death he ordered an enormous quantity of
plate from both Rundells and Lewis. Orders from the latter included objects
in a wide range of styles, such as rococo revival, the seventeenth-century
embossed style and magnificent sculptural candelabra. But his extravagance
was on such a scale that his executors took the unusual (for the royal family

unprecedented) step on his death of arranging for the sale of practically his entire collection at auction in an effort to pay off his debts. For Lewis this was a disastrous turn of events and he was forced to buy back many of the items which he had supplied in an attempt to support his market. Some plate which he bought at a cost of about 12s. an ounce had originally been supplied to his patron at more than twice the price; in other cases the discrepancy was larger still. Lewis continued in business for a number of years after losing his patron, but on a much less flamboyant scale, and thereafter Farrell's work was largely restricted to novelties and products such as tea services decorated with highly embossed scenes derived from Dutch seventeenth-century genre painting.

The developing interest in antiquarianism during this period was naturally also reflected in the growing number of connoisseurs interested in forming collections of such material. Among the most notable of these might be mentioned Horace Walpole (1717–97) and Ralph Bernal (d. 1854), but of particular interest from the perspective of contemporary silver was William Beckford, whose vast gothic mansion of Fonthill was one of the most remarkable buildings of its time. Beckford filled Fonthill with his collection of paintings and antique works of art, but he also commissioned considerable quantities of new silver with which to complete the decorative effect. The earliest dates from about 1781 and, while of exceptionally fine quality, was typical of the fashionable style of the time (see p. 240). His more idiosyncratic commissions date from the early nineteenth century and include both solid plate and an extraordinary quantity of mounted vessels, both new and old. Although his collections were largely dispersed after the sale of Fonthill in 1822, a large part of them was inherited by his daughter, Euphemia, through whose marriage to the Duke of Hamilton in 1810 a group of about fifty pieces have come into the possession of the National Trust for Scotland at Brodick Castle.[10] The early nineteenth-century pieces at Brodick, extraordinarily various though they are, are distinguished by three main characteristics: a consistently high quality, a sense of delicacy and precision and a frequent use of heraldic charges in the decoration. All these features point to an unusual degree of involvement by the patron with the objects that were made for him. Throughout his life he was obsessed by his ancestry and with his unrequited yearning for a peerage. This was reflected in the decoration of Fonthill and also in his plate, much of which is engraved with charges from his arms, such as the ermine cinquefoil or the Latimer cross, decoratively incorporated into the design. He seems to have entrusted dealings with the goldsmiths to his friend Chevalier Gregorio Franchi,

Beaker mounted as a jug, porcelain and silver-gilt, 1820,
maker's mark of James Aldridge, made for William Beckford; $4\frac{1}{2}$ in. high
(National Trust for Scotland, Brodick Castle).

though his keen personal interest is constantly evident in their correspondence. Although he did commission plate from the larger retailers, such as Rundells and Vulliamy and Co., many of his more original commissions were given to smaller concerns, such as those of James Aldridge and Samuel Whitford.

In one sense Beckford was deliberately trying to recreate the world of the Renaissance prince with his 'Schatzkammer' or treasury of precious objects. In that sense he might well be considered an eccentric and little more than a fascinating tributary from the main stream of the history of English plate. Certainly that is how he was perceived by many of his

Bowl, porcelain and silver-gilt, 1816, maker's mark of James Aldridge,
made for William Beckford; 3 in. diameter
(National Trust for Scotland, Brodick Castle).

contemporaries, and when William Hazlitt visited Fonthill prior to the sale he acidly described it as 'a Cathedral turned into a toy shop, an immense Museum of all that is most costly and, at the same time, most worthless in the productions of art and nature'.[11] But in his use of different materials, in his concern to break the mould of the acceptable repertoire of form and decoration, his patronage might well be regarded as a prelude to some of the dominant themes of Victorian silver.

Few buyers of plate, however, were able or prepared to pay the high fashion charges inevitably incurred by the more elaborate objects supplied to the Duke of York or William Beckford. The essence of the revolution in

Pair of sconces, silver-gilt, 1804, maker's mark of Paul Storr,
made for William Beckford; 13 in. high
(National Trust for Scotland, Brodick Castle).

the trade which occurred in the late eighteenth and early nineteenth century
is that mass-production methods lowered the cost of plate and made it
available to a wider public. The advantages were enormous. Spinning, which
had first been developed by Sheffield plate manufacturers, was by the 1820s
widely used for silver and enabled hollow ware such as teapots and cups
to be raised more quickly and thinly than by hammering. The commercial
application of Huntsman's hard crucible steel as early as 1760 was constantly
extended and made it possible to produce strong dies from which clear
impressions could be struck in silver. John Culme quotes an account of a
stamping shop in Elkington's factory in Birmingham in which 'an enormous
stamp ... converts flat discs of metal thirty inches in diameter by the action
of the falling hammer of the stamp ... [into] enormous salvers, dishes and

Chamber candlestick, silver-gilt, 1810, maker's mark LL in script; $6\frac{7}{8}$ in. high
(National Trust, Attingham Park, Shropshire).

meat covers'.[12] But the disadvantages are felt in lower standards of design and workmanship. This was a problem that was increasingly felt as the century progressed and which is discussed at greater length in the next chapter.

Ten

THE VICTORIAN ERA: CRAFT AND INDUSTRY

As recently as 1951 it would have been considered a fair assessment of contemporary attitudes that 'although a nostalgic appreciation for the pretty whimsicalities of the early Victorian period appears to be growing, it is as yet scarcely awarded the honour of academic research or serious aesthetic consideration'.[1] Nowadays such a view is difficult to equate with what is increasingly perceived as one of the most fascinating periods in English silver. The attitude that prevailed until recently was, of course, just part of a more general aversion to all things Victorian which resulted not only in the melting down of large quantities of silver, but the destruction of many country houses and other buildings which would now be considered important examples of nineteenth-century architecture.

Part of the reason for this aversion was the sense of stylistic confusion that characterizes much of the period; another was the evident dominance of the machine, which seemed the antithesis of craftsmanship. But it is a view that fails to do justice to the complexities of the period and to the fact that industrially manufactured silver represented only one aspect, albeit numerically the most overwhelming, of the whole picture. For it is a period of extraordinary contrasts, between the charming and the pompous, the original and the imitation, the beautiful and the banal. Undoubtedly, the greatest tension was between the forces of mass production and individual craftsmanship. Contemporaries were well aware of these contrasts, which were, if anything, heightened by the interaction of artists and entrepreneurs and by the deliberate, almost academic, exploration of new theories of form and decoration which were encouraged by factors as different as parliamentary committees and enlightened patrons.

The middle part of Victoria's reign (1837–1901) has been called the period of the 'battle of the styles', but even by the end of the first quarter of the century it was clear that there was no real consensus over style, or

Milk-jug, silver, 1840, maker's mark of Benjamin Smith the younger
(Victoria and Albert Museum, London).

even a 'typical' style that tended to predominate over others. Publications such as Knight's *Encyclopaedia of Ornament* (1834) and Owen Jones's *Grammar of Ornament* (1857) made a wider range of decoration available to nineteenth-century silversmiths than had existed before, but also reflected the fact that demand for such diversity already existed. In many respects, indeed, the features that are generally regarded as typically Victorian were all evident in embryonic form during the first quarter of the century.

The most obvious of these were stylistic eclecticism; a fashion for large sculptural plate; a dominance of large factories and industrial methods of production; and a tendency for developments of form and ornament to evolve out of a process that had more of the character of a public debate than ever before.

Soup-tureen, silver, 1819, maker's mark of Paul Storr, 1819, 7⅜ in. high (Victoria and Albert Museum, London).

The dominant source of inspiration during the first two decades of the century had been ancient art, whether Greek, Roman or Egyptian, though a freer spirit of eclecticism had begun to show itself after about 1810 with the historicizing plate made for Rundells and Kensington Lewis. During the second quarter of the century a number of quite different styles were promoted simultaneously and with almost equal success, the most important of which were the naturalistic style and the gothic and rococo revivals.

If any one style could be said to typify the second quarter of the nineteenth century, it would be naturalism, for although far from universal, this was undoubtedly the most original of the various stylistic experiments of the period. Evolving out of the use of classical acanthus foliage that figured so prominently in formal Regency plate, it differed fundamentally from the latter in that form and decoration were treated in such a way that, not unlike the rococo at its most fully developed, the decoration became logically integral to the form so that it became impossible visually or

Vegetable dish, silver, 1829, maker's mark of Paul Storr; 9 in. high
(National Trust, Anglesey Abbey, Cambridgeshire).

logically to distinguish between the two. This has been characterized as an 'organic' approach to style and as 'the form becoming the ornament'. A cream jug of 1840 by Benjamin Smith the younger, in the Victoria and Albert Museum, has all the essential features of the style: the classic vase form has given way to one in which the lines have been softened and the entire form treated with a sense of organic growth, of which the decoration is an integral part. Similarly, a covered dish of 1829 by Paul Storr at Anglesey Abbey shows the influence of the style, with its melon-like cover and large vegetable finial. Flaxman seems to have played a decisive role in this innovative movement. Some of his most important designs for Rundells, such as a candelabrum centrepiece of 1812 in the royal collection, show a marked departure from Piranesiesque classicism, with features such as florally entwined branches and candle sockets in the form of open flowers.

A less innovative but equally striking form of naturalism was one in which the aim was not so much to give a sense of living nature as to produce objects that directly copied it. Influential in the development of this style was the publication in 1833 of Knight's *Vases and Ornaments*, which shows vessels formed from sea-shells and the like, supported by clumps of foliage growing up from the base. Within a year of its publication, retailers such as Kensington Lewis were already exploiting its potential. But as with many printed pattern books from the sixteenth century onwards, its author was as much crystallizing and disseminating a fashion that already existed as publishing entirely fresh ideas. Rundells in particular had been producing silver in this naturalistic vein for some years, having almost certainly been influenced by the rocaille pieces by Nicholas Sprimont in the royal collection, of which they were asked to supply replicas. Garrards were also leading exponents of the style, among the most dramatic expressions of which is their pair of candelabra of 1841 at Brodick Castle, which are formed as four discomfortingly lifelike entwined snakes. Grander still is Flaxman's great wine cooler in the Tower of London, which was supplied to George IV in 1822 and which is modelled as a giant clam shell, presumably cast from a real one, and which is supported by rearing seahorses.

Almost the antithesis of the naturalistic style, the gothic revival was pursued with equal vigour over the same period, and again it was the extraordinary versatility of John Flaxman in collaboration with Rundells that was responsible for its first major success. The so-called National Cup was designed by Flaxman and made in 1824 for George IV. Its stem is inspired by fourteenth-century plate such as the King John Cup,[2] and the decoration of the bowl is comprised of the national emblems of England, Scotland and Ireland, with the figures of St Andrew and St Patrick set into gothic niches and the finial formed as St George and the dragon. But the gothicism of the National Cup is more romantic than historical, and the appeal of the more studied gothic silverware of the second quarter of the century hinged essentially on its perceived 'appropriateness', especially in the field of church art. This notion was a powerful force throughout the Victorian period, particularly in architecture. Gilbert Scott's design for the façade of the Foreign Office, for example, was rejected as inappropriate for a building that represented Britain's imperial position in the world (though it did very well when eventually reused for St Pancras Station); a classical

Candelabrum centrepiece, silver-gilt, 1812, maker's mark of Paul Storr; 28 in. high
(Royal collection. Reproduced by gracious permission of Her Majesty the Queen).

building was chosen for that repository of the works of man, the Victoria
and Albert Museum, while a gothic one seemed proper for that of the
Natural History Museum. Similarly, few classical churches were erected
after 1830, the gothic style being deemed to be of a more godly nature
than that of pagan antiquity.

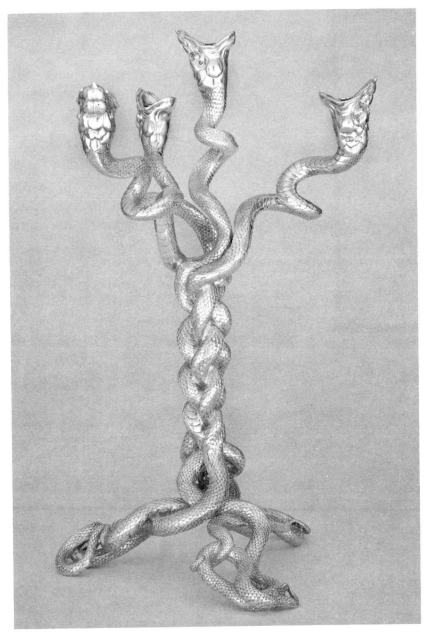

Candelabrum, silver, 1841,
maker's mark of Robert Garrard; 22½ in. high
(National Trust for Scotland, Brodick Castle).

*The National Cup, 1824, maker's mark of John Bridge,
designed by John Flaxman; 19 in. high (Royal collection. Reproduced by
gracious permission of Her Majesty the Queen).*

Dish, silver-gilt, silver and enamel, Birmingham, 1847,
maker's mark of John Hardman & Co., designed by Augustus Pugin; $16\frac{1}{8}$ in. diameter
(Victoria and Albert Museum, London).

The most influential figure in decorative arts of the gothic revival was Augustus Pugin (1812–52), who is said to have been discovered at the age of fifteen, copying drawings and engravings in the Print Room at the British Museum, by John Gawler Bridge. He was immediately engaged by Rundells to design church plate, and most of his designs for silver continued to be in this field until his death, although he did design a certain number of secular pieces, such as a dish of 1847 in the Victoria and Albert Museum. From 1838 most of his work was for the Birmingham firm of John Hardman

*Claret jug, silver and silver-gilt, 1851, maker's mark of
Joseph Angell; 13½ in. high (Goldsmiths' Company).*

and Co. It is characterized by great precision, a fine sense of line and a careful observation of surviving medieval metalwork. His approach, however, was essentially historicizing; he had little interest in innovations of form and indeed condemned the almost inevitable fact that much contemporary plate in the gothic style consisted of 'gothic detail simply applied to a given surface'.[3] But that such plate could be of considerable artistic interest is clear from some of the silver produced by Joseph Angell during the 1850s, such as a remarkable claret jug of 1851 in the collection of the Goldsmiths' Company, in which a general sense of the gothic is suggested by the form, although the decorative scheme as a whole is only faintly reminiscent of the Middle Ages.

The style which seems to have enjoyed the widest and most long-lived popularity of all during the nineteenth century, however, was the rococo revival. Although not coming into vogue on a large scale until about 1815, its origins can be traced to at least the beginning of the century. By the middle of the second decade, Paul Storr was already producing grand rococo silver for Rundells, much of it to royal order, from sources such as François-Thomas Germain, Nicholas Sprimont and Paul Crespin, but as the century progressed there was a growing tendency for debased examples of the style to be produced in the larger factories in an increasingly sloppy and poorly designed manner. The popularity of this style, more than any other in Victorian silver, was a reflection of the greatly expanded market for silver in the mid nineteenth century and, to be fair to the society responsible for its production, it was far from being without its contemporary critics. The *Art Union* complained in 1846 that 'there is a degree of slovenliness engendered by the fact that designers of this kind of ornament know, if they can fill up an angle or a square with two or three large scrolls, throw in a few unnatural flowers and a lot of scrollwork, it will pass current as Old French'.[4]

A similar opinion was expressed in more satirical terms by Dickens, in his description of the silver dinner service that graced Mr Podsnap's table in *Our Mutual Friend*:

Hideous solidity was the characteristic of the Podsnap plate. Everything was made to look as heavy as it could and to take up as much room as possible. Everything said boastfully, 'Here you have as much of me in my ugliness as if I were only lead; but I am so many ounces of precious metal, worth so much an ounce; – wouldn't you like to melt me down?' A corpulent straddling epergne, blotched all over as if it had broken out in an eruption rather than been ornamented, delivered this address from an unsightly silver platform in the centre of the table. Four silver wine coolers, each furnished with four staring heads, each head obtrusively carrying a big silver ring in each of its ears, conveyed the sentiment up and down the table, and handed it on to the pot-bellied silver salt cellars. All the big silver spoons and forks widened the mouths of the company expressly for the purpose of thrusting the sentiment down their throats with every morsel they eat.[5]

As late as 1890 the phenomenon was explained in unambiguous terms by the *Jeweller and Metalworker*, which observed that 'silversmiths do not seem anxious to abandon the Louis XV style, although the revival of that pretty fashion has had a very long run already. It is true that the public encourage them more and more, especially the parvenues, the wealthy bourgeois, who have made their fortune in lines where even the word art is absolutely unknown. They have heard of the reigning style, and, anxious to show their good taste, they absolutely refuse to look at any article in silver which is not offered to them as a remarkable specimen of the rococo.'[6] A more accurate description of Mr Podsnap's position could hardly be imagined.

The general weakening in quality and design that was evident during the second quarter of the century must be seen to some extent in the light of the decline of Rundell, Bridge and Rundell from their position of virtually unchallenged supremacy during the Regency to the final winding up of the firm in 1842. An unpublished manuscript in the Harvard University Library[7] by George Fox, a long-term employee of Rundells, attributes a number of causes to this decline, in particular the death of George IV and an ensuing vacuum of royal patronage, together with Philip Rundell's retirement in 1823, accompanied by the withdrawal of his capital. Hitherto Rundells had been immensely capitalized which, according to Fox, 'enabled the House to execute Orders of the greatest Magnitude and also to accommodate their Customers with unlimited credits so that no house in London up to that time had been able to compete with them with any chance of success'. Some of his most interesting remarks, however, concern the way in which the firm had capitalized on the shortage of silver during the Napoleonic wars and the effect of their conclusion: 'One of the first effects of the transition from War to Peace was the very great and sudden fall in the value of the precious Metals[.] Gold which had been as high as £5-10 per oz. fell to the Average Price of £3-17-10 1/2 per ounce Standard and Silver fell from 7/- per oz. to about 5/2 per oz.' The large stock of gold and silver which the firm carried inevitably hurt them very badly, since it was impossible for them to pass on their losses to their customers.

The field which Rundells had led and in which their departure presented the greatest opportunities was that of grand display plate. From the 1840s onwards the most important manufacturers of large-scale silver were Storr and Co. (which evolved during the next few decades into Storr & Mortimer, Mortimer & Hunt and finally Hunt & Roskell), Garrards, the Birmingham firm of Elkington and Co. and, later in the century, C. F. Hancock & Co. All these manufacturers placed the same emphasis on the fundamental importance of the design department, and in most cases attempted to attract a prominent sculptor to head the team. The most important figures around the middle of the century included the sculptors Edmund Cotterill of Garrards and Alfred Brown of Hunt & Roskell. It was in the prominence given to the design and modelling departments that Rundells' greatest legacy to the Victorian era lay, but it was also inevitable that such an approach to design led display silver to develop a strong sculptural character. A colourful account of the Hunt & Roskell workshop is contained in Beatrix Potter's journal, describing her visit in 1881: '... there was one more thing to see, the designing. In we all went, a little sized studio with skylights, surrounded by curtains, one of which the Frenchman unceremoniously pulled aside to let us in. The work on hand was a large centrepiece, a drawing of which stood on an easel, while the artist was busy at a plaster model.'[8]

The piece in question was the centrepiece of the Ismay Testimonial, which was presented by the managers of the White Star Shipping Line to Thomas Henry Ismay in 1885 and which was designed by G. A. Carter. It has all the character of a public monument on a reduced scale. But in resembling a monument it is at one remove from the type of presentation silver that was especially popular around the middle of the century and of which Cotterill was one of the leading exponents. These were much closer to pure sculpture and tended to have subjects of a patriotic nature or which were derived from sources such as Shakespeare's history plays and the novels of Walter Scott. There can be no doubt as to the popular appeal of such designs, many of which were published in the press, and indeed the *Illustrated London News* proclaimed in 1850 that 'in no branch of the Fine Arts have the artists of this country made greater progress than in the art of modelling [silver] statuettes ... It may indeed be called a national art, and a national manufacture.'[9] But this 'national art', which was probably the most prominent aspect of the British stands at the Great Exhibition of 1851, was not without its detractors. The painter Richard Redgrave, Inspector General for the Government Schools of Design, complained in 1857 that

Centrepiece from the Ismay Testimonial, parcel-gilt, 1881,
maker's mark of Hunt and Roskell, designed by G. A. Carter; 25 in. high.

'many centrepieces, racing cups, and testimonials are treated merely as
groups would be by the sculptor',[10] and the *Journal of Design* complained
in 1850 that 'all beauty of form, all excellence of modelling, is lost in the
glitter of the metal where burnishing is employed, and the compositions
that would have been truly works of art in bronze become almost toylike
when thus wrought'.[11]

The enormous popularity of large sculptural centrepieces was a reflection
at one end of the market of a phenomenon that was equally marked
throughout. The decline in the price of silver and its greater availability

after the exploitation of new mines in Mexico combined with the rapidly expanding middle class to create a greater demand for silver than had ever existed before. Whereas the market for testimonials had largely been created by corporate and political wealth and the desire of companies or political parties to make lavish presentations to their chief executives or representatives, that for domestic silver was mainly in the hands of individuals who wished, much as owners of plate had always wished, to enhance their status through silver. The mid nineteenth century consequently witnessed an enormous expansion in demand for useful as well as decorative plate. While extravagant services such as Mr Podsnap's were certainly produced in large quantities, the greatest growth in demand was not so much for dinner services, which had been superseded in many people's eyes by china ones, as for the matched tea and coffee service and services of flatware. Both these were produced in enormous quantities from the middle part of the century onwards, and an indication of the extent of the demand is given by the fact that one London producer of the mid century advertised a range of no fewer than fifty different patterns of tea services. The key to such large-scale production lay, of course, in mechanization. John Culme[12] quotes a description from 1890 of the process used by the Rhode Island firm of Gorham Company for making silver spoons. It was complicated and involved many stages, but the most significant point is that it was carried out almost entirely by machine, and the procedure in mid nineteenth-century England can hardly have been very different.

An inevitable consequence of these patterns of production was increased specialization; another was a decline in quality. By the beginning of the nineteenth century, Matthew Boulton's company had retired completely from producing silver and made only Sheffield plate; testimonial and large-scale silver was concentrated in a small number of firms, and flatware was almost entirely in the hands of Francis Higgins & Sons and Chawner & Co. The most dramatic example of specialization, however, was that of Elkington & Co. in the field of electroplate. George Elkington had been one of the first to recognize the potential of electroplating as opposed to the fused principle of Sheffield plate. He sponsored the experiments of John Wright and Alexander Parks into plating base metal with silver by electrolysis, and the process was patented by Elkington in partnership with Wright in 1840. Demand was enormous; licences were sold to various other manufacturers, such as James Dixon & Sons and Christofle in Paris, and Elkingtons made such profits that they rapidly rose to be one of the largest producers in the country, both of electroplate and of solid silver.

The most important difference between Sheffield plate and electroplate was that with the former the plating process was done before the object was formed, which made complex relief ornament, let alone sculptural decoration, impossible. With electroplate, on the other hand, the object was entirely formed first, then plated. This gave it the great advantage of enabling worn pieces to be replated; it also enabled electroplate to be made in exactly the same forms as fashionable sculptured silver, and the taste for such objects to filter down to a much lower level of the market. Electroplate was consequently regarded as an ideal means of spreading taste and bringing quality within the means of the masses, but even before its appearance on the market, concern was being voiced about a general decline in the quality of design that had inevitably followed in the wake of mass production.

By 1835 this concern had reached such a level that a Select Committee of the House of Commons was appointed to 'inquire into the best means of extending a knowledge of the arts and of the principles of design among the People (especially the manufacturing population) of the country', the most immediate effect of which was the establishment of the first government School of Design. The report of the Select Committee, published in 1836, was only one of a number of publications around the middle of the century that both criticized contemporary design and suggested various, not always mutually compatible, remedies for the shortcomings. The most fruitful and influential of these was the work of a remarkable civil servant, Henry Cole (1808–82), whose energetic efforts were to lead in the short term to the Great Exhibition of 1851 and later to the establishment of the South Kensington Museum, which came in due course to be known as the Victoria and Albert Museum.

Cole began publication in 1841 of a periodical known under the pseudonym of 'Felix Summerly's Home Treasury'. In response to the widening gulf between extravagant commissioned testimonials and the coarseness of ordinary domestic plate design, he contended in an editorial that 'we desire to see *good Art cheap* ... Art should not be content to minister to the taste of the few alone ... its healthy influence should be felt among *the million* ... grace may be produced as cheaply as deformity. Expensive and intricate detail does not necessarily belong to elegance of form and design.'[13] In 1847 he went further and set up an organization which he called 'Felix Summerly's Art Manufactures', the aim of which was to focus the attention of artists on the design of ordinary domestic plate and 'to revive the good old practice of connecting the best art with familiar objects in everyday use'. He succeeded in securing the co-operation of a number of leading manufacturers, notably Hunt & Roskell and Benjamin Smith Junior. An illustration of the alternative to the purely sculptural silver attacked by Richard Redgrave is a small christening mug which the latter designed under the auspices of Felix Summerly's Manufactures in 1848 and which is embossed with a frieze of angels protecting a kneeling child. The symbolism

Christening mug, silver, 1865,
maker's mark of Harry Emmanuel, designed by Richard Redgrave; $4\frac{3}{4}$ in. high
(Victoria and Albert Museum, London).

is obvious enough, and in many ways it is the exact equivalent of the sort of sentimental Christianity contained in Dickens's earlier novels. But viewed as an example of sculpture combined with useful form, in a way that alludes both to the function of the vessel and that is compatible with its function, it epitomizes the aim of the venture.

Felix Summerly's Manufactures may be seen as the prelude to a number of the most significant artistic developments of the latter part of the century, notably, from the point of view of the silver industry, those led by Christopher Dresser (1834–1904) and Charles Robert Ashbee (1863–1942). But of more immediate importance was the part he played in the events leading up to the Great Exhibition. Under Cole's and Prince Albert's direction, the Society of Arts organized a series of exhibitions of contemporary manufactures between 1846 and 1849, the success of which encouraged the Prince to suggest one on an international scale to be held in London in 1851.

The exhibition was well supported by the main English manufacturers of silver, notably Hunt & Roskell, Garrards and Elkingtons. Pride of place on the former two stands was given to sculptural testimonial pieces that represented patriotic or romantic subjects; other exhibitors showed a variety of pieces in historicizing styles. But the exhibition was held at a time when the battle of the styles was still far from over, and opinions as to the merit of these extravagant pieces differed widely, perhaps the most thunderous

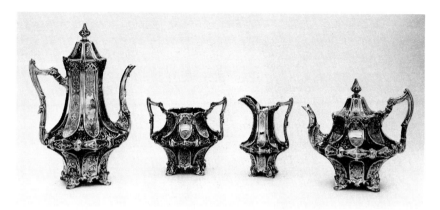

Tea service, silver-gilt and enamel, 1851,
maker's mark of George Angell; height of coffee pot 12¾ in.
(Victoria and Albert Museum, London).

response being that of the *Morning Chronicle*, which pronounced that 'what we want are canons of taste, laws of beauty, principles and axioms of propriety ... The exhibition shows that we are most skilful mimics, that we know how to reprint classics, that we can restore everything. But what do we create?' Nevertheless, it is difficult today to appreciate the enormity of the impact of the series of international exhibitions that followed over the next thirty years. The 1851 exhibition attracted over 6 million visitors, that in 1862 about the same; the Paris exhibition of 1867 admitted over 10 million, while no fewer than 16 million were reported as having attended in 1878. Their power to focus attention on developments in taste and design was therefore immense, and manufacturers responded by producing special pieces on speculation. One of the most imposing of all was the Helicon Vase, made by Elkingtons for the 1871 exhibition[14] and which in fact remained unsold until 1877. But a particularly interesting departure was the series of enamelled vessels produced by George Angell, such as a four-piece tea and coffee service which was made for the Great Exhibition and which is now in the Victoria and Albert Museum.

The decline in purely sculptural testimonial plate that is evident after the middle of the century is in part doubtless attributable to the lambasts of critics such as the *Morning Chronicle* and Richard Redgrave. But it must also in some measure be associated with the presence in England of two remarkable artists, Antoine Vechte (1798–1868) and Léonard Morel-Ladeuil (c. 1820–88), who worked respectively for Hunt and Roskell and Elkingtons. Vechte first met J. S. Hunt in Paris in 1847, and the latter was so struck by his talent as a chaser that he commissioned the Titan Vase which was later acquired by the Goldsmiths' Company. The extraordinary impression made by the vase encouraged Hunt to commission further works from Vechte, who from 1849 to 1862 worked exclusively for Hunt and Roskell in London.

Of equal importance to Vechte was the presence in England of his pupil, Morel-Ladeuil, who worked for Elkington and Co. from 1857 until his death. His first publicly exhibited work was a *repoussé* table shown at the 1862 exhibition in London, but his subsequent works included objects such as the Milton Shield of 1867, the Pilgrim Shield of 1868 and the Helicon Vase of 1871. These works were distinguished by their marked literary qualities and their sophisticated chasing. In his technical command Morel-Ladeuil was by no means Vechte's superior, but the relatively low relief of his designs was particularly characteristic; it invited the eulogy of George Sala that 'he can paint with his hammer'[15] and distinguished his work from that of his master by its obvious inspiration from Renaissance goldsmiths' work. The Milton Shield in particular, although iconographically entirely of its own time, is clearly inspired by an embossed steel shield of about 1570, attributed to Pierre Redon of the Fontainebleau School.[16] Moreover, the techniques reintroduced in both Vechte's Titan Vase and much of Morel-Ladeuil's work, of damascening and contrasting highly polished with oxidized surfaces, were both revivals of sixteenth-century techniques and led the way towards a new taste for silver in the Renaissance style which became increasingly influential during the latter part of the century.

The Renaissance revival would arguably have happened anyway, for reasons that are discussed below, and the main significance of Vechte and Morel-Ladeuil lay in the influence they brought to bear on the development of sculptural silver. During the 1860s and 1870s the other most prominent figures in the field were another Frenchman, Albert Wilms, who worked for Elkingtons, and H. H. Armstead, who by 1862 was working principally for C. F. Hancock & Co. Both responded to the criticism of purely sculptural design by re-emphasizing form. In Wilms's case this meant introducing sculpture as a support for the vessel, in a manner that was reminiscent of

*Titan Vase, silver, silver-gilt and oxidized silver, modelled in Paris in 1847 by
Antonie Vechte for J. S. Hunt; 29¾ in. high (Goldsmiths' Company).*

The Milton Shield,
silver, silver-gilt and oxidized silver, Birmingham, 1867,
maker's mark of Elkington & Co.,
modelled by Léonard Morel-Ladeuil
(Victoria and Albert Museum, London).

*Centrepiece, silver-gilt, Birmingham, 1872, maker's mark of Elkington and Co.,
designed by Albert Wilms; 14 in. long.*

the Parisian goldsmith Jean Baptiste Claude Odiot's late eighteenth-century
neo-classicism, while Armstead's approach was to unite the vessel and
sculptural form in a way that was much closer to Vechte. One of his most
important designs, the Tennyson Vase of 1880,[17] is obviously derived from
the Titan Vase, both in its general design and the balance of high relief and
overall form.

It has been observed that 'in England after the late 1860s, the silver
industry was in decline'.[18] In terms of the trade as a whole, of its rep-
resentation at international exhibitions and of volume of production, that

is certainly true, but in terms of new departures in design it was as interesting as a period, if not more interesting, than that discussed at the beginning of this chapter. The various movements that went to make up the artistic character of late nineteenth-century goldsmiths' work, disparate though they were, were subject essentially to three channels of influence. The first

Decanter, silver, silver-gilt, glass, semi-precious stones, maker's mark of Richard Green, designed by William Burges; 11 in. high (Victoria and Albert Museum).

was the historicist trend that had never been far from the surface and which towards the end of the century became complicated by a growing force in the market, namely the enthusiasm among a growing body of collectors for medieval and Renaissance works of art. The second reflected the extraordinary sense of revelation that swept Europe and America after the opening up of Japan to outsiders in the 1850s; and the third traced its antecedents in the quasi-moralizing writings of Henry Cole and others and its descendents in the parallel movements that were led on the one hand by C. R. Ashbee's Guild of Handicrafts and on the other by the marketing strategy of Liberty and Co.

The leaders of the medieval movement during the latter part of the century were William Morris (1834–96) and William Burges (1827–81), and the work of both was coloured by a more romantic vision of the Middle Ages than Pugin's. Their style accordingly made no pretensions towards archaeological exactitude, but was instead loosely inspired by certain aspects of medieval art, especially the romanesque, such as the combination of different materials and techniques, while drawing freely on the repertoire of ornament.

Although particularly interested in goldsmiths' work, Burges was not a goldsmith himself and much of his more intricate work was carried out by a Danish goldsmith, Jes Barkentin, who worked in London from 1860. His most important client was the 3rd Marquess of Bute, whom he met in 1865 and who commissioned him to rebuild Cardiff Castle. The Marquess had an equal passion for medieval art and instructed Burges to design all the interiors and furnishings for the castle as well. But the growth of antiquarianism and the increasing number of wealthy collectors during the nineteenth century also opened up the opportunity for a different kind of historicizing silver altogether, which was made with fraudulent intent. For obvious reasons, the nineteenth-century fakers, some of whom were extraordinarily skilled craftsmen, are less well documented than their more honest contemporaries. Indeed, some of the most brilliant, such as Salomon Weiniger of Vienna or Reinhold Vasters of Aachen, have emerged only fairly recently and their recognition has inevitably led to the reassessment of objects in private and public collections which had previously been thought to be major works of art from the sixteenth century or earlier.

No faker as brilliant as Vasters has yet been identified in England, although they almost certainly existed. On the other hand, there was a concerted industrial popularization of this antiquarian interest in the form of large quantities of domestic silver in Renaissance styles, such as the so-called 'Cellini pattern' ewer. This was a reproduction of a sixteenth-century pewter model, not in fact made by Cellini, but by the French craftsman François Briot. The tendency during the nineteenth century to associate the name of Cellini with almost any elaborate goldsmiths' work of the sixteenth was symptomatic of the naïve state of that particular branch of art history, and is reflected as much in the hopelessly bad fakes of the period as in the crude pastiches of Renaissance styles that were marketed in the same way as the gothic and rococo styles throughout the period.

It was partly recognition of the decline in the quality and design of industrially produced silver that led to one of the most significant and prophetic developments in the late nineteenth century, namely the industrial aesthetic of Christopher Dresser. Dresser was a botanist, but was also deeply interested in the industrial arts. In 1848 he attended the Government School of Design, and over the next thirty years published a number of influential books, such as *The Art of Decorative Design* and *Principles of Decorative Design*. During the 1870s he produced series of designs for Elkingtons, Hukin & Heath and James Dixon and Sons. In response to what he considered to be the misplaced dominance of ornament in contemporary silver, his designs instead placed emphasis on pure form and the role of the machine. Partly making a social point and partly an intellectual one, they were deliberately conceived with the aim of minimizing costs in order to make 'good' design available to the widest possible market. But in doing so he went far beyond the kind of cooperation between artists and industry that Henry Cole promoted, and developed an entirely new aesthetic which was characterized by an austere, almost brutal functionality, a minimal use of metal and a concern to emphasize the method of construction and the nature of the material by devices such as the prominent use of rivets and screws.

Dresser was a complex figure, and his pioneering role in the design of metalwork is in curious contrast to his equally passionate interest in the arts of Japan, which he did much to encourage in England. In 1882 he published *Japan: Its Architecture, Art and Art Manufactures* which stimulated the interest in oriental art that had gradually been gaining momentum since Japan opened its doors to Western trade around the middle of the century. So often a pioneer, one of the first English silver manufacturers to take a serious interest in Japanese styles was Elkington and Co. English manufacturers were at a disadvantage in this style, since the hallmarking laws made it illegal to combine other metals, such as damascened iron, with silver. The lead in 'Japonaiserie' was consequently soon lost to American firms such as Tiffany and Company; nevertheless, throughout the 1880s Elkingtons produced a special line of wares which were superbly decorated with parcel-gilt decoration in the Japanese manner.

Of all the contrasts and tensions that made the Victorian period so complex, the most fundamental was that between the advocates of the machine and its opponents. At the end of the period this was brought into

*'Cellini pattern' ewer, electroplate,
made by Elkington and Co., c. 1860; 11 in. high
(Victoria and Albert Museum, London).*

stark relief by the conflicting ideologies of Christopher Dresser's industrial aesthetic and the aims and aspirations of the Arts and Crafts movement. C. R. Ashbee was the leading figure in the movement, the silversmiths of which included John Pearson, John Williams, William Hardiman, Gilbert Marks and Nelson Dawson. The first three all belonged to the Guild and

Egg steamer, silver and ebony, Sheffield, 1884,
maker's mark of H. Straford, designed by Christopher Dresser; $7\frac{7}{8}$ in. high
(Victoria and Albert Museum, London).

School of Handicrafts, which Ashbee set up in 1888 at Toynbee Hall in the East End of London. In many ways Ashbee's concerns were similar to Dresser's. He founded the Guild 'with the object of making useful things, of making them well and making them beautiful; goodness and beauty were to the leaders of the movement synonymous terms'.[19] Most silver produced by the Guild of Handicrafts had a simplicity of form and sense of line that in many ways foreshadowed the art nouveau style, but more important was the fact that it was made entirely by hand. Ashbee had a deeply romantic view of the Middle Ages, and invested the idea of craftsmanship unsoiled by the machine with a kind of religious virtue.

It would be tempting to close on the impression that with C. R. Ashbee the story had been brought full circle and that the craft had returned to the sort of innocence in which it was found at the end of the Middle Ages. The myth is one that exercised considerable attraction, and with life for most being dominated by the squalor and filth of the late nineteenth-century city, it is easy to understand why. Liberty's catalogue for 1899 exploited it to the full by claiming that 'in this [hand-hammered] feature of the work

Tray, silver parcel-gilt, Birmingham, 1877,
maker's mark of Frederick Elkington & Co.; 14 in. long.

... there is an echo of those more leisured days when the craftsman not only loved his art for its own sake, but was able to devote his life to it with comparative indifference to the pecuniary result of his labour of love'. But a myth it was, and a particularly transparent one too. The innocent medieval craftsman had never existed in the sense in which he was imagined. Although no less of an art for being so, the art of the goldsmith was, perhaps more than other crafts, governed by economic reality, and in the end the Guild of Handicrafts was driven out of business by other firms who were able to imitate its work at lesser cost. Ashbee's ideological rejection of the machine enabled other manufacturers to undercut his prices with machine-made goods that imitated its appearance.

The most successful of these were Omar Ramsden, who entered into partnership with Alwyn Carr in 1897, and the London retailers Liberty and

Beaker and cover, silver and enamel, 1903, maker's mark of Nelson Dawson; 10 in. high.

Co. The former, both during and after Carr's involvement, produced a wide range of silver, much of which was of a medieval character. Most of Ramsden's silver bears the Latin signature 'Omar Ramsden me fecit', which is, of course, a charming and deliberate 'echo of those more leisured days' and an allusion to the signature on the famous early medieval Alfred Jewel in the Ashmolean Museum. But such an evocation of homely hand-crafted techniques was a deceit, albeit a perfectly harmless one. Ramsden was not himself a practising silversmith, and the hammer marks on his silver were deliberately added to the object after it had been made by labour-saving, mechanized means such as spinning.

The most important artist associated with Liberty's was Archibald Knox, and the wares which were produced under his direction were primarily in the art nouveau style and often decorated with enamel. The name under which they were marketed, Cymric ware, again served to allude to Celtic art, with all its romantic associations of unhurried craftsmanship, even though the goods were in reality made as much with the aid of machine as by hand.

While the closing years of the nineteenth century and the early part of the twentieth were marked by a number of interesting developments in the craft, they made relatively little impact on the trade as a whole. For the majority of manufacturers most domestic silver tended to take the form of reproduction of antique styles, such as Queen Anne and early Georgian, and there was relatively little attempt in England to form and market a 'modern' style. This must be seen, in part at least, as a consequence of the growing interest among the buying public in antiques. For not only were well-off people now much more fully committed to domestic wares in other materials than they had been in the past, but when thinking in terms of silver they were now much more inclined to look to old pieces, which could now be considered as investments, than to patronize modern silversmiths.

In recent years the Worshipful Company of Goldsmiths has done much to revitalize the flagging craft, both by the example it has set with its own collection of contemporary silver and by its organization of trade fairs. But the absence of servants to clean silver, the fear of burglars and the relatively high price of modern hand-made silver in comparison with its antique equivalent, are all very real factors that make it unlikely that silver will ever play as major a role in the everyday life of the future as it has done in the past.

Biographical Appendix

The following list of brief lives is merely a selection of some of the more prominent figures from the period covered by this book. To some extent arbitrary choices have been made, and for each goldsmith that has been chosen there are probably several with equal claim to inclusion. I have deliberately avoided discussing goldsmiths who, although distinguished, are known only by their mark, such as 'T Y L' from the early seventeenth century, and the 'hound sejant' maker from the mid century. In addition to specific sources mentioned at the bottom of individual entries, full acknowledgement is made to Arthur Grimwade's *London Goldsmiths 1697–1837, Their Marks and Lives* (1976) and Charles Oman's *Caroline Silver 1625–1688* (1970).

ADAMAS, Robert (fl. *c*. 1490–1532)
Royal goldsmith to Henry VIII, he came from a family of goldsmiths and was presumably apprenticed to his father, from whom he inherited his working tools and 20 shillings in 1491. In 1503 he substantially improved his position by marrying the granddaughter and heiress of Sir Hugh Bryce, who had been one of the leading goldsmiths of his day. During the early part of Henry VIII's reign he received numerous orders for gold jewels to be sewn on to royal costumes, but in the 1520s the growth of international diplomacy and the custom of exchanging New Year's gifts at court accounted for lucrative business in more substantial plate. Other than the King, his most important client was Cardinal Wolsey. Although nothing survives that may be firmly attributed to Adamas, objects such as the Howard Grace Cup of 1525 or the Barber-Surgeons' instrument case of about 1518 give an idea of the kind of ornamental plate that he would have produced. He evidently ran a large workshop, employing a number of goldsmiths and apprentices among whom was Martin Bowes, who was apprenticed to him in 1513 and who, as Sir Martin Bowes, later presented the Bowes Cup to the Goldsmiths' Company. The key to success in Tudor England lay in patronage, and Adamas was no

exception in his appetite for appointments. On the occasion of the accession of the new King he was appointed Master of the Mint; from at least 1524 he was Master of the Jewels and in the same year he was Prime Warden of the Goldsmiths' Company. There is little doubt that he turned these positions to his own advantage and, in addition to his substantial money-lending activities, it was probably his role at the Mint that was chiefly responsible for the fact that he died reputedly the richest man in the City.

(See Philippa Glanville, 'Robert Adamas, Goldsmith', *Proceedings of the Silver Society*, 1984)

ARCHAMBO, Peter (d. 1767)

Huguenot goldsmith, apprenticed to Jacob Margas (q.v.) in 1710; entered his first mark in 1720. Like his master, he was free of the Butchers' Company rather than the Goldsmiths'. A leading, if not especially daring, exponent of the *Régence* and rococo styles, his most important patron was probably George, 2nd Earl of Warrington, for whom he made a wine fountain in 1728 (Goldsmiths' Company collection) and a wine cistern in the following year, which is still at Dunham Massey.

(See Judith Banister, 'Master of Elegant Silver', *Country Life*, 9 June 1983)

ASHBEE, Charles Robert (1863–1942)

Ashbee was not himself a working silversmith, but he was a leading figure in the Arts and Crafts movement of the turn of the century and in 1888 founded the Guild and School of Handicrafts at Toynbee Hall in the East End of London. The Guild rejected the contemporary dominance of the machine and set out to make small pieces of domestic plate by entirely hand-crafted means in a style that has certain affinities with art nouveau. The school closed in 1895 but the Guild continued until 1908, moving in 1902 to Chipping Campden in Gloucestershire. In 1909 Ashbee published *Modern English Silverwork*, but soon thereafter lost faith in handicrafts and his opposition to the machine wavered. After 1915 he gave up the arts altogether and became an academic.

BATEMAN, Hester (1708–94)

Widow of John Bateman, a gold chain maker who died in 1760, she registered her first mark in 1761. She was not trained in the craft herself, but was evidently a highly competent businesswoman and, in spite of being illiterate, expanded the business into what was probably one of the largest in London. The workshop specialized in domestic wares of ordinary quality and made maximum use of mechanized methods at all stages of production. Her sons Peter and Jonathan took over the business, and the Bateman dynasty lasted well into the nineteenth century. (See David S. Shure, *Hester Bateman*, 1959)

BODENDICK, Jacob (fl. 1661–*c*. 1688)

Married in London and granted denization in 1661, Bodendick was described as a native of Limburg in Germany. Like Wolfgang Howzer (q.v.), he was protected by the King, who instructed the Goldsmiths' Company in 1664 to mark his plate. However, he was not granted the freedom of the company until 1673. Bodendick evidently played an important role in the introduction to England of certain techniques typical of north Germany, and is particularly associated with tankards with cast scroll handles of auricular design and cups with pierced and embossed cagework decoration. One of his most remarkable surviving pieces is a silver-gilt mounted carved walnut wood tankard of 1664 in the Boston Museum of Fine Arts.

BOULTON, Matthew (1728–1809)

Inherited his father's 'toy making' business in 1759 and moved to Soho, outside Birmingham, where he built a large and modern factory employing eventually more than 800 people. He formed a partnership with John Fothergill until the latter's death in 1782, and later with the engineer James Watt. Boulton produced a wide range of metalware, especially ormolu, silver and Sheffield plate. He lobbied intensively for the establishment of assay offices at Birmingham and Sheffield in 1771. His silver is ambitious in design and of fine quality and distinctive style, but was not a commercial success. His most important patron for silver was the society hostess Mrs Elizabeth Montagu, with whom he corresponded extensively and for whom he produced a dinner service in 1776. Production declined towards the end of the century, although the firm remained an important producer of Sheffield plate. (See Nicholas Goodison, *Ormolu: The Work of Matthew Boulton*, 1974)

BOWERS, George (fl. 1661–*c*. 1680)

An immigrant goldsmith who presumably came to England in the retinue of Charles II, since he was sworn 'embosser in ordinary' in 1661. He also benefited considerably from the protection of the King, who requested the Lord Mayor to grant him the freedom of the City of London after his denization in 1664. But such favouritism was resented in the trade, and in 1663 he complained that his workshop had been broken into and goods seized by workmen belonging to the Goldsmiths' Company. Unlike the Mayor, the Goldsmiths' Company resisted the King's interference and he did not receive the freedom of the company until 1667. In spite of these personal details, little is known about Bowers's work. He is not known to have registered a mark, although the fact that Benjamin Pyne (q.v.) was apprenticed to him does suggest that he was fully conversant with all aspects of the craft, rather than being solely a chaser. The mark on an embossed tankard in the Toledo Museum, Ohio, a reversed monogram of G and B, has been attributed to him, as has an unmarked embossed toilet service in the Huntington Collection in California and a similar service at Woburn Abbey.

CAFE, John (c. 1716–57)

One of a number of London eighteenth-century goldsmiths whose workshop specialized in one particular branch of the trade. He was apprenticed in 1730 to James Gould, a fellow Somerset man and specialist candlestick maker, and entered his first mark in 1740. John Cafe and his younger brother William, who was apprenticed to him in 1742, produced candlesticks and candelabra almost exclusively and in particular had a virtual monopoly of one popular type on shaped square base modelled with shells. John Cafe left a substantial sum of money in his will, but his younger brother was evidently a less able businessman: production seems to have declined gradually during the 1760s, and in 1772 he was declared bankrupt. He died between 1802 and 1811, but had evidently retired many years earlier.

(See John P. Fallon, 'The Goulds and Cafes, Candlestick Makers', *Proceedings of the Silver Society*, 1974)

CHAWNER, Henry (1764–1851)

The most prominent member of a large family of goldsmiths, he was presumably apprenticed to his father and registered his first mark in 1786. His workshop produced neo-classical domestic plate, especially tea silver, of a consistently fine quality during the last part of the eighteenth century. In 1796 he entered into a partnership with John Emes.

COURTAULD, Augustine (c. 1685–1751)

A Huguenot goldsmith, brought to England as an infant and apprenticed in 1701 to Simon Pantin (q.v.), he entered his first mark in 1708. Most of his work is well made and well proportioned, but is essentially domestic and with restrained ornament. His most ambitious piece is the 1730 State Salt of the Swordbearer of

the City of London. His half-brother Peter, son Samuel and grandson Samuel were all goldsmiths. Samuel I's widow Louisa inherited her husband's business and formed a partnership with George Cowles in 1768.
(See J. F. Hayward, *The Courtauld Silver*, 1975)

CRESPIN, Paul (1694–1770)
Of French extraction, but born in London, Crespin entered his first marks in 1720 and 1721. He was described as being free of the Longbowstring Makers Company, but no record of his apprenticeship survives. He was one of the most outstanding goldsmiths of the second quarter of the eighteenth century. In 1724 he made a 'curious silver vessel for bathing' for the King of Portugal, weighing 6,030 ounces, and contributed in 1734 to a service for Catherine the Great of Russia. A deep basin of 1722 in the British Museum and a charger of 1727 in the Gilbert Collection, Los Angeles, illustrate his mastery of the *Régence* style. But his most original work dates from the 1740s, when he developed a highly sculptural approach to the rococo which suggests collaboration with Nicholas Sprimont (q.v.). The most remarkable of his surviving plate includes a soup tureen of 1740 in the Toledo Museum, Ohio, and the centrepiece made for Frederick, Prince of Wales in the royal collection. He retired in 1759 and died in Southampton.
(See A. G. Grimwade, 'Crespin or Sprimont?', *Apollo*, August 1969)

DE LAMERIE, Paul (1688–1751)
The most famous English goldsmith of the eighteenth century and head of one of the largest workshops in London. He was born of French Huguenot parents in 's Hertogenbosch in Holland, was brought to London in 1691 and apprenticed to Pierre Platel (q.v.) in 1703. He registered his first mark in 1713 and, presumably through connections formed under his old master, had a number of important aristocratic patrons from quite early in his career, for example the Duke of Sutherland, the Spencer family, Sir Robert Walpole and the Hon. George Treby. His early work is in both the plain Queen Anne and the more sophisticated *Régence* style, epitomized by the Sutherland wine cistern of 1719 (Minneapolis Museum) and the Treby toilet service of 1724 (Ashmolean Museum). From the 1730s he was arguably the leading exponent of the rococo style. Many of his most elaborate pieces suggest that he employed specialist craftsmen and designers whose individual characteristics can be recognized at different periods. In particular, from about 1739 to 1745 he evidently employed a talented but anonymous modeller who was largely responsible for the character of important commissions such as the plate made for Algernon, 6th Earl of Mountrath (Gilbert Collection, Los Angeles, etc.), and the ewer and basin of 1742 commissioned by the Goldsmiths' Company. He also made free and eclectic use of numerous different sources, such

as Dutch auricular silver and printed pattern books. Although occasionally in a highly embossed style, most of his more elaborate designs are in fact standard forms with applied cast decoration.

(See P. A. S. Phillips, *Paul de Lamerie*, London, 1935)

FARRELL, Edward Cornelius (*c.* 1780–after 1835)

No record exists of his apprenticeship, but he registered his first mark in 1815 and was from about 1815 to 1830 supplying plate to the flamboyant and innovative retailer Kensington Lewis. This association was one of the most important elements in the early nineteenth-century historicist movement and resulted in some of the most extraordinary silver of the period, particularly that produced for Lewis's leading patron, the Duke of York. The latter ordered huge quantities of plate through Lewis, perhaps the most splendid of which was a candelabrum of some 1,000 ounces, modelled in the form of Hercules slaying the Hydra. Farrell, however, described himself as a 'silversmith and chaser' and most of his work is embossed in high relief, mainly in seventeenth-century and rococo taste. He would also seem to have been one of the first goldsmiths habitually to 'improve' plain old plate by chasing it up in his characteristic style. It is impossible to tell whether he or Lewis was the dominant force in work bearing Farrell's mark, but it is clear that he had few opportunities to produce large-scale plate after the death of the Duke in 1827; most of his work thereafter is limited to novelties and tea services with heavily embossed decoration inspired by Dutch seventeenth-century genre painting.

(See John Culme, 'Kensington Lewis: A Nineteenth-Century Businessman', *The Connoiseur*, September 1975)

FOGELBERG, Andrew (*c.* 1732–1815)

Born in Sweden and probably to be identified with Andreas Fogelberg, who was apprenticed to Berent Halck of Halmsted. His first mark was entered in London around 1770, but no record of its exact date survives. From 1780 to 1793 he was in partnership with Stephen Gilbert, after which the premises were taken over by Paul Storr (q.v.). Whether produced before or during the partnership, Fogelberg's silver is invariably of fine quality, showing a sophisticated but restrained command of neo-classicism and illustrated by a silver-gilt teapot and stand of 1784 in the Victoria and Albert Museum. Many of his pieces are characterized by the use of silver medallions copied from James Tassie's castings of ancient cameos.

GARTHORNE, Francis (fl. *c.* 1680–1726)
One of the leading native English goldsmiths at the time of the Huguenot influx, and a signatory to the petitions of 1697 and 1711 against 'aliens and foreigners' and 'necessitous strangers'. No records of apprenticeship or the date of his first mark survive, although he is known to have been free of the Girdlers' company. From 1702 to 1723 he was one of the Subordinate Goldsmiths to Queen Anne and George I; he produced a fine ewer at Windsor Castle and a twelve-branch chandelier at Hampton Court. His later work shows an increasing assimilation of the Huguenot style.

HARACHE, Pierre (fl. *c.* 1682–*c.* 1700)
One of the first Huguenot goldsmiths to make a major impact on the craft in England. Thought to be a native of Rouen, his origins have yet to be established. His name appears on the denization lists of 1682 and he became free of the Goldsmiths' Company in the same year. His earliest known pieces date from 1683, although he was obviously a fully trained goldsmith before coming to England. There has in the past been confusion between the work of Harache and that of his son, also Pierre (1653–after 1717). Both goldsmiths produced work of the finest quality, distinguished by relatively squat proportions, remarkably heavy gauge metal and cast and cut-card ornament. Among Pierre I's finest works are a ewer and dish of 1697 in the British Museum and a wine cistern of 1699 made for the Barber-Surgeons' Company.

HEMING, Thomas (*c.* 1725–after 1795)
Apprenticed in 1738 to Peter Archambo (q.v.) and entered his first mark in 1745. In 1760 he was appointed Principal Goldsmith to the King and continued in that position until 1782, when the warrant was withdrawn, apparently on account of his excessive charges. His work is invariably of fine quality, in both a late rococo and early neo-classical style. Some of his most characteristic pieces among the former are a group of two-handled cups and covers with caryatid handles and applied vine ornament. His later silver uses ornament that is derived from classical architecture, but is of a curvilinear form that is in complete contrast to the Adam style. Among the most important of his works are a silver-gilt rococo toilet service of 1766 made for Queen Matilda of Denmark (Kunstindustrie Museum, Copenhagen), another made two years later for Sir Watkin Williams Wynn, a neo-classical bowl made in 1771 for the same patron (both National Museum of Wales) and the Brownlow wine cistern of 1770 at Belton.

HENNELL, David (1712–85)

Founder of a family of goldsmiths that continued in trade until the late nineteenth century and of a firm that is still in existence today. Apprenticed to Edward Wood, a salt-cellar maker, in 1728, he entered his first mark in 1736. Hennell and his descendants specialized in practical domestic silver, especially salt cellars. He retired in 1773 in order to become Deputy Warden of the Goldsmiths' Company (head of the Assay Office).

HOWZER, Wolfgang (fl. 1652–after 1688)

Like George Bowers and Jacob Bodendick (both q.v.), he was presumably a goldsmith in Charles II's service. He came from a family of goldsmiths in Zürich and was apprenticed to his father, becoming free of the guild in 1652. In 1664 he was furnished with a letter from the King instructing the Goldsmiths' Company to mark his plate. The company resented such pressures, but reluctantly agreed to comply, and the mark W H above a cherub has been attributed to him by Charles Oman. A silver-gilt mounted Chinese porcelain vase of about 1670 in the Victoria and Albert Museum bears this mark. His most important surviving pieces, however, predate this and were produced by him through the influence of Sir Robert Viner (q.v.) for Bishop Cozins of Durham's chapel at Bishop Auckland in 1660–61. Some of these pieces were evidently sponsored by Francis Leake (q.v.) and are struck with his mark.

JENKINS, Thomas (fl. c, 1665–1707)

This important goldsmith has long been known from his Britannia standard mark, registered in 1697, but it is only recently that his work prior to that date has been recognized. Jenkins was free of the Butchers' Company, of which he was a prominent member and served as Master in 1699. Over a hundred pieces with his mark have been recorded, the earliest dating from 1668, and they include a pair of tankards of 1671 at Dunham Massey and a large wine cistern of 1677 in the Victoria and Albert Museum. His most productive period was undoubtedly that prior to the introduction of the new standard, and although Jacob Margas (q.v.) was apprenticed to him in 1699, it has been suggested that by this time, like many successful goldsmiths, he was acting mainly in the capacity of a retailer or banker. (See A. G. Grimwade and J. Banister, 'Thomas Jenkins', *Proceedings of the Silver Society*, 1977)

KANDLER, Charles Frederick (fl. 1727– after 1773)

Almost complete mystery surrounds this important maker. He was clearly of German origin and was perhaps related to the Meissen porcelain modeller, J. J.

Kändler, but no record of his apprenticeship or freedom exists and it has proved impossible to establish any significant details about his life. The picture has been further confused by the fact that he would seem to have been known by his first name until 1735 and by his second thereafter. His first mark, C K, was registered in 1727, and his second, F K, in 1735, and it was until recently not unreasonably supposed that the marks were for two separate individuals, a supposition that is *prima facie* supported by the unusual length of his working career. A number of other marks were also registered, including a partnership mark for both sterling and Britannia standards with James Murray in 1727 and two different Britannia standard marks, one in 1751 and another undated and surmounted by a bishop's mitre. His work is of the finest quality and includes some of the earliest soup tureens in English silver, as well as a group of plate from the early 1730s with highly distinctive engraving. But his most important surviving work is undoubtedly the Jerningham wine cistern of 1735 in the Hermitage Museum, Leningrad, which was modelled by the sculptor Michael Rysbrach.

LEAKE, Francis (fl. 1655–after 1683)
Apprenticed to Henry Starkey and free of the Goldsmiths' Company in 1655. Together with his younger brother Ralph, his surviving work reflects most current tastes, especially that for embossed foliage, while the fact that a standing salt from the 1660 regalia in the Tower of London bears his mark indicates that he was among the most prominent goldsmiths of the period. There would also appear to be grounds for supposing that he was prepared to sponsor the work of certain foreign goldsmiths at the Assay Office (see Wolfgang Howzer).

LIGER, Isaac (d. 1730)
A Huguenot goldsmith whose name appears on the denization lists for 1700, he was made free of the Broderers' Company in 1704 and entered his first mark in the same year. Most of his work is domestic plate, usually plain but of excellent quality and heavy gauge, although the toilet service he supplied for the marriage of the 2nd Earl of Warrington's daughter is magnificent by any standards. The largest surviving corpus of his work is among the domestic and chapel plate at Dunham Massey, and his patronage by the Earl of Warrington lasted from 1708 until the end of his working life.

MANWARING, Arthur (fl. 1643–c. 1696)
Completed his apprenticeship under William Tyler in 1643 and was active for over fifty years, his last recorded work being hallmarked for 1696. Manwaring clearly ran a highly successful workshop and probably sponsored other makers' work,

since his work is relatively prolific and suggests command of a wide range of styles and techniques. Among his earliest known works is a porringer and stand of 1655 in the austere Commonwealth style, but the Feake Cup of ten years later in the Goldsmiths' Company Collection shows complete command of the embossed style, which is evident in much of his later work. From 1688, after the death of Sir Robert Viner (q.v.), he received a number of royal commissions.

MARGAS, Jacob (*c.* 1685–after 1730)
Son of a Huguenot goldsmith, Samuel Margas, who had been in London since at least 1687, Jacob was apprenticed to Thomas Jenkins (q.v.) in 1699 and made free of the Butchers' Company in 1706. He registered his first mark in the same year and apparently served as one of the Subordinate Goldsmiths to the King from 1723 to 1730, although he is recorded by Heal as bankrupt in 1725, and Grimwade has pointed out that the fact of several goldsmiths from one family working over the same period has led to some confusion between the different individuals. His known works span the period 1706–25 and are generally in the plain Queen Anne style, one of the best examples of which is a polygonal silver-gilt two-handled cup and cover of 1710 in the Huntington Collection in California. Margas's younger brother, Samuel, was apprenticed to him in 1708 and was free of the same company in 1714, registering his first mark in the following year. He is also recorded as having been Subordinate Goldsmith to the King from 1723–30 and 1732–3.

NELME, Anthony (*c.* 1660–1723)
Apprenticed to Richard Rowley in 1672 and later turned over to Isaac Deighton. He registered his first mark in *c.* 1680 and became one of the leading native English goldsmiths after the arrival of the Huguenots, signing the 1697 petition against 'aliens and foreigners'. He evidently ran a large workshop, and produced a striking range of silver from ordinary domestic wares to large-scale display and ceremonial pieces such as toilet services, maces and pilgrim bottles. Like most successful native makers, his work was of equal quality to that of the Huguenots and gradually assimilated many of the technical and stylistic aspects of the new style. Many pieces from his workshop survive, among the most impressive of which are a pair of large altar candlesticks of 1694 at St George's Chapel, Windsor, and a toilet service of 1691, now dispersed, applied with the monogram of Judith Bridgeman.

PANTIN, Simon (c. 1680–1728)

A native of Rouen, Pantin's name appears on the London denization lists of 1687. He was apprenticed to Pierre Harache (q.v.) and registered his first mark in 1701. The peacock included in his mark is a reference to the address of his first workshop, which was situated in Peacock Street, St Martin's Lane. Much of his work is of excellent quality but simple design, his most important surviving pieces being the Bowes kettle, stand and table of 1719 in the Untermyer Collection, New York, and a soup tureen of 1726 in the Hermitage Museum, Leningrad. Among the most beautiful of his works is a pair of silver-gilt salvers of 1713 in the *Régence* style, made for Sir Henry Featherstone. On his death the workshop was taken over by his son, Simon, who died in 1733 and was succeeded consecutively by Lewis Pantin I, II and III, the last named entering his mark as a goldworker in 1788.

PARTRIDGE, Affabel (fl. c. 1550–80)

Little is known of his early life other than his apprenticeship around 1535 to Richard Crompton, but he was evidently one of the leading goldsmiths of Queen Elizabeth's reign and rose to become Prime Warden of the Goldsmiths' Company. He is mentioned in 1560 and again in 1575/6, together with Robert Brandon, as 'one of her Ma[jest]ies goldsmiths'. The maker's mark here attributed to him is ascribed by Jackson to John Bird, but this can hardly be right, as Heal gives the latter's working dates as 1568–78, whereas the mark is found over the period 1554–78. It is invariably found on pieces of the finest quality, often of a character to suggest the use of continental pattern books or journeymen. That they were made by a goldsmith with connections at court is demonstrated by the Bacon Cups of 1573 (one in the British Museum), made for Sir Francis Bacon from the discarded matrices of the Great Seal of England. The royal associations of the so-called Queen Elizabeth Salt of 1572 (Tower of London), perhaps his most outstanding surviving work, however, are traditional only.

PILLEAU, Pezé (1696–1776)

The first native English member of a family of French goldsmiths dating back at least to 1612. Apprenticed to John Chartier in 1710, he married his master's daughter in 1724. His first mark was entered in, or a little before, 1724. He evidently retired from the trade by about 1755 and his surviving work is comparatively rare, although he would appear to have specialized in jugs with simple but technically sophisticated faceted sides. Like his father, Alexis Pilleau, he is also recorded as a maker of artificial teeth, and it is possible that this occupation formed the main part of his business.

PITTS, Thomas (c. 1723–93)

Apprenticed in 1737 to Charles Hatfield and turned over in 1742 to David Willaume II. Pitts is recorded as a 'goldsmith and chaser', and from his surviving work it is clear that he specialized in the production of epergnes and baskets, many of which were supplied to Parker and Wakelin (q.v.) for retail. His sons William, Thomas and Joseph were all apprenticed to him in 1769, 1767 and 1772 respectively. The first named of these eventually took over the business, entering his first mark in 1781 and forming a partnership from 1791 and 1799 with Joseph Preedy.

PLATEL, Pierre (c. 1664–1719)

Born in Lille and fled with his father and brother to Flanders after the revocation of the Edict of Nantes in 1685. He settled in England in 1688 and entered his first mark in 1699. Platel numbered leading supporters of William III, such as the Dukes of Devonshire and Portland, among his clients, and his most magnificent works include the gold ewer and basin of 1701 at Chatsworth and a silver-gilt toilet service at Welbeck Abbey. These epitomize the style developed by Platel, which often involved more fully worked surfaces and more sophisticated applied decoration and engraving than is found in the work of contemporaries such as David Willaume (q.v.) and Pierre Harache (q.v.). He clearly had a considerable influence over his most illustrious apprentice, Paul de Lamerie (q.v.), whose important early works are in precisely the same style as his master's.

PYNE, Benjamin (c. 1653–1732)

Apprenticed to George Bowers (q.v.) in 1667 and probably working alone from about 1680, when the first mark attributed to him (a crowned P) appears. He was one of the signatories to the petition against the newcomers in 1697, and by the time of the main Huguenot influx after 1685 was clearly well established. By the end of the century there can be no question that he, together with Anthony Nelme (q.v.), was the leading native English goldsmith in London. In 1714 he was appointed Subordinate Goldsmith to the King for the coronation of George I, and rose in 1725 to become Prime Warden of the Goldsmiths' Company. His long career, however, ended in relative poverty, and in 1727 he was obliged to apply for the position of Beadle of the Goldsmiths' Company. Much of Pyne's work shows a relative restraint which balances command of Huguenot techniques with an adherence to native English style. A significant part of his output consisted of church plate and municipal regalia, but among his most important surviving works are the thirty-two-piece silver-gilt toilet service of 1708 made for the Duke of Norfolk and the Earl of Kent's ewers and basin of 1699 (see p. 147).

ROLLOS, Philip (d. 1721)
A shadowy figure whose name appears on the denization lists for 1691, but of whose earlier history nothing is known. He was made free of the Goldsmiths' Company in 1697, but the maker's mark P R in an oblong punch which appears from around 1680 has been plausibly attributed to him. He clearly ran one of the most successful workshops in London and was appointed one of the Subordinate Goldsmiths to both William III and Queen Anne. A number of impressive pieces in the Huguenot style survive with his mark, including the wine-cistern of 1701 at Dunham Massey, another of 1699 in the Hermitage Museum, Leningrad, and a third in the Marlborough ambassadorial plate at Althorp. His son, also Philip, succeeded him in the post of Subordinate Goldsmith to the Crown.

RUNDELL, Philip (1743–1827)
One of the most remarkable entrepreneurs of the early nineteenth century, Rundell was not a practising goldsmith. He was apprenticed in 1760 to William Rogers of Bath, subsequently worked for Theed and Pickett in London, and was made a partner by the latter in 1772. By 1785 he was sole proprietor and by 1803 had brought in John Bridge and his nephew Edmund Rundell as partners of what was now styled Rundell, Bridge and Rundell. Bridge's fortuitous connection with the King is said to have accounted for the firm being awarded the royal warrant in 1797, which in turn led to an enormous increase in business. Rundell employed Paul Storr (q.v.) and other goldsmiths such as Benjamin and James Smith, Digby Scott and Philip Cornman to work exclusively for him and to produce plate exactly in accordance with the specifications drawn up by his design team. By around 1810 the firm was employing over 500 people and entirely dominated the market for extravagant display plate in the Regency style. It was not until his break with Storr in 1819 that Rundell registered his own mark. He would appear to have retired from active business around 1823, when John Bridge entered his mark. He left a fortune of £1¼ million.

SCOFIELD, John (fl. 1776–96)
One of the leading makers of the last quarter of the eighteenth century, although no record survives of his apprenticeship. His first mark was entered in 1776 in partnership with Robert Jones, and his second alone two years later. His work concentrates on domestic silver, especially dinner services and candelabra. It is almost entirely in restrained Adam taste, but is distinguished by superb quality,

especially of chased detail. Among his finest plate are the candlesticks and cruet frame at Brodick Castle, made for William Beckford in 1781 and 1784.

SHARP, Robert (c. 1733–1803)
Apprenticed to Thomas Gladwin in 1747 and became free of the Goldsmiths' Company in 1757. In 1763 he entered his first mark in a partnership with Daniel Smith, which was maintained until 1788, except for a brief period between 1778 and 1780 when a third partner, Robert Carter, was introduced. Smith and Sharp were leading exponents of the Adam style and a number of pieces with their mark are made to designs in Robert Adam's hand, such as a cup of 1764, the design for which is in Sir John Soane's Museum. A magnificent silver-gilt toilet service of 1779 from the partnership is in the Kungl Livrustkammaren, Stockholm.

SHRUDER, James (fl. 1737–c. 1752)
Although he was responsible for some of the most remarkable rococo silver, little is known of this maker, who was presumably of German origin. His first mark was registered in 1737, but there is no record of his apprenticeship or freedom. He is stated by Heal to have been bankrupt in 1749, although a kettle of as late as 1752 with his mark is known. His work is distinguished by the use of spiky Germanic rococo cartouches, and perhaps his most remarkable pieces are a coffee pot and kettle of 1749, engraved with the arms of Okeover, the spouts of which are formed as putti astride dolphins.

SPRIMONT, Nicholas (1716–71)
Born at Liège and apprenticed there to his uncle, Sprimont arrived in London in 1742 and registered his mark in January of the following year, but he only worked as a silversmith for about five years. From about 1747 he became exclusively occupied with the management of the new Chelsea porcelain factory, after which no silver with his mark is known. Beyond these bare details, those of his marriage in 1742 to Ann Protin and the sale of his picture collection at Christie's after his death, little is known of this interesting but shadowy character. Sprimont's silver is extremely rare and its scarcity, together with its individuality of style, suggests that he ran a very small workshop. This small corpus of surviving plate is among the most interesting of all English rococo silver. The most important pieces are the Ashburnham centrepiece of 1747 in the Victoria and Albert Museum, a tea kettle of 1745 in the Hermitage Museum, Leningrad, and the lobster and crab salts

and shell-shaped sauceboats of 1742 and 1743 in the royal collection. In addition it has been suggested that the centrepiece of 1741–2 in the royal collection which is struck with Paul Crespin's mark may have been substantially his work. All these pieces are unusually sculptural and characterized by the use of marine motifs and fluid scrolls.

(See A. G. Grimwade, 'Crespin or Sprimont?', *Apollo*, August 1969)

STORR, Paul (1771–1844)

The most famous silversmith of the Regency period, apprenticed in 1785 to Andrew Fogelburg (q.v.) and free of the Goldsmiths' Company in 1792. His first mark was entered in partnership with William Frisbee in the same year and was followed in 1793 by his first mark alone. In 1807 he moved from his workshop in Air Street, Piccadilly, to Dean Street, Soho, and from then until 1819 worked – apparently exclusively – for Rundell, Bridge and Rundell (q.v.), producing grand, often gilt, display plate precisely to their specifications. Storr became a partner in the firm, but eventually broke away from Rundells and was again independent until forming a partnership with John Mortimer, which lasted from 1822 until Storr's retirement in 1838. Although work with his mark is almost invariably of excellent quality, the evidence suggests that he was not a particularly innovative designer. His early work, such as a pair of gilt baskets of 1798 and other plate made for William Beckford, is superbly executed, but of unexceptional neo-classical design. His finest work all dates from the period of the Rundells association, but is indistinguishable from that made for the same firm by Benjamin Smith, and his work after 1819 generally betrays a decline in design.

(See N. M. Penzer, *Paul Storr*, 1954)

VAN VIANEN, Christian (1598–1666 or later)

Born in Utrecht, Holland, van Vianen was son and nephew of two of the most distinguished seventeenth-century Dutch goldsmiths, Adam and Paul van Vianen. The latter are credited with the invention of the auricular style of ornament, which Christian popularized by the publication of his father's designs in 1650. The younger van Vianen became master of the guild of goldsmiths in Utrecht in 1628, and between 1630 and 1647 spent at least two extended periods in London in the service of Charles I. Nearly all his major works, such as a ewer and basin made for the King in 1635 and the service of altar plate for St George's Chapel, completed in 1637, have been lost, but an auricular two-handled bowl and cover made for the 10th Earl of Northumberland and a basin of 1635 survive from his English period. He apparently never registered a maker's mark and the basin is signed 'C. V. Vianen fecit 1636'.

(See R. W. Lightbown, 'Christian van Vianen at the Court of Charles I', *Apollo*, June 1968)

VINER, Sir Robert (1631–88)

Although not a practising goldsmith, Sir Robert Viner was one of the most influential figures in the craft during the reign of Charles II. He was apprenticed to his uncle, Sir Thomas Viner, and in 1660 succeeded him as royal goldsmith. In this capacity he was responsible for the distribution of royal patronage and played a major part in the promotion of immigrant goldsmiths such as Bodendick, Bowers and Howzer (all q.v.). In a partially successful attempt to win his greater support for native craftsmen, the Goldsmiths' Company brought him on to the Court in 1666 and made him Prime Warden in the following year. It was in connection with the first of these events that he presented the company with a silver-gilt bell for which Paul de Lamerie's (q.v.) inkstand of 1741 was subsequently made. Viner was evidently an influential man in the City (his uncle had been Lord Mayor before him and in 1674 he too was elected Mayor); in 1665 he increased his already considerable wealth by £100,000 through his marriage to Mary, widow of Sir Thomas Hyde. Samuel Pepys visited him in that year and wrote that 'there lives no man in England in greater plenty'. But his massive and unrepaid loans to the Crown led to his downfall: by 1672 he had outstanding debts of £416,000 and in 1682 he was declared bankrupt. His portrait, with his wife and family, is in the National Portrait Gallery.

WAKELIN, Edward (c. 1716–84)

Apprenticed to John Le Sage in 1730 and already in partnership with George Wickes (q.v.) by 1747. He entered his first mark almost immediately afterwards and was free of the Goldsmiths' Company in the following year. From this date he apparently took virtual charge of the running of the silversmithing side of the business. In or after 1758, after Wickes's retirement, he went into partnership with John Parker. This was superseded in 1777 by that between Wakelin's son, John, and William Taylor. The younger Wakelin in turn formed a new partnership in 1792 with Robert Garrard, from which the present-day firm of Garrards is descended. Whether or not Edward Wakelin was a practising goldsmith, there can be no doubt as to his business acumen, and during the 1760s, to judge both from surviving plate and the firm's ledgers in the Victoria and Albert Museum, the Parker and Wakelin workshop was evidently one of the most fashionable in London.

(See Elaine Barr, *George Wickes, Royal Goldsmith*, 1980)

WICKES, George (1698–1761)

Apprenticed to Samuel Wastell in 1712 and registered his first mark in 1721. For much of his career Wickes worked as the sole proprietor of his workshop, but was in partnership between 1730 and 1735 with John Craig (probably a jeweller) and from 1747 until his retirement in 1760 with Edward Wakelin (q.v.). In 1735 he was appointed goldsmith to Frederick, Prince of Wales, a fact which did not in itself lead to very much lucrative royal patronage, but which was immensely prestigious and must have generated business from other clients. He celebrated the fact by incorporating into his mark a coronet in 1735 and the Prince of Wales's feathers in 1739. Wickes was by no means the greatest or most original silversmith of the period, but more is known about him than his contemporaries, thanks to the unique survival of his ledgers, which record the day-to-day details of his business, his patrons and sub-contractors. His work is invariably of excellent quality, but generally of conservative character. Among his most important pieces are an unmarked gold cup and cover made to designs by William Kent for Colonel Pelham in 1736, a large dinner service of 1745–7 made for the Duke of Leinster, and a ewer and basin of 1735 with applied rococo ornament.

(See Elaine Barr, *George Wickes, Royal Goldsmith*, 1980)

WILLAUME, David (1658–1741)

Born in Metz, the son of a goldsmith, and settled in London at least by 1687, when his denization is recorded. He married in 1690 Marie Mettayer, sister of the goldsmith Louis Mettayer. His first known mark was registered in 1697, although he had presumably registered one earlier, since he was free of the Goldsmiths' Company by 1694. Willaume was one of the most outstanding of the 'first generation' Huguenot goldsmiths and his work represents the new style at its best. His patrons included many of the most important nobility, including the Dukes of Devonshire, Portland and Buccleuch, and underscores the concern of those native English goldsmiths who were signatory to the petitions of 1697 and 1711 against immigrants. He probably retired in about 1728, the year in which his son, David II, registered his first mark.

$$\text{---} \quad Notes \quad \text{---}$$

CHAPTER 1

SILVER: THE METAL AND THE CRAFT

1. Although discovered as early as the seventeenth century, platinum's hardness makes it comparatively unsuitable for plate, and it was not used extensively, even for jewellery, until quite recently. A separate hallmark for platinum was not introduced until 1975.
2. Theophilus, *On Divers Arts*, translated by John G. Hawthorne and Cyril Stanley Smith, New York (1963).
3. I am grateful to Mr James R. Curtis, silversmith at Colonial Williamsburg, where eighteenth-century techniques are still used, for this information.
4. On the continent the idea of preserving family plate seems to have been accepted much earlier than in England. For example, in 1565 Duke Albrecht V of Bavaria listed a number of objects that were to be designated hereditary heirlooms of his family in perpetuity. See J. F. Hayward, *Virtuoso Goldsmiths* (1976), p. 32.
5. For a fuller account of the history of hallmarks in England, see *Touching Gold and Silver, 500 Years of Hallmarks* (exhibition catalogue), Goldsmiths' Hall (1978).
6. I am grateful to Mr David Beasley, Deputy Librarian of the Goldsmiths' Company, for this information.
7. See Chapter 6, p. 142.
8. Quoted from a document of 1577 by Robin D. Gwynn, *Huguenot Heritage* (1985), p. 61.

CHAPTER 2

THE EARLY TUDORS

1. Quoted by Ronald Lightbown, *Tudor Domestic Silver* (1970), p. 1.
2. See Chapter 3, p. 56.

3. Although the silver-gilt mounted Chinese porcelain ewer at Hardwick is contemporary with the house, there is no evidence of its presence at Hardwick before the mid nineteenth century (see Gervase Jackson-Stops (ed.), *The Treasure Houses of Britain* (exhibition catalogue) (1985), p. 105).

4. Illustrated by Gerald Taylor, *Silver Through the Ages* (1964), 2nd edition, pl. 1.

5. Joyce Youings, *Sixteenth-Century England* (1984), p. 128.

6. Illustrated by J. F. Hayward, *Virtuoso Goldsmiths* (1976), pl. 41.

7. See Ronald Lightbown, *Secular Goldsmiths' Work in Medieval France: A History* (1978), p. 40.

8. Illustrated by Joan Evans, *Art in Medieval France* (1948), pl. 150.

9. 'Inventory of Archbishop Parker's Goods & C.', *Archaeologia*, XXX, p. 25.

10. 'An Inventory of the Effects of Henry Howard KG, Earl of Northampton', *Archaeologia*, XLIII, pp. 352–3.

11. Quoted by Lightbown (1970), p. 4, from George Cavendish's biography of Cardinal Wolsey.

12. See Philippa Glanville, 'Tudor Drinking Vessels', *Burlington Magazine* (September 1985), pp. 19–22.

13. Illustrated by Michael Clayton, *Christie's Pictorial History of English and American Silver* (1985), pl. 1.

14. Illustrated in *Cambridge Plate* (exhibition catalogue) (1975), p. 23.

15. Illustrated in Carl Hernmarck, *The Art of the European Silversmith* (1977), pl. 71.

16. Illustrated in H. C. Moffatt, *Old Oxford Plate* (1906), pl. 31.

17. Illustrated in *Cambridge Plate*, p. 23.

18. Illustrated in Hernmarck (1977), pl. 294.

19. Illustrated by C. J. Jackson, *An Illustrated History of English Plate* (1911), opposite p. 146.

20. Illustrated by Moffatt (1906), pls. 43 and 33.

21. Illustrated by Moffatt (1906), pl. 65.

22. Illustrated by J. B. Carrington and G. R. Hughes, *The Plate of the Worshipful Company of Goldsmiths* (1926), pl. 14.

23. See A. J. Collins, *Jewels and Plate of Queen Elizabeth I, The Inventory of 1574* (1955), pp. 433, 541, 564, etc.

24. Quoted by Gerald Taylor, *Silver Through the Ages* (1964), 2nd edition, p. 127.

25. Illustrated by Moffatt (1906), pl. 66.

26. See Michael Clayton, *The Collector's Dictionary of the Silver and Gold of Great Britain and North America* (1985), 2nd edition, p. 180.

27. Illustrated by Claude Blair (ed.), *The History of Silver* (1987), p. 76.

28. See Hayward (1976), pls. 32–5. Although thought to have been published around 1540, at least some of its pages had probably been in circulation some years earlier, perhaps in looseleaf form.

29. This was essentially a plagiarism of Jacques Androuet du Cerceau's pattern

book, which was itself derived from one published in Paris in 1530 by Francesco Pelligrino.

30. See Hayward (1976), pls. 211–14.
31. Illustrated by Clayton, *Dictionary* (1985), pl. 425.
32. Illustrated by Charles Oman, *The English Silver in the Kremlin* (1961), pls. 42 and 43.
33. Illustrated by Moffatt (1906), pl. 69, and *Cambridge Plate*, p. 39.
34. Illustrated by Jackson (1911), p. 683, fig. 889.
35. Formerly in the Swaythling collection, sold at Christie's, 6 and 7 May 1924, lot 125, illustrated in the catalogue.
36. Quoted by John Hatcher and T. C. Barker, *A History of English Pewter* (1974), p. 66.
37. William Harrison, *A Description of England* [original title], reprinted *c.* 1921 (undated) by the Walter Scott Publishing Co., p. 147.
38. See Hatcher and Barker (1974), p. 61.
39. See Peter Hornsby, *Pewter, Copper and Brass* (1981), p. 50.
40. Illustrated in *The Worshipful Company of Pewterers of London, Supplementary Catalogue of Pewterware* (1979), p. 19 (S1/104).
41. Illustrated in Chapter 3, p. 80.
42. See Hatcher and Barker (1974), p. 161.
43. Quoted by Lightbown (1970), p. 7.
44. Illustrated in *Cambridge Plate*, p. 17.
45. Cited by Clayton, *Dictionary* (1985), p. 244.
46. Illustrated by Hugh Tait, *The Golden Age of Venetian Glass* (1979), pl. 11.
47. Illustrated by Moffatt (1906), pl. 34.
48. Illustrated by Lightbown (1978), pl. 54.
49. Illustrated by Robert Wark, *British Silver in the Huntington Collection* (1978), pp. 131 and 132.
50. See Norman Gask, *Old Silver Spoons of England* (1926), pp. 81–90.

CHAPTER 3

THE ELIZABETHAN AGE

1. See Christopher Hill, *Reformation to Industrial Revolution* (1967), p. 83.
2. Joyce Youings, in *Sixteenth-Century England* (1984), p. 16, suggests that the book may have been written as early as 1550.
3. William Harrison, *A Description of England* [original title], reprinted *c.* 1921 [undated], by the Walter Scott Publishing Co., p. 118.
4. See Hill, (1967), p. 26.
5. See Roy Strong, *Artists of the Tudor Court* (1983), p. 12.

6. A. J. Collins, *Jewels and Plate of Queen Elizabeth I, The Inventory of 1574* (1955), p. 569.

7. ibid, p. 577.

8. ibid., p. 563.

9. ibid., p. 579.

10. ibid., p. 589.

11. ibid., pp. 549–50.

12. See Robin D. Gwynn, *Huguenot Heritage* (1985), p. 72.

13. Quoted by Ronald Lightbown, *Tudor Domestic Plate* (1970), p. 3.

14. See J. F. Hayward, 'The Destruction of Nuremberg Plate by the Goldsmiths' Company', *Proceedings of the Silver Society*, vol. 2, pp. 195–201.

15. Illustrated by J. F. Hayward, *Virtuoso Goldsmiths* (1976), pl. 650.

16. Illustrated in ibid., pl. 671.

17. Illustrated by Lightbown (1970), pls. 22 and 23. This is the largest of all extant pre-seventeenth-century salts and weighs 58 oz.

18. Illustrated by Michael Clayton, *The Collector's Dictionary of the Silver and Gold of Great Britain and North America*, (1985), 2nd edition, colour pl. 52.

19. Sold at Christie's, 6 and 7 May 1924, lot 103, illustrated in the catalogue.

20. See Collins (1955), pp. 466–7.

21. John Hatcher and T. C. Barker, *A History of British Pewter* (1974), p. 166.

22. See Collins (1955). Compare pp. 358 f. with 416 f.

23. Illustrated by Claude Blair (ed.), *The History of Silver* (1987), p. 70.

24. 'Inventories made for Sir William and Sir Thomas Fairfax', *Archaeologia*, XLVIII, p. 153.

25. Sold at Christie's, 6 and 7 May 1924, lot 121, illustrated in the catalogue.

26. Harrison [1921], p. 89.

27. ibid., p. 90.

28. ibid., p. 90.

29. See Chapter 2, note 3.

30. *Inventory of Robert, Earl of Essex (1588)*; quoted by Hatcher (1974), p. 107.

31. See Muriel St Clare Byrne (ed.), *The Lisle Letters*, Chicago (1981), vol. 6, Appendix E, pp. 189–91.

32. 'Inventory of Archbishop Parker's Goods & C.', *Archaeologia*, XXX, pp. 25–6.

33. 'Inventories made for Sir William and Sir Thomas Fairfax', *Archaeologia*, XLVIII, pp. 153–4.

34. Collins (1955), pp. 523–6.

35. ibid., pp. 515, 522, etc.

36. Harrison [1921], p. 147.

37. ibid.

38. *Inventory of Thomas Yeat, smith of Worcester (1563)*; quoted by Hatcher and Barker (1974), p. 106.

39. Illustrated in *A Short History of the Worshipful Company of Pewterers of London and a Catalogue of Pewterware in Its Possession* (1968), p. 30.
40. See Lindsay Boynton (ed.), *The Hardwick Hall Inventories of 1601* (1971), p. 37.
41. Illustrated by H. Cotterell, *Old Pewter, its Makers and Marks* (1929), pl. XX.
42. Illustrated by Michael Clayton, *Christie's Pictorial History of English and American Silver* (1985), p. 44.
43. 'Cristine Burgh of Richmond, late Prioress of the late dissolved nunery of Nunkylbyng in the County of York (1566)', *Surtees Society*, vol. 26, p. 193.
44. See Charles Oman, *English Engraved Silver* (1978), pp. 47–8.

CHAPTER 4

THE EARLY SEVENTEENTH CENTURY

1. See Christopher Hill, *Reformation to Industrial Revolution* (1967), p. 148.
2. See J. F. Hayward, 'The Destruction of Nuremberg Plate by the Goldsmiths' Company', *Proceedings of the Silver Society*, vol. 2, p. 195.
3. ibid., p. 197.
4. For example, a salver illustrated by Charles Oman, *Caroline Silver* (1970), frontispiece.
5. See J. F. Hayward, *Virtuoso Goldsmiths* (1976), p. 195.
6. 'An Inventory of the Effects of Henry Howard KG, Earl of Northampton', *Archaeologia*, XLII, pp. 351–3.
7. See Ronald Lightbown, 'Christian van Vianen at the Court of Charles I', *Proceedings of the Silver Society*, vol. 2, p. 6.
8. 'An Inventory of Archbishop Parker's Goods & C.', *Archaeologia*, XXX, pp. 25–7.
9. For an illustrated example, see Oman (1970), pl. 7B.
10. Illustrated by Oman (1970), pl. 7A.
11. This is the conclusion reached by Oman (1970), p. 39n.
12. Illustrated by Ronald F. Michaelis, *Old Domestic Base-Metal Candlesticks* (1978), fig. 109.
13. Illustrated by Christopher Peal, *Pewter of Great Britain* (1983), p. 14.
14. Robert Latham and William Matthews (eds.), *The Diary of Samuel Pepys* (1972), vol. 7, p. 10.
15. 'An Inventory of Household Goods, 1612' (of Edward Catherall, a brewer and small farmer of Luton, Bedfordshire), *The Antiquary*, vol. 42, p. 28.

CHAPTER 5

THE RESTORATION

1. See Robert Latham and William Matthews (eds.), *The Diary of Samuel Pepys* (1970), vol. 2, p. 5n. Charles Oman, *Caroline Silver* (1970), p. 12, records that

about 7,000 ounces a year was required for the King's New Year's gifts to peers and senior officers of state.

2. Latham and Matthews (1970), vol. 2, p. 5.
3. See Oman (1970), p. 5n. for tables of the quantities of plate assayed between 1653 and 1662.
4. Illustrated by Charles Oman, *English Church Plate* (1957), pl. 113A.
5. See Oman (1970), pls. 93A and B.
6. See ibid., p. 8.
7. Illustrated ibid., pl. 3A.
8. Illustrated ibid., pl. 9B.
9. For a fuller account of these goldsmiths, see ibid., pp. 32–6.
10. Arthur Grimwade and Judith Banister, 'Thomas Jenkins: The Man and the Master Craftsman', *Proceedings of the Silver Society*, vol. 2, pp. 185–93 and 228.
11. Illustrated by Oman (1970), pl. 37B.
12. See Lindsay Boynton (ed.), *The Hardwick Hall Inventories of 1601* (1971), p. 25.
13. A. J. Collins, *Jewels and Plate of Queen Elizabeth I, The Inventory of 1574* (1955), p. 422.
14. See Oman (1970), pl. 94.
15. Illustrated by Robin Feddon (ed.), *Treasures of the National Trust* (1976), pl. 161.
16. Illustrated by Michael Clayton, *The Collector's Dictionary of the Silver and Gold of Great Britain and North America*, (1985), 2nd edition, colour pl. 64.
17. See Richard Garnier, *The Mostyn Tompion*, Christie's Review of the Season (1982), pp. 228–31. Athough the Chatsworth table was in fact made in Paris in about 1710, Gentot, described but not identified by Oman in *English Engraved silver*, was evidently working in England during the latter part of the seventeenth century.
18. Illustrated by Oman (1970), pl. 40B.
19. Sold at Sotheby's, 13 June 1983, lot 25.
20. For a fuller account of these cups, see Hugh Tait, 'The Advent of the Two-handled Cup', *Proceedings of the Silver Society*, vol. 2, pp. 202–10.
21. Illustrated by Feddon (1976), pl. 160.
22. Latham and Matthews (1972), vol. 6, p. 132.
23. ibid., vol. 1, p. 15.
24. ibid., vol. 9, p. 405.
25. Anthony Wood, Diary, quoted by Oman (1970), p. 45.
26. Latham and Matthews (1970), vol. 1, p. 253.

CHAPTER 6

THE HUGUENOT CONTRIBUTION

1. Robin Gwynn, *Huguenot Heritage* (1985), p. 23.

2. ibid., p. 36.
3. ibid., p. 72.
4. Quoted from J. F. Hayward, *Huguenot Silver* (1959), p. 17.
5. Quoted from *The Quiet Conquest* (exhibition catalogue), Museum of London (1985), no. 332, p. 232.
6. Quoted from Hayward (1959), pp. 20–21.
7. See Christopher Hill, *Reformation to Industrial Revolution*, (1967), p. 174.
8. Quoted from Hayward (1959), pp. 25–6.
9. For a fuller account of George Booth, 2nd Earl of Warrington, and his silver, see J. F. Hayward, 'The Earl of Warrington's Plate', *Apollo*, July 1978.
10. Illustrated by Charles Oman, *The English Silver in the Kremlin* (1961), pl. 11, and Frank Davis, *French Silver* (1970), pl. 18.
11. Now in the collection of the Goldsmiths' Company; illustrated in *The Quiet Conquest*, p. 233. See Chapter 7, note 2.
12. No record of the circumstances of their acquisition exists, although they are known to have been at Blenheim from an early date.
13. See *The Quiet Conquest*, no. 337, p. 234.
14. Quoted from Hayward (1959), p. 82.
15. Illustrated by Hayward (1959), pl. 38.
16. See Hill (1967), p. 237.
17. See Hayward (1959), p. 83.

CHAPTER 7

THE ROCOCO PERIOD

1. See Linda Colley, 'The English Rococo, Historical Background', in *Rococo, Art and Design in Hogarth's England* (exhibition catalogue), Victoria and Albert Museum (1984), p. 10.
2. See *Touching Gold and Silver* (exhibition catalogue), Goldsmiths' Hall (1978), p. 17.
3. See Philippa Glanville, 'Patrons and Craftsman' in *Rococo, Art and Design in Hogarth's England* (1984), p. 324, note 22.
4. In 1738 George Wickes charged £181 1s. for a set of twenty-four plates weighing 488 oz 5 dwt. These were presumably of fairly elaborate design, since the metal alone would have accounted for approximately £135 of the cost, leaving about £46 for the 'fashion'.
5. See Aileen Ribeiro, *Dress in Eighteenth-Century Europe 1715–1789*, New York, p. 202.
6. See *Rococo, Art and Design in Hogarth's England* (1984), p. 259.
7. See Elaine Barr, *George Wickes, Royal Goldsmith* (1980).
8. Arthur Grimwade, *Rococo Silver* (1974), p. 10.

9. Still in the collection of the Goldsmiths' Company; illustrated by Grimwade (1974), pl. 55.

10. Illustrated by Hannelore Muller, *The Thyssen-Bornemisza Collection, European Silver* (1986), p. 99.

11. For an example, see Grimwade (1974), pl. 5.

12. Illustrated in ibid., pls. 45 and 95.

13. Illustrated *Rococo, Art and Design in Hogarth's England* (1984), colour pl. IV.

14. Examples of this type include the centrepiece of 1741 in the royal collection, made for Frederick, Prince of Wales, by Paul Crespin (illustrated Grimwade (1974), pl. 48), and the Ashburnham centrepiece, by Nicholas Sprimont, 1747 (illustrated Grimwade (1974), pl. 50).

15. A full list of this service is given by Charles Oman, *Caroline Silver* (1970), pp. 64–5.

16. Now in the Al Tajir Collection; illustrated by Barr (1980), pp. 197–205.

17. Sold at Sotheby's, 22 November 1984, extensively illustrated in the catalogue.

18. Illustrated Robin Feddon (ed.), *Treasures of the National Trust* (1976), pl. 169.

19. Illustrated Feddon (1976), pl. 152.

20. Christopher Hill, *Reformation to Industrial Revolution,* (1967), p. 247.

21. See David Vaisey (ed.), *The Diary of Thomas Turner 1754–1765* (1985), p. 188.

22. The entire cargo was sold by Christie's, Amsterdam, 28 April–2 May 1986.

23. Both drawing and candlestick are illustrated in *Rococo, Art and Design in Hogarth's England* (1984), E13 and E14, p. 70.

24. The porcelain version of the model is illustrated by Yvonne Hackenbroch, *Chelsea and Other English Porcelain, Pottery and Enamel in the Irwin Untermyer Collection*, Cambridge, Massachusetts (1957), pl. 2.

CHAPTER 8

NEO-CLASSICISM AND INDUSTRIALIZATION

1. Quoted by Helena Hayward, 'English Rococo Designs for Silver', *Proceedings of the Silver Society*, vol. 2, p. 70.

2. Quoted by Robert Rowe, *Adam Silver* (1965), pp. 23–4.

3. ibid., p. 28.

4. Illustrated by Grimwade (1974), pl. 12.

5. For a fuller account of the early history of Sheffield plate, see Frederick Bradbury, *History of Sheffield Plate* (1912).

6. Quoted ibid., p. 30.

7. Robert Rowe (1965), p. 22.

8. Illustrated Bradbury (1912), pp. 398–424.

9. Quoted ibid., p. 2.

10. See *Brass Candlesticks*, privately printed for Rupert Gentle (1973). This facsimile

of a late eighteenth-century brassfounder's catalogue is marked with the price of each model, many of which were available in various sizes.

11. See *Touching Gold and Silver* (exhibition catalogue), Goldsmiths' Hall (1978), p. 17.

12. See Kenneth Quickenden, 'Boulton and Fothergill: Business Plans and Miscalculations', *Art History*, vol. 3, no. 3, p. 277.

13. See Michael Clayton, *The Collector's Dictionary of the Silver and Gold of Great Britain and North America* (1985), 2nd edition, p. 424.

14. The best and fullest account of Boulton's life is in Nicholas Goodison, *Ormolu: The Work of Matthew Boulton* (1974). A more specific account of his silver is contained in Eric Delieb and Michael Roberts, *The Great Silver Manufactory* (1971).

15. Letter to Lord Shelbourne, 1768, quoted by Quickenden, 'Boulton and Fothergill', p. 274.

16. Quoted from Goodison (1974), p. 14.

17. See ibid.

18. See Quickenden, 'Boulton and Fothergill', p. 279.

19. James Keir, *Memorandum of Matthew Boulton* (3 December 1809), p. 1 (Assay Office, Birmingham). Quoted from Goodison (1974), p. 12.

20. Quoted by Quickenden, 'Boulton and Fothergill', p. 280.

21. ibid., p. 281.

22. ibid., p. 282.

23. ibid., p. 281.

24. ibid., pp. 283–4.

25. ibid., p. 279.

26. In this he was far from alone; a set of tea vases by Louisa Courtauld and George Cowles, 1771, formerly at Kedleston and now in the Boston Museum of Fine Arts (p. 214), are exact copies of plates from d'Hancarville. In the following century extensive use was made of Piranesi's prints for copies of the Warwick vase and other classical models.

27. Quoted by Goodison (1974), p. 46.

28. John Culme, 'Beauty and the Beast', *Proceedings of the Silver Society*, vol. 2, pp. 158–64.

CHAPTER 9

THE EARLY NINETEENTH CENTURY

1. See John Culme, *Nineteenth-Century Silver* (1976), p. 33.

2. See J. F. Hayward, 'Royal Silversmiths of the Regency: Rundell, Bridge and Rundell', *Proceedings of the Silver Society*, vol. 2, p. 58.

3. See Culme (1974), p. 65.

4. ibid., p. 63.
5. See Michael Snodin, 'J. J. Boileau: A Forgotten Designer of Silver', *Connoisseur*, June 1978.
6. For a fuller account of the shield, see Shirley Bury and Michael Snodin, 'The Shield of Achilles by John Flaxman, R.A.', in *Art at Auction. The Year at Sotheby's 1983–84*, pp. 275–83.
7. See preface to Christie's sale catalogue, 29 May 1963, 'The Sale of Royal Plate, 1808'.
8. See J. F. Hayward, introduction to *Beckford and Hamilton Silver from Brodick Castle*, National Trust for Scotland (1980) (exhibition catalogue).
9. In 1823 Lewis caused something of a scandal by publicly announcing at the Fonthill sale that a mounted topaz cup, catalogued as the work of Benvenuto Cellini, was not topaz at all, but rock-crystal. For further information on Lewis, see John Culme, 'Kensington Lewis: A Nineteenth-Century Businessman', *Connoisseur*, September 1975.
10. See Michael Snodin and Malcolm Baker, 'William Beckford's Silver', *Burlington Magazine*, November 1980. For a fully illustrated catalogue of the Brodick Castle collection of Beckfordiana, see *Beckford and Hamilton Silver from Brodick Castle*.
11. See Hayward, introduction to *Beckford and Hamilton Silver from Brodick Castle* (1980).
12. See Culme, (1976) p. 13.

CHAPTER 10

THE VICTORIAN ERA: CRAFT AND INDUSTRY

1. Arthur Grimwade, 'A New List of English Gold Plate', *The Connoisseur*, October 1951.
2. See Chapter 2, p. 22.
3. Quoted by John Culme, *Nineteenth-Century Silver* (1976), p. 94.
4. Quoted by Patricia Wardle, *Victorian Silver and Silver-Plate* (1963), pp. 23–4.
5. This passage was also quoted by Patricia Wardle (1963), p. 19, as the preface to her book.
6. Quoted by Culme (1976), p. 216.
7. The quotations given below are taken from a typewritten transcript of the manuscript in the Goldsmiths' Hall library. I am grateful to the librarian, Miss Susan Hare, for making this available to me.
8. *The Journal of Beatrix Potter*, ed. Leslie Linder (1966), also quoted at greater length by Culme (1976), p. 53.
9. Quoted by Wardle (1963), p. 93.
10. Quoted by Culme (1976), p. 105.

11. Quoted by Wardle (1963), p. 94.
12. Culme, (1976), pp. 24–5.
13. Quoted ibid., p. 85.
14. Illustrated by Wardle, pl. 41.
15. Taken from a longer extract, quoted by Wardle (1963), p. 149.
16. Illustrated by Hayward, *Virtuoso Goldsmiths* (1976), pl. 70.
17. Sold at Christie's, 21 October 1981, lot 85.
18. See Culme (1976), p. 206.
19. C. R. Ashbee, *Craftsmanship in Competitive Industry* (1908), p. 5.

Suggested Further Reading

Banister, Judith: *An Introduction to Old English Silver*, London, 1965.

Barr, Elaine: *George Wickes Royal Goldsmith 1698–1761*, London, 1980.

Blair, Claude (ed.): *The History of Silver*, London, 1987.

Brett, Vanessa: *Sotheby's Directory of Silver*, London, 1985.

Clayton, Michael: *The Collector's Dictionary of the Silver and Gold of Great Britain and North America*, London, 1985 (2nd edition).

Clayton, Michael: *Christie's Pictorial History of English and American Silver*, London, 1985.

Drury, Elizabeth (ed.): *Antiques, Traditional Techniques of the Master Craftsmen*, 1986.

Glanville, Philippa: *Silver in England*, London, 1987.

Grimwade, Arthur: *Rococo Silver 1727–1765*, London, 1974.

Grimwade, Arthur: *London Goldsmiths 1697–1837, Their Marks and Lives*, London, 1976.

Hayward, J. F.: *Huguenot Silver in England 1688–1727*, London, 1959.

Hayward, J. F.: *Virtuoso Goldsmiths and the Triumph of Mannerism 1540–1620*, London, 1976.

Jackson, Sir Charles James: *English Goldsmiths and Their Marks*, London, 1921 (reprinted New York, 1964).

Oman, Charles: *Caroline Silver 1625–1688*, London, 1970.

Oman, Charles: *English Engraved Silver 1150–1900*, London, 1978.

Penzer, N. M.: *Paul Storr*, London, 1954.

Phillips, P. A. S.: *Paul de Lamerie*, London, 1935.

Shroder, Timothy: *The Gilbert Collection of Gold and Silver*, Los Angeles, 1988.

Taylor, Gerald: *Silver Through the Ages*, London, 1964.

Glossary

ACANTHUS. Classical ornament in the form of stylized leaf decoration based on the scalloped leaves of the acanthus plant.

ALLOY. An amalgam formed of two or more metals.

ANDIRON. Metal objects, in pairs, with horizontal iron bar for supporting logs in the fireplace and decorative vertical element at the front, in iron, brass or silver. Popular in England until the eighteenth century, when coal generally replaced wood fires.

ANNEALING. Process for restoring the malleability of silver or other metals made brittle by hammering; the metal is heated until red hot and then plunged into cold water. Necessary at frequent intervals during raising.

ANTHEMION. From the Greek word for flower; bands of stylized palmettes and lotus motifs derived from classical architecture.

ARABESQUE. Surface decoration of scrolling and intertwining foliage, tendrils and scrolls. Thought to be of Saracenic origin, first found in northern Europe around the middle of the sixteenth century and popular in English decorative arts during the second half of the century.

ARGYLL. Vessel resembling a small coffee pot and designed for keeping gravy warm while on the table. An inner chamber is filled with hot water which in turn keeps the surrounding gravy hot. First recorded around 1760; possibly originally made for the use of the 4th Duke of Argyll.

AURICULAR. Early seventeenth-century Dutch style characterized by curious lobe-like or cartilaginous forms; developed by Paul and Adam van Vianen of Utrecht. Found in English silver during the second quarter of the seventeenth century. Also known as the lobate style.

BALUSTER. Small vertical moulding of undulating profile and usually of circular section, commonly used for candlesticks and stems and finials of cups, etc.

BRASS. Golden coloured alloy composed of 70–90 per cent copper and 10–30 per cent zinc. Ductile, malleable and capable of taking a high polish. Produced in large

— 321 —

quantities in south Germany and Flanders during the fifteenth and sixteenth centuries; the industry was developed in England in the late seventeenth century.

BRITANNIA STANDARD. Silver alloy composed in the proportion of 95.84 per cent silver to 4.16 per cent of other metals, also expressed as 11 ounces 10 pennyweight of pure silver to 8 pennyweight per pound Troy. The standard enforced in English silver from 1697–1719 and optional thereafter.

BUFFET OF PLATE. The display of rows of precious vessels standard in the dining halls of princes, nobility and great ecclesiastics during the Middle Ages and the sixteenth century.

BULLET SHAPE. Spheroid form popular for teapots during the second quarter of the eighteenth century, with flush cover and tapering sides.

BURNISH. To polish metals by means of rubbing the surface with a hard, smooth object; in the eighteenth century materials such as dogs' teeth and agate were commonly used.

CANDELABRUM. A candlestick with arms and nozzles for two or more candles.

CARAT. Measure of the purity of gold. Pure gold is 24 carats; alloyed with 50 per cent of other metals it is 12 carats. Until the hallmarking act of 1798 all gold plate had to be 22 carat, although marked with the same marks as sterling silver. Legal standards of purity are now 9 ct, 14 ct, 18 ct and 22 ct.

CARTOUCHE. A decorative shield, normally engraved, embossed or cast, and generally containing an inscription or coat of arms.

CASTER. A box or container of variable form but with pierced cover, for sprinkling sugar, salt or ground pepper.

CASTING. A process for making metal objects, or their components, whereby molten metal is poured into a mould and then soldered to other parts. Stronger but more extravagant in metal than raising, it is frequently used in plate for components such as feet, stems, spouts and finials.

CAUDLE CUP. Popular two-handled vessel during the second half of the seventeenth century, alternatively known as a porringer or posset cup and supposedly used for drinking a warm spiced gruel.

CHAMBER CANDLESTICK. A small portable candlestick set on a plate-shaped base with a scroll or ring handle; often equipped with snuffers or extinguisher. Found from the late seventeenth century and throughout the eighteenth.

CHARGER. A large, shallow plate or dish on which meat was served. Sometimes made for purely decorative purposes and unusual after the early eighteenth century.

CHASING. The tooling or surface working of metal to create a relief pattern. Unlike engraving or carving, this involves the repositioning, rather than the removal, of metal.

CHINOISERIE. A frivolous and escapist Western style loosely inspired by Chinese art, usually applied to European forms. Especially popular in silver during the late seventeenth and mid eighteenth centuries.

COASTER. A small tray for circulating food or bottles around the dining table, especially a circular decanter stand with silver sides and turned wood base. A standard form from the third quarter of the eighteenth century.

COMMUNION CUP. The vessel which took the place of the chalice in Anglican communion services after the Reformation, generally with beaker-shaped bowl, knopped stem and circular foot.

CREST. Heraldic device surmounting a coat of arms. Originally worn on a medieval knight's helmet, it is usually displayed on a wreath. Used on silver to denote ownership and often found instead of a full coat of arms.

CRUET. Small bottles, usually with a stopper, used for oil and vinegar in domestic settings and for wine and water in the eucharist; usually of glass, with silver stopper from the eighteenth century.

CRUET FRAME. Silver stand, fitted for cruet bottles, often designed in the eighteenth century for several bottles or for two bottles and three casters.

CUT-CARD. A form of decoration probably introduced by Huguenot goldsmiths in the seventeenth century, whereby patterns cut from silver sheet are applied and soldered to the main surface of the object, thereby producing a sharply defined layered effect.

DIAPER WORK. Pattern of squares or lozenge shapes to create a trellis network of surface ornament. Especially popular during the early eighteenth century.

EGG AND DART. A repeating pattern of alternate egg shapes and arrow heads, derived from classical architecture and often stamped around the borders of late sixteenth- and early seventeenth-century silver.

ELECTROPLATE. Wares made of base metal, generally nickel, and plated with silver deposited by electrolysis; a process used commercially from the middle of the nineteenth century.

ELECTROTYPE. A process patented by Elkington and Co. about 1840 for exactly reproducing forms in electro-plate by means of moulds.

EMBOSSING. A generic term for chased or *repoussé* (q.v.) relief decoration in metal.

ENGRAVING. Surface decoration of metal made by cutting fine V-shaped grooves with a sharp tool. Most commonly used in silver for heraldic decoration.

EPERGNE. The English term, of uncertain origin, for a table centrepiece, usually of silver, composed of branches, baskets and dishes or candle branches. A popular form of plate during the second and third quarters of the eighteenth century.

FLAGON. A tall covered pouring vessel with a handle, usually of cylindrical or pear-shaped form.

FLAT-CHASING. A technique for the surface decoration of metal, resembling engraving, but produced with a hammer and punch and not involving the removal of metal.

FLATWARE. Generic term usually denoting spoons, forks and cutlery. Sometimes extended to other non- 'hollow wares', such as salvers.

FLUTING. Shallow rounded parallel grooves, used on the shafts of classical columns and frequently found on silver.

GADROONING. Convex curves or inverted fluting, often used for the decoration of borders.

HALLMARK. The official mark struck on a piece of gold or silver by an assay office or guild as a guarantee of its standard of purity.

HELMET EWER. A type of ewer reminiscent of an inverted Roman helmet, with ovoid body on low stem; particularly favoured by Huguenot goldsmiths.

HOLLOW WARE. Generic term denoting all vessel forms.

KNOP. A decorative bulbous moulding, usually placed at the mid-point of the stem of a cup.

LAMBREQUIN. A deeply scalloped stylized fringe-like ornament, common in late seventeenth-century French decorative arts and introduced to England by Daniel Marot.

LATTEN. A yellow, copper based alloy similar to brass.

MATTING. A matted texture produced by punching small dots or circles closely over the surface; commonly found contrasting with highly burnished surfaces on seventeenth-century English and German silver and silver-gilt.

MAZARINE. A flat or almost flat plate fitting into a large oval dish and pierced for the purpose of straining off excess water from fish, common in the mid and late eighteenth century and often decorated with elaborate engraving.

MONTEITH. A cooler for wine glasses, resembling a punch bowl, but with notched rim to suspend the glasses by their feet in the water. First found around 1680 and fashionable for about forty years.

MORESQUE. Linear decoration, popular during the mid sixteenth century, and composed of scrolling stylized foliage. Derived from Near Eastern art and similar to the Arabesque, but less tightly arranged.

MUFFINEER. A small, plain caster, found during the late seventeenth and early eighteenth centuries in silver and brass and often with a scroll handle to the side.

PARCEL-GILT. Silver gilded in selected areas.

PATINA. The effect produced either naturally or artificially by oxidization on the surface of the metal or, especially for bronze statuettes, by the deliberate application of a lacquer.

PENNYWEIGHT. A unit of weight for precious metals; one twentieth of a troy ounce.

PEWTER. An alloy consisting principally of tin and lead or bismuth. The Pewterer's Company required that an alloy of not less than 94 per cent tin and 6 per cent of other metals be used for the finest quality English pewter,

PLANISH. The first stage in finishing the surface of plate before polishing; the removal of hammer marks which occur during raising, by the use of a special flat-headed hammer.

PLATE. Generic term for wrought silver and gold, derived from the Spanish word *plata*, meaning silver. Not to be confused with Sheffield plate (q.v.).

PORRINGER. A small shallow circular vessel with one or two flat handles, in silver and pewter, found in pewter from the mid sixteenth century. Also a deeper vessel, often covered, with two scroll handles, occurring mainly in silver, but sometimes in base metal and pottery, from mid to late seventeenth century.

REEDING. Decorative moulding composed of narrow parallel convex threadlike forms; usually restricted to borders.

REPOUSSÉ. Relief decoration on metal produced by hammering from the reverse so that the decoration projects, then to be finished from the front by chasing.

SALVER. A tray or plate, sometimes footed, for serving food or drink; often with moulded border and decorated with an engraved coat of arms in the centre.

SCONCE. A wall-light consisting of a bracket candlestick with mirror or polished back-plate to reflect light; normally of brass in the sixteenth and early seventeenth centuries, popular in silver during the late seventeenth and early eighteenth.

SHAGREEN. (From the Turkish *saghri*.) The granulated grey-green skin of sharks and rays, used since the seventeenth century for covering small boxes or tea caddy cases.

SHEFFIELD PLATE. Wares made of copper fused between thin sheets of silver under rollers, used as a substitute for solid silver; first developed in Sheffield during the third quarter of the eighteenth century.

SILVER-GILT. Silver plated with a thin layer of gold.

SKILLET. English medieval term for a saucepan with round bowl, three feet and a long handle, found in bronze from the fifteenth century. Silver skillets survive from the mid seventeenth century.

SNUFFERS. An instrument of scissor form with a box at the end, for trimming candle wicks; a redundant form after the invention of the self-consuming wick at the end of the eighteenth century.

STANDISH. Early term for an inkstand, usually fitted with inkwell and sand box and, until the mid eighteenth century, often with a bell.

STERLING STANDARD. Silver alloy commonly used in England, composed in the proportion 92.5 per cent pure silver to 7.5 per cent of other metal (11 ounces 2 pennyweight to 18 pennyweight per pound Troy).

STRAPWORK. Form of decoration resembling cut and curling strips of leather, first used for the decoration of François I's palace at Fontainebleau and very popular in English silver and other decorative arts during the second half of the sixteenth century.

TANKARD. A mug with hinged cover, usually for beer.

VERMEIL. The French term for silver-gilt.

WARWICK CRUET FRAME. Design of cruet frame, usually consisting of three casters and four glass bottles on cinquefoil frame with central handle; popular during the second quarter of the eighteenth century.

General Index

Italics indicate illustrations

Index of Goldsmiths and Manufacturers

Adam, Charles, 180
Adam, Robert, 214, 216–17, 232, 242
Aldridge, James, 254
Angell, George, 275
Angell, Joseph, 268
Archambo, Peter, 150, 152, 181
Armstead, H. H., 276–9
Ashbee, C. R., 274, 281–2, 284–5, 281
Auguste, Robert-Joseph, 247

Ballin, Claude, 192
Bamford, Thomas, 180
Barketin, Jes, 281
Barnard, Edward; Edward Barnard and
    Co., 250
Bateman, Hester, 238–40
Bodendick, Jacob, 116
Boulton, Matthew, 223, 230–36, 241,
    272
Bowers, George, 116
Bradbury, Thomas and Sons, 223
Braithwaite & Fisher, 250
Brandon, Robert, 55
Bridge, John Gawler, 243, 266

Cafe, John and William, 180
Callard, Isaac, 181
Carr, Alwyn, 285–7
Carter, John, 238
Cellini, Benvenuto, 281

Chawner, Henry; Chawner and Co.,
    272
Christofle et Cie., 272
Cobbold, William, 53, 64
Coker, Ebenezer, 181
Collaert, Adrian, 89
Cooper, Robert, 121
Cotterill, Edmund, 270
Courtauld, Louisa, 214, 215
Cowles, George, 214, 215
Crespin, Paul, 175, 177, 183, 192, 198,
    209

Daniel, Jabez, 180
Dawson, Nelson, 284
de Lamerie, Paul, 150, 156, 177, 181,
    183, 186, 188–90, 192, 197–8,
    202, 208, 210
Dixon, James and Sons, 272, 282
Dresser, Christopher, 274, 281–4

Elkington, George; Elkington and Co.,
    256, 270, 272, 274–6, 282

Farrell, Edward, 251–3
Farren, Thomas, 190–207
Fothergill, John, 232

Garrard, Robert; Garrards Ltd, 262,
    270, 274

Index of Collections